Also by
EMILY MARCH

The Christmas Wishing Tree
The First Kiss of Spring
A Stardance Summer
Christmas in Eternity Springs
Reunion Pass
Heartsong Cottage
Teardrop Lane
Dreamweaver Trail
Miracle Road
Reflection Point
Nightingale Way
Lover's Leap
Heartache Falls
Hummingbird Lake
Angel's Rest

Jackson

EMILY MARCH

St. Martin's Paperbacks

First published in the United States by St. Martin's Paperbacks, an imprint of St. Martin's Publishing Group

JACKSON

Copyright © 2019 by Geralyn Dawson Williams.

For information address St. Martin's Publishing Group, 120 Broadway, New York, NY 10271.

www.stmartins.com

ISBN: 978-1-250-31491-8

Our books may be purchased in bulk for promotional, educational, or business use. Please contact your local bookseller or the Macmillan Corporate and Premium Sales Department at 1-800-221-7945, ext. 5442, or by e-mail at MacmillanSpecialMarkets@macmillan.com.

Printed in the United States of America

St. Martin's Paperbacks edition / July 2019

10 9 8 7 6 5 4 3 2 1

*For Terri Hendrix, singer songwriter extraordinaire.
Thank you for your kindness, sharing, and support.*

*For Becky Beal, a fan of Eternity Springs and the
mother of Texas musician Brady Beal. Thank you and
Brady both for helping me bring Jackson to life.*

*And as always, for my readers. You continue to spend
time in Eternity Springs, and in doing so, allow me to do
this work I love. Thank you! How about we adopt a
theme song? I suggest the great Texas singer songwriter
(and Aggie) Robert Earl Keene's "The Road Goes On
Forever and the Party Never Ends."*

Prologue

ETERNITY SPRINGS, COLORADO

The envelope arrived in the morning mail and sat unopened on Boone McBride's desk like a rattlesnake coiled to strike. He'd thought—he'd prayed—that he'd left the trouble behind when he moved to Eternity Springs. The arrival of the certified letter three hours ago suggested otherwise.

Despite the fact that it was only two in the afternoon and Boone rarely drank anything stronger than beer, he rose and crossed to the antique sideboard where he kept drinks to offer visitors. He reached past the soda and bottled water to the liquor decanters. Pouring a shot of bourbon into a crystal glass, he muttered, "Liquid courage," and tossed it back.

Fire burned down his throat. He splashed two more fingers of liquor into his glass and as he lifted it to sip, his gaze strayed back to his desk. Maybe instead of drinking he should make a quick visit to the nearest church and say a few prayers. If the excrement was hitting the fan in Texas again, he'd likely need some divine intervention.

A buzz from the intercom sounded a reprieve. The receptionist downstairs asked if he was available for a visitor who did not have an appointment. Could he see Celeste Blessing?

"Absolutely." His lips twisted with a grateful smile. Looks like the divine intervention had come to him.

Boone was inordinately glad of this interruption, not only because it gave him an excuse to delay the opening of the letter, but also because something about Celeste Blessing simply lightened his heart. A woman somewhere upward of seventy, she exuded a magnetic radiance and displayed an energy that defied her age. The laugh lines at the corners of her crystal blue eyes and the constant smile on her face gave her a perpetual happy look that begged a similar response from whomever she encountered. Celeste owned and operated Angel's Rest Healing Center and Spa, the local resort that attracted visitors from all over the country to Eternity Springs. She always had kind and often wise words to share.

Heaven knows, he could use those today.

Boone had just enough time to hide his glass of whiskey behind a photograph of his parents and two sisters before a knock sounded on his office door's frosted glass. Feeling a combination of relief and welcome, he answered it. "Celeste, please come in. This is a nice surprise."

"I'm sorry to drop by unannounced this way," she said, her manner unusually distracted. "Do you have a few minutes to spare, Boone? I'm in need of advice."

Celeste Blessing needs advice? At that, the world seemed to tilt on its axis.

Boone gave his visitor a closer look. Celeste didn't look like her usual serene self. A worry frown deepened the creases on her brow, and the customary twinkle in her sky blue eyes had most certainly dimmed.

Concerned, he spoke with conviction. "I absolutely have time for you."

In addition to the sideboard and his desk, Boone had furnished his office with a seating area that included a small sofa, a coffee table, and two chairs. He motioned toward the chairs and asked, "May I get you something to drink?"

"Sparkling water, if you have it, please," Celeste replied, sinking onto the sofa as if she carried the weight of the world around with her.

"I do." He left his bourbon hidden away as he filled two glasses with ice from the ice bucket and added sparkling water from his sideboard. He handed his visitor one of the glasses. Celeste tossed back her water like he'd done his whiskey moments before.

Concerned, Boone brought the bottle of water with him and set it on the coffee table as he took a seat to the older woman's right. "What can I do for you, Celeste?"

She folded her hands prayerfully in her lap. "It's my cousin. She's in a bit of a mess. Actually, she *is* a bit of a mess. She usually has good intentions, but her decision making sometimes leaves much to be desired. Recently she has landed in some trouble and needs legal representation. I'm hoping you are able to refer us to someone."

So, Celeste has a cousin? From what Boone could recall, she rarely mentioned family, and no family member had ever visited Eternity Springs. "I'll certainly try. I'll need more information. Is it a civil or criminal issue? And in what state?"

"Virginia. Nothing criminal. Well, perhaps a little bit criminal. Angelica is passionate about her interests and causes, and that can be a very positive thing. Unfortunately, this time her passions led her to involvement with a group who stepped over the proverbial line and caused some . . . well . . . I guess one could call it vandalism. Angelica admitted responsibility for her part in the debacle. She made reparations, but now she's being threatened with a personal injury lawsuit that she claims is frivolous. And, there's something about her being forced from her home. I advised her to seek representation from the beginning, but she didn't listen to me." Celeste rubbed her temple with her fingers and added, "She never listens to me!"

Not too bright of Angelica. Boone had been around Eternity Springs long enough to know that when Celeste talked, people should listen.

"Virginia. Hmm. Not my usual stomping grounds." He picked up the green bottle of sparkling water and re-filled Celeste's glass as he mentally reviewed his contacts in the state. "I don't have a name for you on the tip of my tongue, but I'm happy to make a few calls. I should be able to have a recommendation or two for you by the close of business today. Will that be all right?"

"That will be fabulous. Thank you." Celeste smiled with relief, but when she continued, exasperation riddled her tone. "Some people truly are trouble magnets. Have you noticed that? And almost every family seems to have one."

Boone sneaked a longing glance toward the sideboard where his drink remained hidden. *Oh, yeah. I've noticed. In my family, the trouble magnet is me.*

Celeste continued, "That sounds uncharitable, and I don't mean to be unkind. Angelica truly is a good person whose heart is in the right place. You'd like her. Everybody does. But the woman is stubborn. More granite in her head than in all the mountains of all of Colorado. And when Proverbs says 'Idle hands are the devil's workshop,' the Good Book might as well be talking about my cousin. As long as she has a project keeping her busy, she does all right. It's when she's bored that she gets into mischief and manages to land herself in these situations. In the heat of the moment, she won't listen to good advice. Too many times she's her own worst enemy."

Boone rolled his tongue around his mouth. Sounded more and more like he and Angelica had a lot in common.

"About this referral. Is your cousin ready to seek legal counsel?"

"Oh, yes. She's at the end of her rope, otherwise she'd never have stooped to ask me for help. She said that she knows she must have an attorney, and that she probably shouldn't call someone out of the yellow pages." Celeste paused a moment and pursed her lips. "Do they still even print a yellow pages?"

"I honestly don't know."

"Well, that's neither here nor there." Celeste gave a dismissive wave. "The bottom line is that any assistance you're able to give us will be very much appreciated."

She took one more sip of her water, then set the glass on a coaster on the coffee table and stood. "Now, I've taken enough of your time, and Gabe is expecting me upstairs at his office. We have plans to review. We're remodeling the outdoor living spaces for the cabins at Angel's Rest. He's doing the design for us, of course."

Gabe was Gabe Callahan, a landscape architect and a distant cousin of Boone's. Gabe had been the first member of the Callahan family to settle in Eternity Springs. Now his brothers and father had summer places on a large section of property out on Hummingbird Lake, and his nephew was a full-time resident here in town.

Boone walked her toward the door. "I'll be in touch as soon as I have a name to refer."

"Thank you, dear." Celeste lifted her head and looked him directly in the eyes, her gaze suddenly and unusually intense. "And remember, Boone, the trick to breaking the chains of the past is to reject it as your master and embrace it as your teacher."

Boone froze. *What does she know?*

She gave his hand a squeeze. "Have a lovely afternoon, Boone. Goodbye."

She left him standing with his mouth slightly agape as she exited his office. After a moment of stunned silence, he gave his head a shake. Here was a perfect example of Celeste being Celeste.

Carefully and quietly, he shut his office door. He strode toward his desk and picked up the rattlesnake with the return address of his former law firm in Fort Worth. *Reject the past as your master and embrace it as your teacher.*

He filled his lungs with air, then exhaled a heavy breath and used a letter opener to slit the envelope open. He unfolded the single sheet of paper inside and began to read. By the third sentence, the dread churning in his gut had evaporated. This wasn't what he'd thought it was. Not at all.

After reading the letter through twice, he dropped the page onto his desk. "Huh," he said aloud into the empty office. "Looks like I'm headed back to Texas."

Part One

Chapter One

NASHVILLE, TENNESSEE

Bang. The judge's gavel fell and officially crushed Jackson McBride's heart. He closed his eyes. Bleak despair washed over him. Up until this very moment, he hadn't believed she'd take it this far.

He'd thought she'd come to her senses. He'd thought she would recognize that this proposal was not only nonsense, but truly insane. He'd believed that somewhere deep inside of her, she still had a spark of humanity. That she wouldn't do this to him. To them. He'd been wrong. Damn her. Damn her and the yes-men she surrounded herself with. Damn them all to hell and back.

The enormity of what had just happened washed over him. *Oh, God, how will I survive this?*

On the heels of his anguish came the rage. It erupted hot as lava, and it fired his blood and blurred his vision with a red haze of fury. He'd never hit a woman in his life. Never come close, despite plenty of provocation from her direction. In that moment had she been within reach, he might have lived up her accusations.

It scared the crap out of him. *That's what she's brought me to.*

Abruptly, he shoved back his chair so hard that it teetered, almost falling over. He strode toward the courtroom exit. "Jackson? Jackson, wait!" his attorney called, hurrying after him.

Jackson waved her off and didn't stop. There was nothing left to be said. Nothing left to be done. No place left to go.

No little girl waiting at home to hug and cuddle and kiss good night.

The tap on the toes of Jackson's boots clacked against the tile floor of the courthouse as his long-legged strides ate up the hallway. He shunned the elevator for the stairs and descended three flights at a rapid pace, then headed for the building's exit. In a foolish bit of positive thinking, he'd driven his SUV to the courthouse this morning. Now the sight of the safety booster seat in the back seat made him want to kick a rock into next week.

He didn't want to go home to a quiet, empty house. He shouldn't go to a bar. Alcohol on top of his current mood could be a dangerous combination. Somebody probably would get hurt.

He got into the car and started the engine. For a long moment he sat unmoving, staring blindly through the windshield, his hands squeezing the steering wheel so hard that it should have cracked. When his phone rang, he ignored it.

A couple of minutes later, it rang a second time. Again, he ignored it. When it happened a third time, he finally glanced at the display to see who was calling. His cousin. Okay, maybe he would answer it.

"Hello, Boone."

"How did the hearing go?"

Jackson couldn't speak past the lump in his throat, so he said nothing.

Following a moment's silence, Boone got the message. He muttered a curse, and then said, "I'm sorry, man. So damn sorry."

"Well, it is what it is."

"You can take another run at it."

"Yeah." In three years. Three years. Might as well be three decades. He cleared his throat and changed the subject. "So, how are things in Eternity Springs?"

"Good. They're good. My friend Celeste Blessing visited my office a few minutes ago and spoke of her granite-headed cousin. Naturally, I thought of you."

"Naturally," Jackson dryly replied. But he felt a little less alone.

"Do you have plans this weekend? I could use your help with something."

Pretty convenient timing. Knowing Boone, he had a spy in the courtroom. But Jackson wasn't in the position to ignore the bone he'd been thrown. "I'm free. Whatcha got?"

"I'd like you to meet me at home."

Jackson straightened in surprise. "You're going back to the ranch?"

"No. Not there. I'm never going back there. However, I am talking about Texas. The Hill Country in particular. A little town west of Austin called Redemption."

"Redemption, Texas?" Jackson repeated. For some weird reason, his heart gave a little skip. "Why there?"

"It's a long story. Too long for a phone call. I'll give you the entire skinny when I see you. When can you get there?"

After today's debacle, Jackson had absolutely no reason to remain in Nashville. "When do you want me there?"

"I'll be in later today. I'm in Austin now. I've been helping a friend with a project. I have a flight back to Colorado Sunday evening. The earlier you can get here the better, but I'll make anything work."

Jackson figured the distance and the drive time. "I'll meet you tomorrow afternoon. Where?"

"Great. I'll text you the info when we hang up. Bring camping gear."

When a sound behind him had Jackson glancing up into the rearview mirror and the booster seat caught his notice, he made an instant decision. "Can't. I'll be on my bike."

"You're gonna ride your motorcycle all the way from Nashville?"

"Yes, I think I am."

"Okay. I'll bring stuff for both of us." Boone hesitated a moment and added, "Hang in there, Jackson. It'll get better."

No, I don't think it will. "I'll see you tomorrow."

Jackson ended the call and finally put his SUV in gear and backed out of the parking place. With the distraction of the call behind him, fury returned, and by the time he reached home, he felt like a volcano about to explode.

He threw a handful of things into his tail bag, filled his wallet with cash from his stash, and ten minutes after his arrival, he fired up his bike and took his broken heart and headed out of Nashville. He left behind his home, his work, and his one reason for living, his six-year-old daughter, Haley.

As the motorcycle picked up speed, he recalled their last goodbye when he'd dropped her off at her mother's at the end of their regular weekend. The nanny met them at the curb, as usual. Haley had given Jackson a hug, then taken the nanny's hand and walked up the hill toward the mansion's front double doors.

Jackson always waited to leave until she was inside. She always watched until the door completely closed. This time, she'd held the bright pink stuffed rabbit she slept with at his house in her arms. Bunny-Bunny. Ordinarily, she left him at Jackson's, but last Sunday, she wouldn't leave him behind.

He thought he'd probably see that flash of neon pink every time he closed his eyes for the next six months. For the next six months while Haley and Bunny-Bunny traveled the world. Six long interminable months before he'd be allowed to see his sweet baby girl again.

AUSTIN, TEXAS

Caroline Carruthers covered her mouth with her hand as she watched her husband of twelve years lean over and tenderly kiss the cheek of another woman. Caroline knew all about the woman. Her name was Gina. She was twelve years older than Robert's forty-eight. She was a widow with two children and five grandchildren. Holding hands and smiling, Robert and Gina walked away from Caroline on their way to the community room.

Caroline blinked back tears. Her beloved husband was in love with another woman. Intellectually, she was okay with that. Emotionally, some days, she couldn't deal. It was too much to see him flirting like a teenager with someone else. Today was one of those days.

Today was her wedding anniversary.

Her husband didn't have a clue who she was.

Caroline turned on her heels and fled the Easterwood Memory Care Center where Robert Carruthers had been living for the past four months. Most days when she visited, she could look beyond her own heartache and be thankful that he was comfortable and happy, but she simply didn't have it in her today.

She missed him so much.

Tears blurred her eyes as she signaled the attendant

at the door to release the lock so she could leave the building. It was a blustery spring morning with temperatures in the mid-seventies and thunderstorms forecasted later in the day.

Lost in her own misery, she narrowly avoided bumping into a silver-haired woman who rounded the corner of the sidewalk. "Excuse me," Caroline said, dodging out of the way at the last minute.

The woman looked at her with cloudy blue eyes. "I'm sorry. My fault. I wasn't watching where I was going. I just . . . I don't feel well. I . . . oh." The woman swayed, and then her eyes rolled up and her knees gave out and she started to collapse at Caroline's feet.

Caroline gave a horrified gasp and lunged for the older woman, managing to catch her below the shoulders and ease her to the ground. "Ma'am? Ma'am?"

Was this a heart attack? A stroke?

Caroline touched the woman's face. *She feels warm.*

Caroline gazed around quickly. Had anyone noticed? Was help already on the way? She needed her purse . . . her phone . . . to call 911. She'd dropped it when she'd grabbed for the lady. There. It had fallen just beyond reach. "Ma'am?" she repeated as she reached for her bag.

The woman's eyes opened. Brilliant blue, but cloudy. She blinked rapidly, repeatedly, and struggled to sit up. "Oh, dear," she said, her voice weak. "I'm so sorry. I got a little dizzy."

"Careful. Hold on. Why don't you stay down? Let me get help."

"No, no, no. Not necessary. I know what the problem is." Her smile was wan, but reassuring. "You need not be concerned that I've exposed you to something vile, my dear. I suffer from a recurring fever—Lyme disease—and I suspect I'm having a bit of a flare. I just need to get back on my feet, and then I'll find a shady spot and sit a spell. I could probably use a glass of water. Dehydration can be a problem in the elderly, you know."

Caroline took the older woman's hands and gently levered her up. She gasped in pain.

Immediately, Caroline supported the woman's weight. "You're hurt."

"My ankle, I'm afraid."

"Is it broken? Let's set you back down. I'll call nine-one-one."

"No, no, no. It's not broken. Just a little tender. I fell on it wrong. I think if I get ice on it for a few minutes, I'll be fine."

"Still, let's sit you back down. I'll run inside and get a wheelchair."

"Oh, no. No, no, no. A wheelchair isn't necessary. I can walk. I see a bench over there beneath that lovely magnolia tree. Perhaps you can help me over there?"

"But ma'am—"

"Celeste. I'm Celeste. Celeste Blessing." She patted Caroline's hand and asked, "What's your name, dear?"

"Caroline."

"Caroline, have you noticed how life has a way of knocking one's feet out from underneath one?"

What? She couldn't help but give a little laugh as the vision of her husband and his new love flashed in her mind. "Oh, yes. Yes I have."

"Well, if you'll indulge a bit of advice from someone who has, shall we say, extended experience in the area of life, sometimes getting mobile again does require a wheelchair. Sometimes climbing in and letting someone else take charge is exactly the proper response. You just have to sit back and roll with it."

"Okay." Caroline wanted to insist that now must

surely be one of those moments. *What do I know? I must
be forty years younger than her.*

Celeste leaned heavily on Caroline and hobbled
forward toward the bench she'd pointed out. "Now,
other times, it's possible you can lean on someone and
limp along. That's okay. Sometimes that's the way it's
gotta be. Life throws injuries at you that flat-out hurt,
and the support of family and friends is exactly what
you need to enable you to take those necessary steps
forward."

"Lean on me as much as you need, Ms. Blessing."

"Call me Celeste, dear. Please. And before we go any
farther, may I trouble you to pick up my bag for me?"

Now Caroline finally noticed the tote on the ground
and the small bottles and bars of soap that had spilled
from it. "I'll come back for it."

"No, no, no. I can stand by myself. I practice dili-
gently." She gave Caroline's arm a little squeeze that
summoned her attention. The blue eyes that had been
hazy moments before now appeared clear and crisp as a
winter morning as she directly met Caroline's gaze and
said, "You see, dear, sometimes wheelchairs and leaning on others *aren't* the right solutions. Sometimes when
life knocks you down, the best thing you can do for
yourself is to stand on your own."

Caroline flinched and drew back.

"Because, when you stand on your own, you stand
tallest. When you're standing tall with your chin up, you
see your future, and your future sees you." Celeste gave
Caroline's arm a second squeeze, then released it, encouraged her with a warm, friendly smile, and then
made a shooing motion with her hand toward the spilled
tote.

Oh, jeez. The way my luck is running today, she'll

tumble again the moment I'm out of arms reach. Caroline dashed for the bag, bent and scooped the contents back into it, then rushed back to Celeste. She didn't relax until she'd once again taken hold of the older woman's elbow. "That soap smells wonderful."

"Isn't it fabulous? It's handmade by a friend of mine. Heavenscents Soaps. We were exhibiting her products at the trade show of the innkeepers' conference at the hotel down the street. It ended at noon. We like to donate our leftover samples to nursing homes at the end of the event. I saw this memory care facility and thought it would be a good choice."

"That's a lovely thought. I'm sure they'll appreciate them." Caroline looked closely at the woman. Her cheeks were rosy and her eyes had gone hazy again. *Bet she is feverish.*

"I'm so sorry to cause all this trouble."

"No trouble."

"Sure, I'm trouble. But don't worry, Caroline. When I'm involved, everything always turns out fine in the end. Oh, my. I am hot. Distract me, dear. Tell me about yourself. You live in Austin?"

"I do."

"It's a lovely city. I live in Colorado now, and I make regular visits to the Dallas/Fort Worth area, but this is my first visit to Austin in years and years. I've enjoyed my stay so much. People have been so kind."

"I'm glad we gave a good impression." Having finally reached the bench, Caroline settled Celeste and helped her prop her ankle up. "I'm going to run inside and get you some ice for your ankle."

"Bless your heart. You're so kind, Caroline. By the way, I do love your pearls. Such a classic look."

"Thank you." Caroline swallowed hard. "They were

a gift from my husband." For their first anniversary. She hurried up the front steps, buzzed the intercom, and once inside, made her way to the onsite medical office where she explained the situation to the nurse.

A few minutes later, while the nurse went outside, Caroline ducked into the community room to get Celeste something to drink. Robert was sitting on a sofa with his Gina, watching TV and holding hands. Caroline filled a paper cup with sweet tea and thought longingly of a gin martini.

It was her anniversary, after all.

She wiped new tears off her cheeks as she returned to the bench outside to find the nurse wrapping Celeste's ankle with an ace bandage and saying, ". . . bring down the fever. I suggest you spend the rest of today in bed. Resting your ankle and keeping it elevated will make it happy, too."

"Oh, dear." Celeste sighed heavily. "I'm supposed to drive over to the Hill Country this afternoon."

"That's out of the question," the nurse replied.

Celeste worriedly clicked her tongue. "This is frightfully inconvenient. I promised to help an industry colleague out of a bind and now *I'm* in one! We have appointments set up for tonight and tomorrow in Redemption—it's a lovely little tourist town a couple hours west of here—to research an article for an industry publication that is due Monday morning. My colleague's daughter went into early labor this morning, and I told her I'd take the meetings and write the article. Oh dear oh dear oh dear. What to do, what to do, what to do? This is going to inconvenience a lot of people." Celeste looked hopefully from the nurse to Caroline. "Have either of you ever been to Redemption, Texas?"

"Not me," said the nurse.

"I'm afraid not," Caroline said.

"I'm told it's a lovely little town." Celeste folded her hands prayerfully. "I feel so terrible. They were counting on me. How can this problem be solved?" She lifted her gaze, met Caroline's, and held it.

Caroline heard herself say, "I'll do it."

Celeste's brows arched innocently. "Oh?"

"I'm a writer. It's what I do for my job. I write travel articles. I could do this for you if you'd like."

Celeste beamed and clapped her hands. "Oh, Caroline. That would be fabulous. Simply fabulous. Although, like I said, these meetings are today and tomorrow. Could you clear your schedule?"

Caroline thought of Robert and their wedding day and how he held Gina's hand. "Celeste, this project could not come at a better time for me."

The angel wing earrings dangling from Celeste's ears sparkled in the dappled sunshine beneath the magnolia tree as she said, "In that case, what a fortuitous fever this is. God truly does work in mysterious ways. You just never know when leaning on a friend can change the course of one's life, do you? And isn't there such power in climbing back up onto your feet and standing tall and strong?"

Caroline didn't know why a shiver ran down her spine at that moment, but it did. Fifteen minutes later when she left Easterwood Memory Care Center for a second time that day with a mission and a notepad filled with details, her spirit was lighter than it had been in months. As she climbed into her car, she blew a kiss toward the center. "Happy Anniversary, Robert. My love."

Then Caroline drove home, packed a bag and headed west, leaving half of her heart behind.

Chapter Two

Jackson rode into Redemption on a Harley, feeling mean. He'd made the fourteen-plus hour trip from Nashville in a little less than twelve, traveling through the night, driving recklessly, half hoping he'd hit an oil spot and lose control. He wouldn't consciously try to kill himself, but the idea held some appeal. He needed something to put an end to this hell.

As he passed the sign that read: REDEMPTION. CITY LIMIT. POP. 1373, he began watching the street signs for the turnoff to the bed and breakfast where his cousin had booked rooms for tonight. A B&B. The thought of that didn't improve his mood at all. Hope it wasn't all ruffles and cabbage roses. Jackson had stayed in too many hotels and motels to count over the years—it was part of the business—but he couldn't recall ever staying at a B&B. He wasn't the B&B type.

Apparently, Redemption was a B&B type of town. Founded by German immigrants in the mid-1840s, today the town had a thriving tourist industry. Visitors were attracted by its history and architecture and to the food and festivals that were heavily reflective of its heritage. In a state where chili cook-offs and barbecue festivals filled the culinary calendar, Wurstfest added a nice bit of variety.

Jackson had visited Redemption on two different occasions years ago. What he remembered most about those trips were the local pastries served in the breakfast bar at the motel where he'd stayed. *Wonder if Boone's B&B serves local pastries?*

If not, he might have to scope out a bakery.

Spying the street sign that read Travis Avenue, he turned right and began watching for Erlösung Gästehaus. He'd promised to meet his cousin in the bar there at six thirty. A quick glance at his watch showed he'd made it to town with an hour and fifty minutes to spare, enough time to check in to his room and steal a nap before meeting Boone.

Jackson looked forward to seeing his cousin again. It had been too long. He'd have preferred that the reason for the meeting not been such a mystery, but this was typical Boone. The man kept secrets like nobody's business.

Two blocks off the main drag through town, he spied his destination. With its crossed beams and dark shutters and window baskets full of flowers, the inn looked more like it belonged in an alpine village rather than the Texas Hill Country. Pulling into the drive, Jackson felt good about his chances for those Bavarian pastries, so he wasn't feeling quite as mean when his gaze snagged on a sight as pretty as a Parker County peach—the woman approaching front porch steps of the stately B&B.

See that girl. The thought drifted through his mind and stuck. Like a lyric.

A lyric.

Jackson grew abruptly still. This was the way it used

to happen for him. A thought or a phrase would ghost into his mind and hang around until he did something with it. Sometimes, words went so far as to don a pair of boots and start two-stepping across his brain, demanding a tune. But when his marriage started falling apart, the words and the tunes began to dry up. He hadn't written anything better than decent since the divorce four years ago. However, since Sharon blew up his world eight months ago by proposing these ridiculous changes to their custody agreement, the only thoughts dancing through his head were plots of revenge.

But now . . . something. There was something there.

See that girl.

Jackson gave her a slow once-over. Slim, sleek, and sophisticated and a little out of place with her tailored blouse, pencil skirt, and three-inch heels. She wore her dark hair smoothed away from her face and tamed into a knot at the nape of her long neck. Big brown eyes. Cheekbones. What glorious cheekbones. Thin, patrician nose. Full lips.

See that girl. Skinny skirt. Red lipstick and a string of real pearls.

Whoa. What the heck was that? Emotion stirred inside him, something that felt a little too much like hope.

Hope? That he'd get his music back? At this point in his life why would he even care? What did it matter?

Maybe because you need something to get you through the next six months.

Getting his music back damn sure would be a gift, but Jackson wasn't about to get his hopes up. As far as he could tell, hope's only purpose was to set you up to get crushed.

The woman disappeared inside the inn, and Jackson released a breath he hadn't realized he'd been holding. Then, because it somehow seemed like the right thing to do, he pursed his lips and blew a soft, politically incorrect wolf whistle.

Minutes later, he sauntered toward the entrance of Erlösung Gästehaus, his mood just a bit more mellow, his step a little bit lighter, and possibly . . . just possibly . . . the beginning of a song in his heart.

Caroline smiled with delight as she followed the innkeeper into her room at Erlösung Gästehaus, the Yellow Rose suite. Decorated in a springtime pallet of green, yellow, and gold, the room was oversized with a fireplace, a sitting area, and a queen-sized four-poster bed. A peek into the attached private bath revealed a soaking bathtub and separate shower. "It's lovely," Caroline told her hostess.

"Be at ease," the innkeeper replied. "We'll be serving complimentary hors d'oeuvres and wine from our local vineyards at five in the parlor if you care to join us. Breakfast is served from seven to nine in the morning, though coffee and rolls are available twenty-four seven. Bobby will be right up with your bag and ice. If you need anything at all, please don't hesitate to ask."

"Thank you." Just as Caroline began to shut the door behind the innkeeper, she saw a young man start down the hallway carrying her suitcase and an ice bucket. After she closed the door behind him a few minutes later, she opened the room's French doors and stepped out onto a balcony that overlooked a flower garden bursting with blooms in a rainbow of colors. As a cacophony of birdsong floated to her ears and the perfume of roses drifted past her nose, Caroline closed her eyes and reached for peace. And reached. And reached.

A single tear escaped to roll slowly down her left cheek. *Only one tear. Okay. You're making progress, Caro.*

Celeste Blessing's voice echoed through her mind. *When you stand on your own, you stand tallest.*

"I'm trying." Behind her, she heard her cell phone play her sister-in-law's ringtone. For the briefest of moments, she considered ignoring it, but duty and love propelled her back inside to pick up her phone. Bracing herself, she said, "Hello."

"Caroline, where are you? I called and called and called. Why didn't you answer your phone?"

"I'm sorry. I forgot to put it on the charger last night. I didn't realize it had died until a little while ago."

"That's so irresponsible. How typical of you."

She closed her eyes. "What do you need, Elizabeth?"

"Nothing now. It's your own fault that Robert was asking for you."

Everything inside her stopped. "What?"

"Your husband was with us. He was asking for you."

"He's aware?"

"He *was* aware. He isn't any longer. He's gone again and you missed it. On your wedding anniversary at that!"

He'd come back. He'd come back and she'd missed it! A tidal wave of despair washed over Caroline. She'd missed him.

This did happen in occasional spurts, but it hadn't happened in months. Not since before Valentine's Day, and it had been almost a year since Robert had a full day of clarity where he'd recognized her and his sister and their friends. It had been the most joyous day, and for long afterward, she'd waited for it to repeat, but when so much time passed, she'd abandoned hope. "If you have nothing else for me, Elizabeth, I'm going to call Dr. Theimer."

Her sister-in-law paused a moment, then said, "You reap what you sow, Caroline. If you had kept Robert home where he belonged, he wouldn't have developed a fixation on that woman."

Caroline didn't try to stop the tears that filled her eyes, and she didn't attempt to defend herself. It would be a waste of words. "Goodbye, Elizabeth."

The conversation ended, as had so many others during the past year—in a cloud of anger and pain and guilt and despair. Once upon a time, Caroline and Elizabeth had been friends despite the fact that she was the same age as Caroline's mother. They'd bonded while cochairing a fundraiser for the Cystic Fibrosis Foundation when Caroline had been in college. Elizabeth had been the person who introduced her to Robert.

Not to say that she'd been thrilled when her younger brother started seeing Caroline. Elizabeth had never approved of her May-December romance with Robert. She'd never understood how Caroline could have fallen in love with a man fifteen years her senior. She never trusted Caroline not to fall in love with someone else and break her brother's heart.

"Well, the joke is on me, isn't it, Elizabeth?" She tossed her phone onto her bed with a little more force than advisable and it bounced off the plump mattress and fell onto the floor. As was her luck, the screen cracked.

Caroline glared at the cell a long moment before she picked it up and placed a call to Robert's doctor. Miracle of miracles, he actually heard his nurse take her message and took the call. The conversation eased her heart a bit, the physician giving her the absolution her sister-in-law absolutely would not do. This time when she tossed the cell phone onto the bed, she did it with a gentler touch.

Then because endorphins were her drug of choice when it came to dealing with stress, and she had plenty of time before her first appointment, she opened her suitcase and pulled out her running clothes and shoes. Five minutes later, she headed downstairs and took the exit that led into the flower garden.

She stopped briefly to smell the roses—literally—and the sultry fragrance elicited a flash of memory of her first date with Robert. *The ring of the doorbell, a pause before the entry hall mirror to check her lipstick, swinging the door open with a smile, and the blast of perfume from the huge bouquet he extended toward her with his own smile.*

Moisture flooded Caroline's eyes at the bittersweet memory, and she continued along the garden path. She really, *really* needed this run. Walking with her head down and her ear buds looped around her neck, and staring at her phone screen while she attempted to gaze past the cracks and her tears to her music app, Caroline didn't pay attention to where she was going.

Until she ran into a wall.

"Whoa there, pretty little lady." Large hands came around her waist to steady her. His voice was a deep, resonant rumble that skidded along her nerves.

Caroline was already embarrassed for having plowed into the mountain of a man, and her nerves were on edge from Elizabeth's phone call. While she was girly enough to appreciate being called "pretty," she didn't like "little lady" under any circumstance. Consequently, she had starch in her spine and scissors on her tongue as she lifted her face. Her gaze collided with mesmerizing green eyes, and she promptly forgot all about being annoyed or embarrassed.

As the moment stretched, concern dawned in the big man's gaze and when he spoke, his voice seemed to reach down inside of her and stroke her nerves. "You all right, ma'am? You're not hurt, are you?"

"I am."

"You are?"

"Oh, no. I'm sorry. No. Y-Y-Yes. No. I'm fine. I, um, I apologize. I didn't see you."

He released her and took a step backward, then gave the phone in her hand a significant look.

Caroline winced and embarrassment flooded back. She wanted to explain that poor cell phone etiquette was a particular pet peeve of hers, that she wasn't one of those people always staring at a screen and ignoring the world around her and running into someone and missing out on life because they were glued to the Internet. Life was too short, too fleeting, and too precious.

A lump of emotion lodged in her throat. Tears flooded her eyes. She stammered. "I'm s-so s-sorry."

The man took another step back. His hands came up in a gesture of surrender. "No problem. I was a tad distracted myself. Garden sure is pretty. Flowers are nice."

"Yes."

"Makes me think of my grandmother. She had a flower garden and loved to be out in it digging in the dirt. Guess I'll um . . ." He gave a crooked smile and gestured vaguely toward the inn.

Blinking rapidly, Caroline shoved her phone into the pocket on her running shorts. "I'll get on with my run."

"Well, you have a nice afternoon for it. Enjoy. Glad you're not hurt."

For just a moment, Caroline watched him go. Dark hair worn a little long. A maroon T-shirt stretched across broad shoulders, faded jeans, and scuffed boots. An easy, confident, long-legged stride.

Robert used to have a confident stride. Now he shuffled. He shuffled and had come back briefly on their anniversary and she'd missed it because she'd acted like a jealous teenager and run away.

Caroline choked back a sob and headed for the garden gate, picking up her pace so that she was jogging by the time she reached it. She turned north, running hard, her hands fisted as her arms pumped. The stranger had been right, she wasn't hurt. But she was broken. Heartbroken.

Today she had missed the chance to hear Robert say her name once more.

See that girl. Bambi eyes. Heart breaking, it's the end of her world.

"Well, hello stranger," drawled a familiar voice.

Thoughts of the teary-eyed beauty in the garden disappeared as Jackson turned to see the cousin who was older than him by one month striding toward him, a wide grin on his face. Boone McBride, Uncle Parker's only son. The two men shook hands, clapped one another on the shoulders, and then embraced. "Damn, Boot," Jackson said, using the old nickname. "Colorado obviously agrees with you. I haven't seen you this relaxed since that long weekend in Jamaica the year you finished law school."

"Ah, yes." Boone schooled his features in a wistful look. "The Blankenship twins. What a trip. You know, I haven't been able to look at a mango in quite the same way since."

Jackson smirked, and deep inside him some of his tension eased. No matter what other crap went on in his life, he knew he could count on his cousin. Family always had his back.

Boone hooked a thumb over his shoulder and continued, "I have a table in the back room. A surprise, too. Follow me."

Immediately, Jackson went on high alert. He might not have seen his cousin in months, but like their grandfather used to say, dogs didn't change their spots. Jackson had been down the surprise path with him in the past. Boone had something up his sleeve. So when he turned to lead the way toward the back room, Jackson stopped him by grabbing his shoulder. "If you've brought some woman for me . . ."

"No. No." Boone held up innocent hands. "Nothing like that this time. You'll like this surprise, I promise."

"Better not be jerking my chain," Jackson grumbled. He followed his cousin toward the darkened back section of the tavern. A quick glance around upon entering the space revealed an empty room. "Where—" he started to ask until a figure moved out of the shadows. Jackson gaped when he recognized the man. He could not have been more shocked.

Tucker McBride, his younger cousin by a month. "Well, I'll be damned."

The tall, suntanned man wore fatigues and his hair cut military short. He flashed a smile that was eerily similar to Jackson's own. "Jeez, Jackson, you need to find a barbershop."

And then they were sharing a swift, hard hug. Jackson's throat had closed around a lump of emotion, so he had to work to get his question out. "What are you doing in our neck of the woods? Have you gone AWOL? We're not going to have to hide you from the MPs are we?"

"Nah." Tucker's rueful smile dashed Jackson's hope. "I'm back on official business. Had something at Fort Hood that needed tending to and it gave me an excuse to attend this little soirée Boot has arranged."

Fort Hood was the huge military base about an hour north of Austin. Tucker was back from . . . well . . . somewhere in the world. He never said where he was stationed. The family had no clue as to what his job in the Army was, either, because he dodged the question any time he was asked so everybody quit asking. Well, except for Aunt Ruth. She never hesitated to ask anybody anything.

Thinking about family led him to ask, "Do your folks know you're stateside?"

"No, not yet. I figured I'd call them when we're done here. If I give them too much advance warning they'll kill the fatted calf, and I'd just as soon avoid all the nonsense."

"I wouldn't mind a nice veal dinner," Boone observed.

"Then you should pay a visit to Fort Worth while you're in Texas," Tucker fired back. "Your parents would kill the whole herd if you'd ever go home."

In reply, Boone shot Tucker the bird and changed the subject. "So, are y'all ready to hear why I asked you to meet me in Redemption, Texas?"

Jackson shot Tucker a look. "You don't know, either?

His cousin shook his head, and without taking his gaze off of Boone asked in a casual tone, "Need us to kill someone for you?"

Tucker's question was a joke, Jackson thought. Probably.

"Nope. Let's sit down. My beer is getting warm." Boone led the way toward a booth at the very back of the room where a pitcher and three pint glasses sat on the table.

Tucker took a seat with his back to the wall, and Jackson slid in beside him. Since two of the glasses on the table already held beer, he filled the empty third and took a sip. A Kölsch. Jackson liked it. Boone then called the meeting to order by raising his glass and repeating the cousins' traditional toast. *"Un pour tous, tous pour un."*

One for all. All for one. Straight out of *The Three Musketeers.*

"Un pour tous, tous pour un," Jackson and Tucker repeated. They clinked glasses, took sips of their beer, and then waited expectantly for Boone's explanation.

He started out with a family history lesson. "Gentlemen. Do you recall the stories Granddad used to tell about his family reunions? About the crazy aunt?"

"Great-Aunt Mildred," Jackson said.

"Yes. Great-Aunt Mildred."

"She's the one who had a hissy fit about the Super Bowl, isn't she?"

"Yep. She cut off all contact with Granddad's side of family because our great-grandfather didn't invite her to join him in his suite at Super Bowl XXX."

"Cowboys versus Steelers," Tucker recalled.

"She was quite the Cowboy fan, but apparently in her later years, she switched her allegiance to baseball. When she died, the Astros owned her heart."

Jackson asked, "How long ago did she pass?"

"She died six weeks ago at the age of ninety-six, so she got to see them win the Series. Better luck than I've had with my Rangers." Boone sighed and took a sip of his beer before continuing. "Apparently the Astros' success soothed her ruffled feathers over the great Super Bowl suite sin because she remembered our branch of the family in her will."

"If crazy Great-Aunt Mildred left us a houseful of cats, I'm bailing right now," Tucker declared.

"Not a houseful of cats. Though I expect there's probably a cat or two roaming the area. Big ones. You see, when Great-Aunt Mildred wasn't watching baseball, she spent the last two decades of her life purchasing real estate. Her goal was to buy back land that had originally been part of the first Mildred McBride's holdings, land that had been sold out of the family over time. She closed on the final piece of property ten weeks before she died. She told her lawyer that she'd been ready to pass on for a couple of years except she couldn't kick up her toes before—and I quote—'that old goat Edward Dillon croaked because he wanted to die in his own bed, in his own house, on his own ranch.' She bought the ranch from his heirs the day of old man Dillon's funeral."

"Wait a minute," Jackson said. "Are you saying crazy Great-Aunt Mildred left us a ranch?"

"Yes and no. She put the property into a trust that prevents the land from being sold outside of the McBride family tree, and she named the three of us the sole trustees."

Boone gave his cousins a moment to absorb the news before continuing, "I'm told it's beautiful land, a canyon with a spring-fed river and plentiful game. It's just shy of three thousand acres."

Jackson pursed his lips and gave a soft whistle. "Three thousand acres? Near here, I assume?" At Boone's nod, he added, "I'm familiar with Hill Country land prices. Great-Aunt Mildred must have had some serious scratch."

"Mailbox money," Boone replied, using the colloquial term for oil-and-gas royalties. "Also, I'm told she was a voracious reader who loved being able to buy her books online, thus she invested heavily in Amazon shortly after their IPO."

"Sounds like we'd better stop using the word 'crazy' when speaking of Great-Aunt Mildred," Tucker suggested.

Jackson nodded. "Good point. 'Crafty' is more like it. That said, why us? We never met her."

"Apparently, that's not true. Our parents took us to her birthday party when we were nine years old. We charmed her."

"We did?"

Boone pulled an envelope from his pocket and removed a two-page handwritten letter from inside. He handed it to Tucker who started reading and passed each page to Jackson when he finished. Once both men had completed reading the letter, they sat in stunned silence a moment until Jackson burst out in a laugh. "I remember that day. That pasture. That whipping Dad gave me afterward—I couldn't sit down for days."

"It's the day we gave you your nickname. Your dad kept saying he was gonna put a boot in your ass. Didn't realize it was Great-Aunt Mildred's birthday."

"Me either," Boone added. "Where did we get those firecrackers, anyway?"

"We stole them out of somebody's truck." Jackson rolled his tongue around the inside of his cheek as he thought back to the day under discussion. "Stole the matches from the barbecue supplies."

"Whose idea was it to blow up the cow patties?" Tucker asked. Boone and Jackson pointed at each other, and Boone added, "But it was your idea to lure my sisters over near the cow patty when we blew them up."

"No!" Tucker protested.

"Yes!" his cousins fired back simultaneously.

Tucker's lips twitched and he asked, "Do you remember their screams?"

"I do," Jackson replied. "I swear my ears rang for a week." He paused a moment and added, "I can't believe she's kept up with us all these years."

"I can't believe Branch Callahan never mentioned it," Boone added. "When it comes to family, that man meddles like nobody's business."

"How are we related to him again?" Jackson asked.

Boone grinned. "I know this one by heart. He mentions it every time he introduces me to someone. His wife's great-grandfather is our great-great-great-grand-father's brother."

"And that makes us family?"

"To the Callahans it does."

Tucker lifted the pitcher and refilled his glass. "So back to this canyon, tell us more."

"Well, it's definitely off the beaten path. Aunt Mildred and Dillon both ran a few cattle primarily to get the agriculture tax exemption. It hasn't been hunted in forever and is chock full of wildlife."

"Oh yeah?" Jackson hadn't the opportunity to hunt for years, but back in the day, it had been a pastime he'd enjoyed. Venison breakfast sausage was hard to beat.

"Here's the coolest part," Boone continued. "One I'm anxious to explore. Apparently there's a ghost town at the south end of the canyon, a nineteenth-century outlaw enclave named Ruin."

"An outlaw hideout? Seriously?"

"Yep."

"Awesome," Tucker said. "I look good in a black hat."

More than a little bemused at the news his cousin had passed along, Jackson clarified, "So do I have this straight? You're saying we own the road to Ruin?"

"Or, the road to Redemption, depending on your point of view."

Definitely Ruin from where he was standing, Jackson decided. "What's it called? The ranch?"

"Enchanted Canyon Ranch."

"Sounds like something a marketing department came up with."

"I don't know that the Comanche had one of those," Boone drawled. "We're not far from Enchanted Rock. Apparently you can see it from certain spots within the canyon."

Jackson pictured a map. Enchanted Rock was north-west of here, a high hill with a granite dome that rose more than four hundred feet above the surrounding terrain. Jackson and his cousins had camped there a few times in their teens. He remembered being captivated by the Native American legends of the place. The ghost stories in particular had him sleeping uneasily as a fifteen-year-old.

"Enchanted Rock," Tucker mused. "I was talking about that place with a buddy only a month or so ago. There's this mountain in Afghanistan that—" He broke off abruptly and shook his head. "Never mind. But there's a word for what Enchanted Rock is. A weird word. I was trying to recall it and I couldn't."

"Monadnock." Jackson lifted the pitcher and topped off his beer. "Enchanted Rock is the largest pink-granite monadnock in the United States."

His cousins shared an eye roll, and then Boone said, "Of course Jackson remembers it."

Tucker nodded in agreement. "Guy has more useless information filed away than anyone I've ever met."

"Not so useless. It came in handy to know right now, didn't it?" Jackson tried to recall details about the land surrounding Enchanted Rock. "Hardscrabble" was the term that came to mind. Lots of rocks and cedar trees and sunflowers in the summer. Land that wouldn't support a whole lot more than a few deer and lots of rattlesnakes.

Of course, the world within a canyon could be a whole lot different from what was above it. Enchanted Canyon could be a veritable Eden for all that he knew. He seriously doubted it, but he could be wrong. "What are we supposed to do with it? The ranch?"

"That's what this trip is all about. We're going to have to figure out a way to make it produce enough each year to at least cover the taxes. Great Aunt Mildred didn't leave much in the way of liquid assets."

Tucker used the pad of his thumb to wipe away a bead of moisture slipping down his glass. "You're saying we're land-poor?"

Boone shrugged. "I don't think we'll have that answer until we take a gander at what we've got. Y'all up for a campout?"

"I thought we were staying here at the B and B," Jackson said, his thoughts returning briefly to the runner he'd bumped into in the garden and the way she'd stirred the music inside him, be it ever so faintly.

"Tonight, yes. I brought gear so we could stay in the canyon tomorrow night if y'all are up for that."

Tucker and Jackson shared a look, then nodded. Tucker said, "No sense in my getting accustomed to a bed at this point. It'd just make the real world that much harder."

"This isn't the real world?" Boone asked.

Tucker snorted. "I wish." He paused a moment, then added, "I'm on board with camping tomorrow night as long as we get German food tonight. I've had my mouth set on schnitzel since I woke up this morning."

"Camping works for me," Jackson said. "So does German for dinner. And breakfast. I'm counting on pastries in the morning."

"You two still think about your stomachs above everything else, don't you?"

Out of the corner of his eyes, Jackson spotted movement in the garden. He turned his head to see the runner returning and, once again, the faintest thread of melody drifted through his mind.

See that girl.

"Not everything else, Boone," he corrected.

His cousins' smirks conveyed their belief that he referred to another organ, but that wasn't it at all. After the hell his ex-wife had dragged him through for more than four years, sex was way down Jackson's list. Way down. Intellectually, he knew it was stupid to paint all women as black-souled witches just because the one to whom he'd given his heart had clawed it from his chest and stomped it into a gooey pulp beneath her stilettos, but his big head wasn't driving this particular bus. His little one simply wasn't much interested these days.

Who knew, maybe someday his libido would return, and he'd jump back into the hook-up scene he'd quickly tired of following the death of his marriage. Right now he didn't really care one way or another.

But as his gaze locked on the crepe myrtle hedge behind which the runner had disappeared, he wondered if maybe, just maybe, another vital part of him still had a spark of life left, after all. What if he could get his music back?

Hell, he just might survive the next six months, after all.

Chapter Three

Caroline ran until she was drained. Returning to the B&B, she showered, then dressed in a simple navy sheath for her dinner meeting with members of the Redemption Chamber of Commerce. She looped the gold locket that had been her sixth-anniversary gift from Robert around her neck, slipped her feet into a pair of navy slingback pumps, grabbed her purse and a sweater in case the restaurant air-conditioning was set to arctic, and headed downstairs where she was scheduled to meet the Chamber president in—she checked her watch—two minutes.

Punctuality was important to Caroline. She thrived on order and organization. All the food in her freezer was marked with labels and dates. On any given day, her closets looked good enough to be featured in a *Southern Living* magazine photo shoot, and everything in her kitchen junk drawer had a place of its own.

That aspect of her personality didn't serve her well in the chaos that had become her life.

Well, she'd taken steps there, hadn't she? For the past four months since moving Robert to Easterwood, she didn't wake up to find shoes in the toilet or broken glass all over the kitchen floor. Her home was clean and neat and . . . like living in hell.

In that moment, Caroline hated herself more than her sister-in-law ever could.

Halfway down the stairs, she spied the Chamber president, whom she recognized from the photo on the town's website waiting in the lobby. Maisy Baldwin's short blonde hair framed pixyish features and big blue eyes. She wore a cream-colored blouse with romantic, flowing sleeves, black slacks, and simple black flats. Stylishly professional, Caroline thought. *I'd better up my game.*

She paused and took a moment to trap her raging emotions inside a casing of ice. It was the only way she'd managed to get through her days since Robert's diagnosis. Continuing down the stairs, she smiled as she extended her hand and approached her visitor. "Ms. Baldwin?"

"Call me Maisy, please." Maisy Baldwin offered Caroline a bright, friendly smile.

"I'm Caroline."

"It's a pleasure to meet you, Caroline. It's so nice of you to step in and save the day. Celeste Blessing spoke so highly of you when she called to explain the situation."

"I'm glad I could help."

"I'm a fan of your work," Maisy continued. "I'll admit to googling you after Celeste called. That article you wrote for *Texas Monthly* about the ghosts in the Baker Hotel in Mineral Wells gave me goose bumps as I read it. You're a fabulous writer. I cannot tell you how pleased I am that you'll be writing this piece about Redemption."

"Thank you. I'm looking forward to learning about your city. I'm embarrassed to admit that this is my first visit to Redemption—and I live less than three hours away."

"We are definitely off the beaten path, and to be perfectly honest, that's been part of the attraction for many of us who live here. However, Austin and San Antonio have been growing in our direction, so we're not quite as isolated as we used to be. Our population has decided to embrace the change and hopefully guide it along in order to ease the inevitable growing pains."

"That's a smart approach."

The light in Maisy Baldwin's eyes turned impish. "Like my grandma says, progress is gonna progress. Might as well try to throw a collar around it and hook up a lead. Now, I hope you've brought your appetite with you to town. The chef at Otto's has a treat planned for us tonight."

"Fabulous," Caroline said. "I've been looking forward to this meal all afternoon."

It wasn't a total lie. Once upon a time, she and Robert had been real foodies, but as his memory faded, so too did her appetite. She'd lost twenty pounds she didn't need to lose in the past three years. Six months ago, she'd started making a real effort to eat properly and she'd put five pounds back on, which made her doctor happy.

"The restaurant is a block and a half away. If you don't mind the walk, I'll take the opportunity to point out a few points of interest along the way."

"I'd love to walk."

Maisy Baldwin proved to be an excellent and engaging tour guide. They detoured into the Pioneer Museum and loitered over an exhibit of nineteenth-century textiles. Soon Caroline was making notes. By the time they joined three more members of the Chamber, her mood had improved. Distraction was excellent medicine to treat the blues.

Even before she'd needed an escape, work had always provided one for her. She loved the research and the writing process. She loved words. Robert had often teased her about her obsession with perfect, nuanced word choice.

The Chamber president introduced Caroline to the mayor, a gift shop owner, the manager of one of the wineries in the area, and the president of the local historical society, Henry Bittner. Dinner was delicious farm-to-table German cuisine and the first meal Caroline truly enjoyed in a long time. This being her wedding anniversary, she considered that a victory.

Following dessert—a flourless chocolate torte called Schokoriegel—and coffee, the historian suggested they adjourn to the back patio to enjoy a nightcap. "The thunderstorm is going to stay north of us, but it's putting on quite an entertaining light show."

Caroline perked up at the news. The less time she spent alone in her room tonight, the better. "That's a lovely idea."

Chairs squeaked against the wood floor as the diners rose from their seats and followed Henry toward the door leading to the patio at the back of the restaurant. Passing the hallway that led to the restrooms, Caroline touched the Chamber president's arm to gain her attention. "I'll join you in few minutes."

"We'll order for you. A brandy? Something else?"

"Brandy sounds nice. Thank you."

When she stepped onto the patio a few minutes later, she paused to give her eyes time to adjust to the deepening shadows. A burst of male laughter attracted her attention. She turned toward the sound and locked gazes with the man from the guesthouse garden.

The intensity of his look unsettled her.

He sat at a table with two other men. Brothers? Maybe. They shared a definite resemblance. The same dark hair, prominent cheekbones, and thin noses. One wore a solid white sports shirt, the second wore a plaid one. Garden Guy was dressed in a forest green chambray work shirt that complimented his dark green eyes.

"Caroline! We're over here."

She tore her gaze away from the stranger and focused on Maisy, who waved at her from the benches placed in a U around a fire pit in one corner of patio. Walking toward her party, Caroline tangibly felt the weight of the stranger's gaze and reacted instinctively by draping her sweater over her shoulders. Why in the world did she feel like she needed an extra layer of . . . what? Protection? She sensed no threat from the man.

But the way he looked at her shook her. It was as if he were trying to see down into her soul.

Maisy scooted over on the bench to make room for Caroline, and they all looped her into the current conversation, a discussion about repeated requests for a local stargazing tour to take advantage of the area's dark sky. Caroline withdrew a small leather notebook from her purse and made a note to contact a friend of hers, an astronomy professor at the University of Texas who might be able to help with the project. As she set down her pen, the mayor said, "Oh, there's the new owner of Enchanted Canyon, Boone McBride. Looks like he's just finished dinner. That gives me an idea. Caroline, you need to know about Ruin as background for your article."

"Ruin?"

"It's our local ghost town." Maisy lifted both a hand and her voice and called, "Mr. McBride!"

Three men turned their heads toward the sound—the man from the garden and his companions. The man in white smiled in recognition toward Maisy, and Caroline surmised that he was Boone McBride. Garden Guy skimmed his gaze over the Chamber president before settling on Caroline. His lips quirked up in a grin. The third man returned his attention to his wallet. He placed a stack of cash into a leather folio and left it on the table before following the two men headed their way.

Maisy beamed up at the man in white. "So you decided to take my restaurant recommendation I see. I hope you enjoyed it."

"That was some of the best German food I've ever had," Boone McBride responded. He then introduced his companions.

Not brothers, Caroline learned, but cousins. They were shared owners of the place called Enchanted Canyon, and Garden Guy's name was Jackson McBride.

"We're having an after-dinner drink and sharing the skinny about Redemption with Caroline because she's writing an article about the town for a national innkeeper industry publication," Maisy continued. "Would you care to join us?"

Boone McBride said, "Thanks, but—"

"Sure," Jackson interrupted. "We'd love to."

Even as his cousins shot him a look of surprise, he took a seat on the bench beside Caroline and quietly asked, "How was your run?"

His gaze was once again intense, and she felt the warmth of a blush stain her cheeks. "Nice. Very nice."

Jackson's cousins pulled up chairs as Maisy signaled the waiter. All three men ordered a beer. Jackson never took his gaze off Caroline. "You're a travel writer? Is it your full-time gig? I've always thought that sounded like a dream job. So, do you travel all over the world doing research?"

"No, not at all. I rarely leave south Texas for work trips. I freelance and write about Texas almost exclusively, usually for the Texas Travel Industry Association."

"I told her she really should see Ruin," Maisy said to Boone. "That and the Last Chance are spectacular pieces of this area's history."

"What's the Last Chance?" Jackson asked.

Maisy nodded toward the historian, who explained, "The Last Chance Saloon sits at the halfway mark between Redemption and Ruin. The brothel next door went by many names through the years."

"A brothel?" Tucker repeated.

"And a saloon," Maisy said with a grin as she lifted her glass in a cheerful toast. "Redemption's settlers made sure that succumbing to temptation took real effort."

The historian relayed a story about a stagecoach robbery that led into a discussion about some of the villains of Ruin. The mayor, the winery manager, and the retailer finished their drinks and took their leave. The historian rose to follow them a few minutes later. "We have a collection of letters in our files from a traveling minister who preached at Ruin that you might be interested in," Henry Bittner said. "Let me know if any of you would like to read them."

"We'll do that," Tucker said, answering for all three of the McBrides.

"I have your card, Henry," Caroline said. "I don't have time this trip, but I'll be sure to give you a call before my next. They sound fascinating."

In the wake of the historian's departure, Boone said, "Now I'm even more anxious than before to see Enchanted Canyon. We're headed out there to explore tomorrow. Planning to camp overnight."

"Oh yeah?" Maisy perked up. "There's a great camping spot just a little beyond Last Chance. I swear it's gotta be one of the best swimming holes in Texas. It's on a spring that flows into the river, just beyond a bend that—" She broke off. "It'll be easier if I draw you a map. Caroline, may I use a piece of paper from your notebook?"

"Of course."

Caroline flipped to a blank page, tore it out, and handed it and her pen to Maisy who sketched as she spoke. "The Last Chance is still in pretty good shape. Or at least it was the last time I was out there, which was probably seven or eight years ago. Mildred McBride and my grandmother were great friends. When I was growing up she hosted picnics and campouts with my family in the canyon. My brothers and I played hide-and-seek in the buildings at Ruin until our mom put a stop to it after we stumbled across a rattlesnake nest."

Caroline winced. "I hate snakes."

"Me too. That's why I wear snake boots whenever I'm out and about in the boonies." Maisy scooted her map toward Boone and used the pen to point out landmarks. "I'm not much of a cartographer, but this is the river, this is the saloon, and this is the campsite I recommend."

Boone frowned at the page. Jackson glanced at it, then over to Maisy before he suggested, "You should come out tomorrow and be our tour guide. Caroline might be able to use the ghost town in her article."

The notion of an outlaw hideout and the Last Chance on the road to Redemption stirred Caroline's imagination. With material like that, this travel article would all but write itself. She really wanted to see it except . . . "I don't have snake boots."

Maisy waved away the suggestion. "I have an extra pair that should fit you. That's a great idea. I have an appointment set up for us in the morning and we have a lunch date. We could drive out after that. Meet at the Last Chance. Say around two? Would that work?"

"Sure," Boone said. "Sounds good."

Caroline slipped her pen back into its customary slot

in her notebook. Glancing up, she noted that Jackson's gaze was focused on her left hand. Reflexively, she wiggled her fingers. The diamonds on her wedding set sparkled in the firelight.

Jackson's whiskey voice said, "Feel free to bring your husband along."

The pain was swift and sharp. *If only I could.* "He's not with me this weekend. He's at ho—" She cut off the word, tucked away her notebook into her purse, then finished. "He's in Austin."

When Caroline lifted her gaze to meet Jackson Mc-Bride's, the tender concern in his eyes all but took her breath away. "You love him," he said, his tone soft and gentle.

"I do. Very much."

He briefly touched her hand. "I love a girl who I can't be with right now. Being apart from her rips my guts out."

Caroline offered Jackson McBride a trembling smile. *He understands.* For the first time in a very long time she didn't feel totally alone.

"So what was that all about?" Tucker demanded as they exited the restaurant headed for the guesthouse. "Why were you hitting on a married woman?"

Jackson scowled at Tucker. "I wasn't hitting on her."

Boone scoffed. "Well you were damn sure doing something. I haven't seen you that interested in a woman since you first introduced us to Sharon."

Tucker nodded. "I have to agree with Boone. You were hitting on pretty Ms. Caroline."

"No. I. Wasn't. Look, I ran into her—literally—in the garden at the guesthouse earlier. It would have been rude to ignore her tonight."

Boone said, "That's never bothered you before. Not in the past four years, anyway. I've seen you turn on the arctic winter on more instances than I can count, and I only see you a handful of times every year."

"Lay off." Jackson picked up his pace and walked half a dozen steps in front of his cousins. He didn't have to explain himself to them. Hell, he couldn't explain himself to himself.

It was true that he had a head case where women were concerned, but after what he'd been through, who could blame him? His ex, her lawyers, his lawyers, even the damn judge all had been women. Gave him nothing but trouble. The only girl he wanted to have anything to do with was Haley, and look how that had turned out.

And yet *See that girl* was there, ghosting around his head. Maybe this development had nothing to do with Mrs. Caroline Carruthers. Maybe the long hours spent on the motorcycle had done the trick, or perhaps coming back to Texas had made it happen. Maybe it was nothing more than getting the hell out of Nashville. He couldn't know. His creative process was a peculiar thing, and he'd learned years ago not to question it.

He did have to work at it, though. Except for rare occasions when magic happened, songs didn't write themselves. He still approached songwriting like a job and put in regular hours at it, but he'd been spinning his wheels. His music had evaporated.

Lately, he'd been thinking about getting a job, a traditional nine-to-five sort of thing. Between the legal bills and his creative dry spell, his bank accounts were on life support. He'd played a few gigs hoping to work himself out of his funk, and while the work had helped pay the bills, he'd known he hadn't given the crowd his best. That only made him feel worse.

An elbow jabbed him in the side. Boone asked, "Does that work for you?"

"Huh?"

"Calling it a night and making it an early morning."

"I'm whipped," Tucker said. "Time-zone changes have caught up with me."

"Yeah. Sure. Sounds good." Though of course, it didn't. Jackson's workday meant that ten p.m. was still middle of the day for him. His body clock ran on night-owl mode.

An hour later, he was sitting in the dark on the balcony of his second-floor room watching the distant flash of lightning and enjoying the perfume of roses drifting up from the garden when he spied the lovely Mrs. Carruthers returning to the guesthouse. Muted lanterns and light from the nearly full moon illuminated the garden path that she strolled.

See that girl. Crystal tears. Frozen smile. But there's rage in her eyes.

His cousins had been wrong in their assumption that he'd been hitting on the woman. He hoped that she hadn't suffered under the same misconception, but he didn't think so. That wasn't the vibe he'd picked up from her. She'd been polite enough and maybe no one else had noticed, but she'd been distracted the entire time they'd sat together. He'd noticed her wedding band right away, of course, but the comment about her husband had been a shot in the dark. He scored a direct hit.

He wondered why the woman was in emotional turmoil. His cousins might not have seen it, but to Jackson it much was obvious. "Takes one to know one," Jackson softly murmured. Then he rose from his chair, went into his room, and took a seat at the desk to begin his nightly journal entry.

He wasn't allowed to text. Wasn't allowed to call. Wasn't allowed to send a damn snail mail letter. Not that he'd know where to send it since Sharon planned to haul her all over the world for the next six months. But by all that was holy, some day his daughter would know that he thought of her every damn day. He wrote the date and the words, "Dear Haley."

Chapter Four

Morning arrived when a cold, wet towel landed on Jackson's face. "What the hell?" he growled in a sleep-graveled voice. Dragging the towel off his face, he flung it at Tucker.

"You suck at security, cuz. Left the connecting door between our rooms unlocked."

"Did not."

"Don't call that little switch you flipped a lock. Didn't take me five seconds to get past it." Tucker swirled one end of the towel around in preparation of popping it.

Jackson lowered his brows. "Do it and die."

Tucker laughed. "Move your ass, Jackson. The Jeep is loaded, and Boone and I are ready for Ruin."

Having tossed and turned most of the night, Jackson failed to recognize the allure of the ghost town at that particular moment. He shut his eyes and pulled his pillow over his head. "Go ahead. I'll catch up later."

"Nope. The Three Musketeers ride together or not at all." Tucker paused a moment, then added, "I have coffee and homemade pastries in my room."

Pastries. Coffee. Jackson looked at his cousin from beneath the pillow. "Maybe I won't kill you."

"Like you could. You have five minutes."

"I'll be there in ten."

"Five."

He took a quick shower, eschewed his razor, and sauntered into Tucker's room in eight minutes to find his cousins bent over a paper map. "Getting into the spirit of the weekend with old-fashioned technology?"

"Better believe it," Boone replied. "Manly men don't screw with GPS."

Without looking up, Tucker added, "Can't count on Google Maps working in the boonies."

"Don't you have a super-secret decoder ring that has maps?"

"Uncle Sam doesn't like me bringing it along on vacation."

"Grab a cup of coffee and let me show you where we're going," Boone said. "I assume you're planning to take your bike? You're welcome to ride with me in the truck."

Jackson veered toward a tray of pastries and a paper cup of what he deduced was his coffee. "I'll take my own ride. Knowing the way you camp, you probably can't afford the space."

"True that," Tucker observed as Jackson took his first glorious sip of coffee. "Boot always has liked his creature comforts. Remember that year we went to scout camp, and he packed his duffle so full that the zipper broke and his love letters from Annalise Mulvaney fell out?"

"Oh, stuff it," Boone muttered.

"Don't mind if I do." Tucker snagged a pastry from the tray and ate half of it in one bite.

Jackson laughed, bit into a sweet roll, and turned his attention to the map of Texas spread out on the table. Boone traced the route with his finger. "We head south for a little over three miles, then turn north on this farm road for a mile and a half and then west for another two miles. I'm told the tricky part is finding the turnoff to the canyon. It's on the left, a gravel road that's not marked. If we reach the fourth cattle guard, we've gone too far."

"Better make Tucker point man," Jackson suggested. "He never gets lost."

Tucker snorted. "If you only knew."

Next Boone gave Jackson a rundown of the supplies he'd procured. It was a ridiculous amount of gear, considering they planned to spend but a single night in Enchanted Canyon. Boone responded to Jackson's questioning look with a sheepish grin. "I know. I packed like one of my sisters heading off for college. I swear I don't know what got into me."

Neither did Jackson. While it was true that Boone liked his luxuries, he usually managed to acquire them on a budget. The man took after their grandfather, a notorious penny-pincher who liked to proclaim, "I'm so tight that I'll squeeze a nickel until the buffalo squeals."

"Maybe the canyon's enchantment got to you," Tucker drawled.

"From fifteen miles away?" Jackson pointed out. "Pretty strong mojo."

"Hey, at least we'll be comfortable. Y'all ready to go? Daylight's a-wastin'."

Jackson grabbed another roll and headed toward his room. "I need to throw my stuff in my bag and check out. Meet you downstairs in five."

Back in his room, he tossed his clothes and toiletries into his duffle. He made a final sweep of the area, then paused in front of the window and stared down into the empty garden.

Caroline Carruthers with her Bambi eyes and glittering wedding band had said she'd ride out to Ruin today with the Chamber president. Jackson hoped she'd show.

He wanted to discover why she of all people stirred his music.

A few minutes later, he tossed his duffle bag into the back of Boone's truck. When he started to sling his leg over his Harley, Tucker stopped him. "Hold it. You forgot your guitar."

Well, crap. He'd hoped they wouldn't notice. "I didn't bring one with me."

Boone and Tucker turned to look at him as if he had suddenly grown two heads. Boone asked, "You didn't bring your travel guitar? How come? You always have that with you."

"Not this trip, I don't." Jackson snapped, and then dismissed the subject by climbing on his bike, firing up, and revving the motor.

Within minutes, they headed out. Tucker led the way on the H-D Road King he'd ridden from San Antonio, with Boone following in the pickup and Jackson bringing up the rear on his Harley Fat Boy. Traffic was heavy on the highway as visitors took advantage of the nice weather and fled the cities for the peace and tranquility of the Texas Hill Country. Even the farm roads were busy, clogged with cyclers and bikers and even a tour bus or two apparently hitting the vineyard tasting rooms early.

Despite the traffic, they made good time, and twenty minutes after leaving Redemption, Tucker turned off the farm road onto a rutted, narrow dirt road. His cousins followed. Their tires stirred up dust, so both Boone and Jackson dropped back a bit allowing the space between them to lengthen. Jackson slowed to little more than a putter as he surveyed the surrounding land. Great-Aunt Mildred had been the crazy aunt, after all. This might not technically qualify as desert, but it surely was the next thing to it. Rocks and scrub vegetation.

Rattlesnake land. No wonder Maisy Baldwin included snake boots in her wardrobe.

"Wonder if we could get our rooms back at the B and B?" Jackson grumbled aloud as he approached a bend in the road. Rounding the curve, he instinctively slammed on his brakes. The earth had fallen away. Below him stretched Enchanted Canyon.

Whoa.

In that moment an elemental knowledge drifted over him, surrounded him, seeped into the marrow of his bones like a cold mist on a winter day. It was ancient and primitive and beyond understanding. Jackson couldn't have explained where it came from or how it worked had his life depended on it. All he knew for certain was that in that instant, his life had irrevocably changed.

It's like another world.

It was as if God had plunged his fingers into the flat, barren land, ripped it asunder, and breathed life into it. Rock walls rose hundreds of feet above a canyon floor green with lush vegetation. Big cypress trees and huge, ancient pecans hugged the river bottom where the spring-fed ribbon of green flowed wide in some spots and narrow in others. Jackson watched a red-tailed hawk launch from his perch halfway up the north-facing wall and beat his wings majestically once, twice, three times before settling into a circular sail, a predator on the hunt.

When Boone climbed out of the truck and walked toward the drop-off, Jackson and Tucker both switched off their motors and followed him. The three men stood side by side by side in the silence of the morning and stared down into the canyon.

Tucker blew a soft whistle. "I don't think I've seen so much green since my last visit to Ireland."

"Why am I suddenly thinking of the Garden of Eden?" Boone observed.

"Because it's verdant." A smile flirted on Jackson's lips as he turned in a slow circle. "Maybe you'll run into a naked Eve—whoa."

Surprised at his reaction, his cousins shot him a look. Then they, too, spied the breathtaking site rising above the far end of the canyon. "Now I understand how the canyon got its name."

Enchanted Rock. The massive pink-granite dome rose majestically above the canyon, a solid, steady, un-yielding sentry guarding the playground.

And once again, Jackson's music stirred.

Boone said, "Okay. I'll admit it. I'm stoked about this new asset of ours. Let's go explore, shall we?"

Tucker nodded. "Let's do it."

Jackson didn't speak. He wasn't certain he could.

The road down to the canyon floor was narrow and full of switchbacks. Jackson could see why Wild West outlaws would have used this place for a hideout. Plus, the men of Redemption must have had a powerful thirst to brave a visit to the Last Chance Saloon and brothel. Jackson tried to recall the last time he'd ever been that thirsty. Maybe that road trip he'd taken with Tucker and Boone when they'd lost their virginities in that cat-house in Nuevo Laredo.

Halfway down, Tucker braked to a stop and pointed toward what at first glance Jackson thought was a cave in the limestone cliff. Not a cave, though. He identified a slag heap. "A mine?" he called out above the rumble of their motors.

"Hey, maybe we inherited Jim Bowie's lost silver mine!" Boone called.

One of the tall tales in Texas history was that some years before his death at the Battle of the Alamo, Jim

Bowie worked alongside a tribe of Lipan Apache to mine a rich vein of silver somewhere in the Hill Country. In a region of non-mineral-bearing limestone, fortunes and lives were spent chasing the chimera.

"Boone McBride. A legend in his own mine," Jackson quipped.

The cousins continued on their way to the canyon floor. As the road widened, Jackson spied a trio of buildings set on a rise above the river. One was a typical Queen Anne Victorian–style house, three stories tall with towers and turrets, wraparound porches on both the ground and second levels, and gingerbread everywhere. Freestanding next to it was a two-story structure with the word "Saloon" built into its brick front edifice. As intriguing as Jackson found that, what captured his attention was the third building.

Faded and peeling white paint covered a clapboard exterior with a two-story middle section and single-story wings. Positioned in the center, three wooden steps rose to a screen door hanging crookedly from a broken hinge. The eave of the high-pitched tin roof protected the sign that Jackson read aloud: "Last Chance."

They pulled to a stop in front of that third building and cut their engines. Boone asked, "Is it a church, you think?"

Tucker responded. "Next door to a saloon and brothel? I doubt it."

Jackson thought he knew the answer, and it gave him a jolt of excitement. He asked Boone, "Do you have keys?"

"I do. Look at this." Boone leaned into the truck and pulled a large brass key ring containing half a dozen ornate keys from the center console.

"Reminds me of the fake skeleton key you had when we were kids," Tucker observed.

"The pirate key. I remember that," Jackson said with a laugh. "It had a skull and crossbones on the top."

"I still have it," Boone said. "Maybe I'll add it to this key ring. Seems like it belongs. This whole adventure has a make-believe feel to it."

Tucker nodded. "Makes me feel like a little like a kid at Christmas. So, gentlemen, where do we start?"

"The house," Jackson responded and headed in that direction. For some reason, he wanted to save the mystery building for last.

"Watch yourself," Boone said to him as they climbed the front steps. "That second step looks to be almost rotted through."

He hadn't noticed. Jackson stepped nimbly around the soft section of the board then took a closer look around. The porch appeared to be in decent shape, though he spied three different shades of paint where weathering had occurred.

Boone tried five different keys in the front door lock before one worked. Then the three McBride men stepped across the threshold and into the dusty, musty past.

The staircase dominated the entry, beginning proudly with an elaborately carved newel and rising to a landing where a stained-glass window depicted Eve in the Garden of Eden. Sheets covered furniture in the parlors opening off to either side. Jackson strode to the nearest piece and tugged the covering. Dust rose in a sneeze-producing cloud as a rosewood sofa upholstered in red damask was revealed. It remained in surprisingly good shape.

"Wonder if all the properties remain furnished," Tucker mused. "If so, it's possible we could have a small fortune in antiques."

Boone pulled a second sheet aside to reveal a player piano. "We will have to get an expert in to evaluate."

Upstairs they discovered bedroom after bedroom furnished only with a bed frame and a single, simple chest. Jackson was relieved they wouldn't have to deal with mattresses, although a quick peek into the attic revealed a space packed to the rafters, so his assumption could yet prove to be wrong.

With the initial cathouse tour complete, they headed next door to the saloon where again, Boone sorted through the ring of keys to find one that fit the lock on the oversized double doors. The McBrides stepped inside and halted in reverent wonder. "It's right out of a movie set," Jackson murmured.

The bar was carved wood, brass, and mirrors and still held a handful of glass bottles, though all stood empty. An ornate metal cash register decorated the center. Ladder-back chairs surrounded a dozen round tables scattered around the room.

"Look at this," Tucker said, striding toward a cabinet set against one wall where wooden poker chips stood alongside decks of playing cards. "If this isn't the coolest damn thing. I remember seeing a cabinet like this in a museum."

"This whole place is a museum." Jackson wandered toward the opposite side of the room where an upright piano stood against the wall. He opened the lid and pressed an ivory middle C. It sounded surprisingly in tune. He tried a few more keys that didn't fare as well, the notes jangling in his ear until Boone's exclamation summoned his attention.

"Well, I'll be damned."

Jackson glanced around to see his cousin standing behind the bar. He held a glass stopper in one hand and a bottle half full of amber liquid in the other. "Jack Daniels Old Number Seven."

"That is *not* leftover booze from the eighteen hundreds."

"No. But there's a newspaper dated nineteen fifty-eight beside it. Bet it was somebody's stash. Kids, probably. But I smelled it. I think it's the real deal. I think we need to give it a try. What do you say?"

Jackson and Tucker shared a look and a shrug.

Boone strolled outside and returned a few minutes later with three red plastic cups. He poured two fingers of whiskey into each and passed them out. "Who's gonna be brave enough to go first?"

"All at the same time," Jackson said as he held up his glass in salute. "*Un pour tous, tous pour un.*"

They clinked cups and, holding one another's gazes, each man took a sip.

"I'll be damned," Boone repeated.

Tucker nodded. "Nice."

"Smooth as silk." With the taste of whiskey clinging to his tongue, Jackson felt a sudden urge to see the last stop on their Last Chance tour. He swooped up the bottle and turned toward the door. "I want to check out the dance hall now."

Tucker said, "Dance hall? Is that what it is?"

"Yes, I believe so. I've played enough of them through the years."

"A brothel, saloon, and dance hall. How cool is this?"

His cousins followed him out of the saloon and moments later, following another round of trial and error with the ring of keys, they stepped into the third structure. Unlike the other two buildings, this one was primarily empty. It was also huge. Five to six thousand square feet, Jackson guessed. There was a small bar in front, a stage in the back, and side flaps that could be lifted to provide for open-air dancing. Tin advertising signs graced the walls: Lone Star Beer, Pearl Beer, Jim Hogg Cigars, and dozens more.

Beside him, Boone released a soft whistle. "Big place. I wonder which came first—the house, the saloon, or the dance hall?"

"Seems kinda weird to have a dance hall next door to a cathouse," Tucker observed. "Dance halls are family places."

"This building is newer than the saloon." Jackson spied a chalkboard mounted on the wall near the stage and he crossed to read it while saying, "It might have opened once the cathouse closed. What do we know about the history of Last Chance, Boone?"

"I don't know anything. What digging into history I did focused on Ruin. The conversation last night with Maisy was the first I'd heard about Last Chance."

Jackson drew close enough to read the writing on the chalkboard. It was faded and smeared in places, but he could make out some of what was listed. Week of October third, nineteen . . . was that thirty-three? Or thirty-eight? Thursday night was the Specht's Polka Band. Friday, Redemption Community Band. Saturday afternoon was reserved for traveling salesmen, and Saturday evening advertised the Ruin Review. That sounded like a burlesque show.

"We're going to have to find out the scoop on this place," Jackson said as he spied a balled-up newspaper beneath the steps leading up onto the stage. He scooped it up and smoothed it open. Not a newspaper, but a playbill advertising the Juan Lobo rodeo taking place in Enchanted Canyon. Juan Lobo rodeo. That sounded vaguely familiar to him. Frowning, he checked the date. May 1940. A long time after the Wild West rode off into the sunset. What was it about the Juan Lobo rodeo that stuck in his brain? "In nineteen forty," he murmured aloud. "Huh."

"What is it?" Boone asked.

"A rodeo playbill from nineteen forty." He glanced around hoping to discover further clues, and his gaze snagged on an item propped against the wall at the back of the stage. An acoustic guitar. Jackson repeated, "Huh."

Jackson had not picked up a guitar since Sharon served him with papers for this latest custody crap, but here in an old dance hall deep in the heart of Texas his fingers began to itch. His feet began to move. Soon he stood staring down at the coiled rattlesnake that was a guitar. His mouth went as dry as a drought.

The squeak of the screen door caused him to look up as his cousins turned. Maisy Baldwin walked into the dance hall followed by Caroline Carruthers.

See that girl . . .

In that instant, something clicked inside of Jackson. He knew why the Juan Lobo rodeo rang a bell. The great Hank Williams had entertained at and possibly participated as a cowboy at the Juan Lobo rodeo in Texas in 1940. Without taking his gaze away Caroline, Jackson picked up the guitar and picked out the chorus of Hank's hit "Hey, Good Lookin'."

Chapter Five

"Hey, cuz. You're playing my song!" Boone said, giving Caroline and Maisy a flirtatious wink.

"No," Jackson replied, and without missing a beat he launched into something Caroline didn't recognize.

"Hey!" Boone protested with a scowl that was all for show since he had a twinkle in his eyes when he explained, "Old joke. It's supposed to be Van Halen's 'Fools,' although you can't recognize it."

Caroline smiled as she glanced around the building. "I'll bet this is the first time these walls heard Van Halen."

Jackson quit playing, but held on to the guitar as he hopped down from the stage and strode toward them saying, "Considering that was a badly out-of-tune acoustic guitar, it is probably safe to say they still haven't heard it. This is a nice surprise, ladies. We didn't expect to see you until this afternoon."

Maisy gave him an apologetic smile. "I hope you'll forgive us for showing up early. The appointment we had for this morning got rescheduled for the afternoon. We took a chance and came on out."

"Glad to have you," Boone responded.

"Thank you. I'll be honest, I didn't want to miss my

chance to see inside these buildings. They've always been locked during my previous visits to the canyon. I've tried to peek through the windows, but they're too grimy to see inside." Taking an avid glance around the room, she exclaimed with delight, "Look at that old cash register!"

"Wait until you see the one next door," Tucker said. "It's a lot fancier."

Boone walked toward the bar. "It occurs to me that we didn't check them for money. Let's look."

While Tucker and Maisy followed Boone toward the bar, Caroline turned in a slow circle and studied her surroundings. She jotted a few notes in a spiral notebook, and then looked up at Jackson. "This is a fabulous building. I toured a number of Texas dance halls for an article I wrote a few years back. It was a lot of fun. So much history." She glanced at Jackson. "Mind if I take a few pictures?"

"Be our guest."

In addition to the notebook she rarely left home without, Caroline had come prepared with her camera bag. She was a good photographer, having studied with professionals and attended numerous classes. She usually submitted photos with her articles, and they were often used. She suspected she would want to include photographs of the Last Chance Hall in her piece about Redemption, so she took care setting up her shots.

Boone's discovery of three buffalo nickels in the cash register sent him, Maisy, and Tucker on a mission to check out the one in the saloon, which left Jackson and Caroline alone in the dance hall. Caroline took a few wide-angle shots, and then knelt beside her camera bag to change lenses.

"That is quite a bag of goodies you have there," Jackson observed.

She smiled up at him. "A gift from my husband for our ninth anniversary."

"Nice."

"I was thrilled—and a little intimidated. Luckily, the gift included lessons, too. I'm still learning, but I enjoy it." She started to rise, and he gentlemanly offered his arm to assist. "Thanks. You know, it's a shame I didn't have my camera out when Maisy and I walked in here. I'd love to have a shot of you on the stage playing that guitar. Would you mind recreating it for me?"

A strange look flitted across Jackson's face before he shook his head. "I don't think that would be a good idea."

"But—"

"No," he interrupted. "What would be better is if I return this guitar to the spot where I found it and you take a photo of that. Look, I didn't even wipe off the dust." He held the instrument out for her to see, then without waiting for a response, turned around and strode back toward the stage.

Caroline had no choice but to follow him, and when she saw the shot he was suggesting, she nodded. "You have a good eye."

Sunlight beamed past the iron bars on a dusty window and cast jail-cell shadows upon the wood floor next to the spot where he'd propped the guitar. "Photography is like music and writing in that it's just another method of storytelling."

She considered that and smiled. "You know, I've never looked at it like that, but you're right."

She took a few shots, and then because his observation had lit a creative spark inside her and the story she wanted to tell was incomplete, she said, "I want your boots. Maybe your hand, too. Would you stand beside the guitar?"

Frowning, he hesitated. "You won't take my face."

Now she glanced up at him, her curiosity piqued right along with her creativity. His tone of voice brooked no argument. She wondered why. "Well, that's not the shot I have in mind. Just your boots and your hand resting on the head of the guitar."

"Okay then."

He moved into position, and she lined up the shot. While she worked, she said, "You know, Jackson, it *is* a very nice face. Rugged and handsome. I feel like I can say that because you called me pretty yesterday. You look right at home here in a Texas dance hall."

"I'll admit I've spent a considerable amount of time in dance halls." His mouth twisted in a self-deprecating smile. "Good thing my cousins aren't here—they'd give me grief about the 'rugged' and 'handsome' part. Of course, they're just jealous."

Caroline laughed. "I don't know why. The three of you look enough alike to be brothers." She lowered her camera and took one more glance around. "I think I have everything I need here. Thank you, Jackson."

"You're very welcome."

While she packed up her camera bag he exited the stage, then gentlemanly supported her arm as she climbed down the steps. "Make I carry that for you?" he asked.

Bemused, she handed the case to him without comment. Men with old-fashioned manners seemed to be a dying breed. She liked that quality in a man. Robert used to be that way.

Caroline's heart gave a little twist at the thought as she walked beside Jackson toward the door. When he asked her how long she'd been a travel writer, she grasped the topic like a lifeline. "About six years now. I was a technical writer for a defense contractor and I submitted my first article on a whim."

"What did you write about?"

"Barbecue." She smiled at the memory. "My husband was forever in search of the best barbecue in Texas. He'd hear about a little place and the next thing I knew, it was road-trip time. I updated it every year." *Until last year.*

"Oh, man. Now I'm hungry. You know, I've been away from Texas for a long time, so my personal list of great barbecue joints is dated. Any chance I could get a copy of your most recent list?"

"Absolutely. Give me your email address, and I'll send it."

He rattled off an address that was a bit too generic for Caroline to count on remembering, so she opened her notebook and jotted it down. As she finished, she heard Maisy call from the doorway of the saloon, her voice vibrant with delight. "You must see this, Caroline. The only thing missing is John Wayne."

They spent the next half hour touring the saloon and the house, then all five of them piled into Maisy's SUV for the drive to Ruin. Caroline sat in the back seat between Jackson and Tucker, Boone having called "Shotgun" to beat his cousins out for the front passenger seat. "You sound like my nephews," Maisy observed wryly as the three men indulged in a little back-and-forth bickering. "They're six and eight."

The expressions of all three McBride men turned sheepish.

About a mile away from the Last Chance structures, Maisy veered off the main road for fifty yards or so until she braked to a stop at the campsite she'd recommended. The McBride men piled out of the SUV. Caroline grabbed her camera bag and followed. At her first sight of the swimming hole, she released a long, admiring sigh.

The deep green pool snuggled against a tall rock cliff

on one side and lapped up against a grassy bank on the other. A mallard drake and hen floated lazily on the water's mirror surface. When movement and a flash of red above caught Caroline's notice, she spied a cardinal flitting from the branches of a maple tree to those of a cottonwood. It was a lovely, peaceful place. A little Eden.

Caroline pulled out her camera and took a series of shots while Tucker observed, "Now *that's* a swimming hole. Look at that cottonwood with the branch stretched over the creek. Cries out for a rope swing."

"You're right," Jackson said. "It does."

Boone nodded his agreement. "When we finish our tour, I might have to go for a dip. This is one thing I miss about Texas. Our lake in Eternity Springs is beautiful to look at. It's a great place to fish and go sailing in the summertime, but it'll darn sure turn your . . . toes . . . blue if you try to go swimming, even on the Fourth of July."

"It gets even better," Maisy told them. "Unless something has changed since the last time I was here, when we have a decent rain, there's a waterfall. You'll see them all around the canyon, in fact."

Jackson picked up a flat stone and skipped it across the water. "I love it. Thanks for showing us this place, Maisy. I doubt we'd have found it on our own. Not today, anyway."

"You're very welcome. You do realize I'm aiming for an invitation to come swimming here myself, don't you?"

Boone clapped her gently on the back. "You're welcome anytime."

"Fabulous. Now, shall we continue on the road to Ruin? Caroline is going to want to take a lot of pictures of the ghost town. I don't want to rush, but I also don't want to be late to our meeting in Redemption."

They climbed back into the SUV, and Maisy returned to the main road, heading toward Ruin. A few minutes later, an unexpected sound split the morning. Repetitive honking. Boone leaned forward to look in the passenger side mirror and spoke the obvious. "Car's coming fast."

Everyone in the back seat turned to look. Actually, the vehicle was a truck rather than a car, a big red dually with a powerful engine and horn. "Uh-oh," Maisy murmured, pulling to the side of the narrow road. "This can't be good."

She rolled the window down as the truck braked to a stop beside them. Its window lowered. A man leaned toward the opening. "Maisy, phones have been ringing all over town looking for Mrs. Carruthers. Family emergency."

For a moment, everything inside her froze. Then Caroline's heart dropped to her knees. She grabbed for her purse. Plunged her hand inside in search of her phone. Grasped it. Pulled it out.

No bars. No service. She leaned forward and demanded of the driver, "What sort of emergency?"

"It's your husband, ma'am," the driver said, his eyes kind and his voice soft with sympathy. "I'm sorry to tell you your sister-in-law says he's suffered a heart attack."

"What?" She was confused. "There must be some mistake. Robert doesn't have heart disease."

"Sorry, ma'am. That's the message."

Caroline brought her hands to her mouth. A heart attack. A heart attack? No! She tried to think. She couldn't think. She needed to do . . . . something. What? Her head was spinning. Fear clawed at her. *Robert. Please, God. Please God. Please God.* "I have to go home."

Her tone calm and reassuring, Maisy said, "We'll turn around and head back to Redemption immediately. I'll get you there as fast as possible." She nodded toward the messenger. Thanks for the effort, Johnny."

"Glad to help. Good luck."

Caroline sat stiff as a statue as Maisy whipped the SUV around and headed back the way they'd come. "I'll have you to a place where there's cell reception in ten minutes, honey."

A lump had formed in her throat. Unable to squeeze a word past it, Caroline acknowledged the news with a nod.

She lost all sense of time or place as her thoughts flew to Austin and her husband. She was vaguely aware that she'd begun to wring her hands. At some point Jackson took hold of one of them and gave it a comforting squeeze. It barely registered when Maisy slowed down as they approached Last Chance. Or when the SUV stopped and the McBride men got out. Except for Jackson.

Caroline did manage to rouse herself from her stupor when she heard him say, "She can't drive. Wouldn't be safe. I'll take her in to Austin."

"But, you're on a bike," Tucker pointed out.

"I'll drive her car."

"Good plan. You can rent a car to get back here." Boone leaned in. "Good luck, Caroline. We'll be pulling for you."

"Saying a prayer, too," Tucker added before stepping back, shutting the doors, and thumping the side of the SUV, signaling for Maisy to take off.

Jackson stayed seated right beside Caroline, holding her hand, offering her silent support. The tiny part of her who remained here in Maisy's back seat instead of in Austin with Robert recognized that Jackson's offer went above and beyond the call of a person she'd only just met. However, she didn't have it in herself to object. He was right. It wouldn't be safe for her to drive right now. And besides, she didn't want to be alone.

I'm so alone. Please, God. I've lost him, but I can't lose him. Not now. Not yet. Please, God.

She checked her phone. Still no bars. She croaked out, "How much longer?"

"Any minute now, honey."

As anxious as she was to connect with those at home, she almost asked Maisy to turn around. A heart attack. She didn't know if she could bear to face the worst.

Brrrring. Brrrring. Caroline thumbed the green button on her screen and brought her phone to her ear. *Please. Please. Please.* "Hello?"

"Caroline!" Elizabeth said. "Robert needs you and you aren't here! You're never here. You've let him down again."

Jackson watched what little color remained drain from Caroline's face and wanted to curse. Poor little thing. What lousy timing to have this happen when she was out of cell range. Not that there ever was a good time to receive news like this.

And just how bad was this news?

"What happened?" she asked, and then listened for a good two minutes. Halfway through, she closed her eyes and slumped a little bit. Then she drew a deep breath and blew it out softly. Relief? He wasn't sure.

"Okay. Okay. That's good. Okay."

She paused to listen, and Jackson watched her left hand make a fist, relax, then repeat the motion over and over again. "This happened when?" Pause. "I see. Well, that's a blessing." Pause. "I know, Elizabeth. I was out of cell phone range." Long pause. Tight voice when she said, "I will get there as fast as I can." She licked her lips. "Probably a little over two hours. Depends on traffic coming into Austin. Please, keep me apprised of any new information or if anything changes."

When the call ended, she closed her eyes and let her head fall back. Maisy looked into her rearview mirror and met Jackson's gaze. Her voice gentle, she observed, "Sounds like you got some good news, Caroline."

"He's alive. He's still alive. The doctors told my sister-in-law that the next twenty-four hours are critical."

Conversation fell silent as they drove the final miles to Redemption. As they passed the city limits sign, Jackson suggested, "When we arrive, when don't you run up and pack, and I'll see about getting you checked out."

"Yes." Caroline finally looked at him. "Thank you. Every minute counts."

"Is there someone we can call for you? A family member who could meet you at the hospital? Family?"

"No. My mom . . . I lost her two years ago."

"How about a friend?"

Tears flooded her eyes. She closed them and shook her head.

Surely there was someone, Jackson thought, but he chose not to pursue it. He was a little surprised that she didn't attempt to protest his plan to drive her. For her own safety and that of other drivers on the road, he would have insisted—she looked like she might pass out any moment—but he was glad to avoid the argument.

Moments later, Maisy pulled into the parking lot at the B&B. "That's your BMW, isn't it?"

"Yes."

Maisy whipped in beside the car and parked. Jackson helped Caroline from the SUV, grabbed her camera bag, and then asked, "May I have your keys?"

"Oh. Yes." Caroline dug in her purse, and then handed

a key ring with four keys and a fob to Jackson. Maisy gave her a quick hug goodbye, wished her well, and Caroline dashed to her room, as Jackson hurried to the office. Less than ten minutes later, they were on the road.

Caroline didn't speak for the first twenty miles, and Jackson took the cue to remain silent. When a glance her way revealed tears flowing down her face, he grabbed a tissue from the box in the console and handed it over. She accepted it without comment and wiped her cheeks. Five miles later, she said, "I met Robert when I was still at UT. He and Elizabeth—she's his sister—they're family friends of one of my professors. We all worked together on a project for the Cystic Fibrosis Foundation. He is fifteen years older than me."

Whoa. That's quite an age difference, Jackson thought.

"People can be cruel. Just because I was on scholarship and my mom was a single mother. I wasn't after his money. He wasn't a father figure to me. It was never that way. He's a kind and generous and loving man. He has the biggest heart. He was shy and so sweet. Yes, I was young, but I knew my heart. I fell in love with him. We fell in love! Neither one of us expected it, but that's what happened. We fell in love." Her voice cracked. "I love him."

They traveled another eight miles before she spoke again.

"He has early-onset Alzheimer's. I did the best I could at home. Even with private caregivers, home wasn't the safest place for him any longer. There were accidents. In December, I made the decision to place him into a residential memory care facility. It's been good. He's comfortable and happy. He is! He doesn't know who I am."

Oh, hell, Jackson thought. Now he understood the Bambi eyes.

"Yesterday he had a period of clarity, and I wasn't in town to be there with him. He was upset. He wasn't at home and I wasn't there to soothe him and tell him it's okay that he . . . well . . . that I still love him. Now today he has a heart attack. My sister-in-law says it probably a result of stress from yesterday."

"Did the doctors tell her that?"

"No, but—"

"Then don't go there, Caroline. Take it from some-one who's a pro at the self-blame game. If stress caused your husband's heart attack, you'll have plenty of time later to punish yourself. Although, if I can throw in my two cents . . . you'd be a fool to do so. You love your husband, and you made an informed decision, one that you believed was best for him. Am I right?"

"Yes, but—"

"No buts. You shouldn't second-guess yourself on this one, Caroline. And you sure as hell shouldn't listen to his sister."

She closed her eyes at that and they rode for a few more miles in silence before she asked, "What do you blame yourself for?"

Whoa. Jackson winced. The question was a shiv to his ribs. *Should have thought this one through a little better, McBride.*

And yet, something about the raw misery of the story she'd shared got to him. It made him want to recipro-cate. He knew from personal experience that sometimes focusing on other peoples' problems lightened the bur-den of your own.

But telling her would be a big step. Jackson had never shared the entire story with anyone he wasn't paying for legal advice. Not even Boone and Tucker knew all the gory details. So why was blabbing even a consider-ation?

See that girl. Trudging down the road. Thinking life is over and dreading what's in store.

"You want the long version or the short?"

She glanced around and tried to get her bearings. "How long until we reach Austin?"

"About forty-five minutes."

"How about the long version?"

He nodded. "Okay then. Give me a moment to organize my thoughts." On the drive from Nashville to Texas, he'd passed a billboard advertising a church service and a quote had caught his attention. He'd spent a good twenty miles or so thinking about his situation in a different light. "I tangled with the seven deadly sins and lost."

Caroline gave him a sharp glance. "Obviously, you don't mean gluttony."

His grin was quick. "Hey, I can pack away a good chicken fried steak when I have the opportunity. But I will admit that gluttony is not in my top three."

"What are?"

"Pride and anger are one and two. Sort of a toss-up for the third spot between envy, greed, and lately, sloth."

"Sloth? Admittedly I've just met you, but you don't strike me as a slothful person. That's six . . . what have we left out?"

"Lust."

"Oh. Yeah. Forgot that one." Embarrassment stained her cheeks, but then she darted him a look and asked incredulously, "That's last?"

"Pitiful, I know, but yes. A byproduct of divorce."

"Ahh. Ugly, was it?"

"Ugly doesn't begin to describe it. If we were going with the short version of the story I'd tell you that she sank her claws into my chest and ripped my heart out, then sliced it into little pieces, and then set the pieces on fire."

"That's certainly descriptive, but I don't see the connection with the seven deadly sins."

"It's an old story. A cliché. I discovered she was cheating on me with a guy I considered a friend. In hindsight I recognized that our marriage wasn't healthy to begin with, but at the time, it caught me by surprise. Poked my pride and stoked my anger. I filed for divorce. That in turn caught her by surprise. She claimed she wanted to reconcile, but I had that pride and anger thing going on, and absolutely no forgiveness in my heart. Still, if I'd stopped there with a divorce, I think everything would have been okay."

Caroline watched him steadily, silently asking the obvious question: *What did you do?*

"I didn't cheat on her, if that's what you're thinking. I never cheated. I believed in fidelity—and unfortunately, getting even. I wanted to hurt her as bad as she'd hurt me, so I did something phenomenally stupid. See, my ex and I worked together. I not only ended the marriage, but then I walked away from our working relationship, too. Then I sued her."

"For what?"

"Intellectual property theft."

Caroline gave a startled blink. "Okay, I didn't see that coming."

Jackson shrugged. "I was a songwriter. She's a singer. When we started out, we wrote together, but over time she concentrated on vocals while I did all the writing. We continued to credit her for my work. I didn't care. The work itself was always what mattered to me—not recognition—and I figured it all went into the same pot, anyway. But when the personal stuff turned ugly, well, here come two of the seven deadlies. Pride and anger. I dealt with her manager, but when she threw her new creative guru at me, I was done. They put her name—only her name—on a project that was entirely my own work and gave me some BS about how I'd agreed to it. I decided that crossed a line and I filed the lawsuit. It cost me more than I ever imagined."

"You lost."

"Yes, absolutely, but not the way you think. When I filed a lawsuit against her, I managed to wipe away the guilt she felt, and I handed her the prize of victimhood. She was justified in her turning her legal dogs loose on me." Jackson suspended his tale while he focused his attention on passing a pickup pulling a horse trailer on the narrow, two-lane road. Once he completed the maneuver, he continued. "Now, I'm paying a wickedly high price for my sins. I have a daughter. Haley. She's six now. After I got pissy about work stuff, my ex got nasty about custody and visitation."

"Oh, Jackson."

He sighed heavily and shook his head. "I should have seen it coming, but I honestly never thought she'd go there. Sharon loves Haley, and she knows it's important for me to be in my daughter's life. She was the custodial parent, but we'd shared custody pretty much fifty-fifty since we separated. Once she decided I was the bad guy, she started hacking away at my visitation. About a year ago, she decided to go scorched earth on me. I was in court for that earlier this week. I got my ass whipped."

"Why? Because she's the mother?"

"That's certainly part of it. Primarily, it was . . ." Jackson rubbed his fingers together in the universal sign for cash. "She has a close-to-unlimited supply. And, she was willing to say anything. Use anything against me. Accuse me of vile things."

Caroline looked at him, the question in her eyes, but she didn't verbalize it. Jackson's grip tightened on the steering wheel. Why the hell had he started down this road? He didn't want to say it. It killed him to say it. But he'd gone this far. No sense stopping now. Besides, he'd darn sure accomplished what he'd set out to do, hadn't he? She wasn't thinking about her Robert or Alzheimer's disease or heart attacks.

See that girl. The weight of the world is on her shoulders. The heart of her soul is in her eyes. Keepin' her chin up as she's takin' on the haters.

Watch your step, Bambi eyes. Watch your step, Bambi eyes.

Keep lookin' up, you just might end up fallin' down.

Huh. *I can work with that. If I had my guitar I could— whoa.*

Jackson blinked. He stole a second glance at Caroline. She was patiently waiting for him to finish. *Don't wuss out on the lady now.* "My ex accused me of physically abusing our child."

Caroline gaped at him, shock filling her eyes. "What? Oh, Jackson, how cruel! How could a mother lie about something like that?"

She'd said "lie." No hesitation. No question. No debate. She didn't know him at all. She'd just met him yesterday. She couldn't know how much her belief in him meant.

Jackson's death grip on the steering wheel relaxed. Bitterness laced his tone. "Technically, I couldn't deny it. Not long after Haley started walking I took her on one of those moving sidewalks at an airport. Stupid thing to do. I was young and dumb and didn't think. I held her hand and when we reached the sidewalk's end, I lifted her off by her arm. I jerked it out of its socket. Let me tell you, I felt like a child abuser at the time."

"It was an accident."

"Yes, it was. But with the right attorney and judge and

people whispering in her ears and that bottomless checkbook of hers, it was enough to label me an abuser. I am allowed one phone call every five weeks with Haley, so I'm not entirely cut off from her."

"Five weeks! Why five weeks?"

"It's a long story. Stupid reasons."

"Well, I'm appalled. Your poor daughter. Children need their fathers. How can a mother do that to her child?"

"Sharon has always been ruthlessly ambitious. Her career means everything to her. I embarrassed her. She hit back hard."

Jackson slowed down as the speed limit lowered at the approach to a small town. Ahead, a light turned red and he braked to a stop. Conversation lapsed and in the minutes that followed, he brooded about the events surrounding his divorce. His daughter's absence from his life left a yawning, aching hole inside him. Sharing his story with Caroline might have given her a much-needed distraction, but it hadn't done himself any favors.

Or had it? *Watch your step, Bambi eyes.*

"What sort of music do you write?"

"Lately, nothing. I haven't been working." *She stole more than just a song. She stole my music.* "I've got that seven deadly sins thing going on. I'm practicing my sloth."

With that, Jackson decided that he'd talked enough. Some wounds were still too raw. He switched on her stereo, and the classical music station to which it was tuned suited him. He bumped the volume up, thus discouraging further conversation.

Talking about his troubles had made him feel sorry for himself, and that only made him ashamed, because his little girl was happy and healthy. Caroline Carruthers's husband was dying.

Well, he had distracted her as he'd intended. He'd done some good. God knows there should be a silver lining somewhere in this debacle of his custody fight.

Traffic grew heavier the closer they got to the interstate that would take them into Austin. He got caught behind a large group of bicyclists, which necessitated a slowdown. The delay made Caroline visibly antsy. When she turned her head and focused on him, studied his profile with narrowed eyes, he could see the next question coming from a mile off.

He smothered a sigh when she blurted out. "You're a celebrity, aren't you? That's why you didn't want me to take your picture. I'm afraid my taste in music is mostly limited to classic rock and show tunes, so I'm not familiar with contemporary music artists. I mean, you could be someone who sells out the Cowboys' stadium and I wouldn't recognize you. It's embarrassing."

It's refreshing. "Show tunes? Seriously?"

She smiled for the first time since receiving her sister-in-law's phone call. "Love me some *Les Mis., Chicago, Wicked*."

That smile made Jackson feel like he'd won a prize. *See that girl. Smiling through her heartbreak, she's the best of his world.*

Damn, I'm really getting something. I might actually want to take notes.

"So, are you? Famous?"

"No. Not really. People outside of the business don't know me at all. I played bass guitar. Was a backup vocalist. Definitely not a household name."

"But your ex is?"

Jackson drew in a deep breath. "Yeah. Her name is Sharon." They covered a good two miles before he spoke the name that tasted bitter on his tongue. "She goes by Coco."

Caroline looked at him sharply. "I know who she is. She's a pop star, right? You married a pop star?"

"I married a girl from my hometown who shared my interest in music. The pop star thing came later, and pop isn't really the right term. She's more crossover. Started out as pure country then moved to a mix of Americana and pop with a heavy blues influence. It is its own sound."

"She had one song I know I really liked. A ballad. Something about a songbird."

"Songbird Alley."

"Yes, that's it. Is it one of yours?"

He nodded.

"It's a beautiful song, Jackson. Hauntingly beautiful. Full of emotion."

Full of heartbreak. "Coco has the range for it."

Caroline tilted her head to one side as she studied him. He anticipated the question she would ask next. He'd heard it often enough. *What's the story behind "Songbird Alley"?* "I wrote it after we lost Haley's little brother in a second-trimester miscarriage."

"Oh, Jackson. I'm so sorry."

"Me too." In hindsight, it had been the beginning of the end of his marriage because it had opened his eyes to the true callousness of Sharon's nature. She hadn't been pleased to discover she was pregnant again so soon after Haley's birth, and from what he could tell, she hadn't grieved. She'd scarcely missed a beat resuming her touring schedule. And her reaction to the commercial success of "Songbird Alley" had literally repulsed him. She'd all but stated aloud that losing Patrick had been worth it!

He wanted . . . needed . . . to change the subject. "Do you have any children, Caroline?"

"No. I'm afraid not. I always—" She broke off when

her phone began to ring. Caroline cast a tense, fearful glance his way as she brought her phone to her ear.

Once again, her sister-in-law was calling. Once again, Caroline began to cry. Jackson bumped the cruise control speed up a few more miles per hour and prayed he wasn't driving a new widow home.

He wasn't. Her sister-in-law had called for an ETA.

The phone call effectively killed the conversation, and Caroline spent the balance of the drive lost in thought. Jackson followed suit, his memories of his little girl and the son who never had the chance to live weighing his heart like a rock. It wasn't until the hospital came into view that he was able to shake off his blue thoughts. "Almost there."

Caroline's hands shook as she reached for her purse. "I can't thank you enough, Jackson. You've been so kind. Let me give you money to rent a car for the trip back."

"No. Absolutely not."

"But—"

"Caroline, my mother would disown me if I took money for doing a kindness. Leave your wallet in your purse."

He made the turn into the hospital drive and saw that they offered valet parking. Good. He zoomed up to the valet stand, shifted into Park, opened his door, and hopped out. He was around to help her before she'd managed to exit the car. She paid no attention to him at this point, her anxious gaze locked on the hospital front door. Jackson dealt with the valet, then handed her the ticket. "Here you go."

She tore her gaze away from the door and offered him a tremulous smile. "I really appreciate all you did for me today, Jackson. It was a pleasure to meet you. Maybe someday I'll get to finish my tour of Enchanted Canyon."

"Maybe someday," he repeated. He gave her hand a

quick, comforting squeeze. "I was glad to help. I hope all goes well, Caroline. I'll be thinking of you and your husband."

"Thank you."

Then, without a backward glance, she was gone.

Chapter Six

Caroline's nerves stretched like taffy on a pulling machine as she approached the cardiac ICU. Through the clear glass wall of the waiting room, she saw a crowd of familiar faces. Oh, joy. Elizabeth must have called every one of their mutual friends. Bet they'd all had a field day discussing Caroline's absence. Talk about running a gauntlet.

Well, she didn't really care, she thought as she entered the waiting room. The only thing that mattered was Robert's health.

She spied her sister-in-law by the coffee bar at the center of a group of six. "Elizabeth?"

"Finally!" exclaimed the woman dressed in her usual, stylish St. John, her voice frosty, her eyes blue ice. She gave her head a little disapproving toss as she lifted her nose into the air, which sent her chin-length silver hair swaying.

Seven years older than Robert, Elizabeth Garner took her role of big sister seriously. Their mother had died young, when Robert was in elementary school, so she'd filled that role, too, for much of their lives. She'd never really approved of her brother's relationship with Caroline. The age difference had always bothered her.

However, because Robert loved them both and they both loved him deeply in return, the two women had made an effort to get along.

The events of the past year had slowly eroded that co-operation, and Caroline's decision to place Robert in a memory care facility had wiped it out completely.

Ignoring the sharp comment, Caroline asked, "What's the latest?"

"They are doing a test at the moment, and they asked me to step out. Someone will come get me when it is okay to go back in."

Us. They'll get us. "What sort of test?"

"I don't recall," Elizabeth responded, waving a hand. "Something that ends with *phy.*"

Caroline worked to swallow her annoyance at her sister-in-law and the frustration at the timing of her arrival. The need to see Robert—and to see him now— was a living, breathing thing inside her.

Another voice spoke up. Caroline identified Elizabeth's BFF, Lorraine Hayman. "Exactly where were you when this terrible thing happened, Caroline? Why were you unavailable to answer the phone during this emergency?"

"I was out of town doing research for an assignment. The area has no cell phone service."

"I see," she drawled with syrupy doubt.

Caroline set her teeth. "It's a place called Enchanted Canyon. It has no cell phone service."

"Mm-hmm. And who accompanied you to Enchanted Canyon?"

"A very nice woman named Maisy Baldwin who is the president of the Chamber of Commerce in Redemption. Now if you'll excuse me, I think I'll get some coffee." With anger simmering inside her, she turned toward the refreshment bar where she filled a Styrofoam cup with black coffee.

"Carruthers family?"

Caroline forgot all about her drink as she turned toward the nurse standing in the doorway.

"You are welcome to come back now. Room seven."

Elizabeth bumped into her in her rush to be the first person through the ICU door. Caroline didn't care. Elizabeth and her judgmental friends didn't matter. Nothing mattered except her husband's health. Her heart in her throat, she stepped into room seven, unable to stop the tears from flooding her eyes. Robert lay still and pale.

Pale as death.

Please God. I'm not ready.

Jackson caught a ride back to Enchanted Canyon with a friend who owed him a favor. He arrived to find camp set up, but his cousins were nowhere around. Hiking somewhere, he figured, since both the Jeep and Tucker's motorcycle stood parked at the campsite. He decided to do some exploring himself, and he followed the road to Ruin.

The ghost town was a collection of dilapidated buildings right off a movie set. A grin twisted his lips as he pictured horses at the hitching posts and black-hatted cowboys wearing low-slung gun belts pushing through swinging saloon doors. If the walls could talk. He thought of the famous photograph taken in Fort Worth of Butch Cassidy and the Sundance Kid. Wonder if those two had ever made it down to Ruin?

He poked around for a little while and in the process, scared off a couple of rabbits, disturbed a grazing axis deer, and came way too close to stepping on a rattlesnake. Throughout the exercise, his thoughts bounced around between memories of his marriage, the events of today, the drive with Caroline Carruthers, and the possibilities of the future, namely, what could he and his cousins do with Enchanted Canyon?

A ghost of an idea began to shimmer in his mind.

Upon finishing his tour of Ruin, Jackson turned his motorcycle around and thus took the road to Redemption. As he approached camp he saw that his cousins had returned while he was at Ruin. He parked his bike next to Tucker's, switched off the engine, and the roar of the motor faded away. Tucker observed, "You're back faster than I expected."

"Called in a favor from a friend. He picked me up at the hospital and brought me back."

Boone asked, "How's Caroline's husband?"

"Not really sure. I didn't hang around once we arrived at the hospital, but he didn't die during the drive to Austin, thank God."

"I'm glad you didn't have to deal with that."

"Me too. Believe me." Jackson gestured toward the campsite. "Looks like you two have been busy."

Tucker nodded. "Yep. Had to unload the Jeep in order to get to the cooler for lunch, so we figured we might as well set up camp. After that, we did a little more exploring. Wait until you see what we found in the cathouse."

"I'm almost afraid to ask," Jackson responded as Boone opened the Jeep's door, removed a box from the passenger seat, and handed it to him. The box contained three items—a leather-bound journal, a gold pocket watch, and a harmonica. Jackson picked up the harmonica and studied it. It was a Hohner, an old one. He ran the pad of his thumb across the name etched into the metal.

"Why don't you try it out?" Boone suggested.

"Not until I clean it. No telling what's growing inside it."

"I don't think spit germs would survive for a hundred years," Tucker observed.

"Maybe not, but I'd just as soon not get a mouth full of spider eggs."

He returned the harmonica to the box and picked up the watch. He depressed the catch, and the cover flipped open. *For my love* was engraved in script, and the numbers on the clock face were in Roman numerals. The second hand ticked off the seconds. Boone said, "We wound it. Keeps perfect time."

"It's beautiful." Jackson set down the box and picked up the journal. He opened the book and thumbed through the pages. "Whenever I see handwriting this perfect, I always wonder how much practice the writer had to do in order to produce it. Did y'all read any of this?"

"The first part of it. I'm looking forward to diving into it later on. A woman who must be an ancestor of ours, Ellie McBride, wrote it. It says she came to this area in the eighteen fifties and was number sixteen of seventeen children."

"Whoa." Jackson said. "Busy guy."

"Three wives."

"Idiot."

"That's the way it worked back then," Tucker observed. "Women had babies until they died."

"I'm not saying women didn't have it bad. I'm saying the idea of having three wives chills my blood."

Tucker nodded. "Can't disagree with you there."

Boone smirked and continued, "In the introduction to the journal, Ellie wrote that she intended to record the stories that her father had relayed to her and her siblings about the Comanche raids, outlaw deeds, and cattle drives of his youth."

"Very cool. A journal like that probably should be in a museum."

"The watch and the harmonica, too," Tucker said. "I'd like to find out who the watch belonged to, though. Maybe it'll say something about it in the book."

Jackson returned the journal to the box and handed it back to Boone. "So what other exploring did you do while I was gone?"

Boone answered. "Hiked. Found an animal trail that we followed for a couple miles. Some pretty views. We planned to come back here and try out the swimming hole."

"Sounds good to me," Jackson said. Then, because cousins do what cousins do, he yanked his shirt up and off and bent to untie his boots while he said, "Last one in has to do the dishes."

The water was cool and clear, the swimming hole deep enough to dive in places and shallow in others so that they could stand and talk once they quit splashing and dunking like the old days. Tucker shared a little bit about his work, enough to make Jackson believe he was no longer stationed in the "sandbox"—aka the Middle East—but nothing that gave his cousins a clue as to where he was assigned. Boone spoke about life in Eternity Springs.

"I like it. It's slow paced and low stress. People are friendly and they've made me feel a part of the community."

"You sinking roots there?" Tucker asked him.

"Maybe. I'm not sure. I sort of thought I was, but . . ."

When Boone's voice trailed off, Jackson prodded, "But what? You having second thoughts about running away from Fort Worth?"

"I didn't run away," Boone snapped.

Yeah, right. Jackson and Tucker both shot skeptical

looks his way. "I did not run away," Boone repeated. "I chose to strategically retreat."

Jackson met Tucker's gaze and shared a smirk. Boone remained almost as closed-mouth about what had sent him fleeing Fort Worth as Tucker did about his work for the Army, but Jackson knew him well enough to know that he'd moved to Colorado in order to lick his wounds. "Well, we're here for you, Boot. You decide to go kick some ass, you can count on us to stand beside you."

"Well, maybe a little behind," Tucker clarified. "Let *him* get the broken nose next time."

Boone flipped him the bird and all was right in the McBride family world.

They roasted German sausages over a campfire for dinner and broke out a bottle of bourbon to sip while Boone read aloud from the journal, relaying what was supposedly a Comanche legend about the Ghost Riders of Enchanted Canyon. They turned in to the music of howling coyotes, the lingering scent of cedar rising from the campfire coals, and a sky filled with stars. Jackson drifted off to sleep contented in a way he hadn't been in years.

He dreamt of angels riding horses and awoke in the morning with the idea that had simmered beneath his consciousness the previous day developed into a full-blown plan.

"Hey, guys?" Jackson said as he put biscuits into an iron skillet to cook over the fire. "I know what we should do with Enchanted Canyon."

Part Two

Chapter Seven

THE FOLLOWING SPRING

Her heart pounding, her mouth dry, Caroline made one last slow circle, studying the empty building and imagining the possibilities, before she licked her lips and told the real estate agent, "Let's make the offer, Sam."

"Excellent." Sam Willis, the sixty-something real estate agent dressed in khakis and a golf shirt, grinned. "I have it all written up and ready to submit." He flipped back the cover on his tablet, opened an app, and in seconds, it was done. "Knowing the owner, unless he's on the golf course I expect we'll hear back within an hour."

"Good. That's good." Caroline gave him a nervous smile. "Tell me again that you think I have a good chance to get it."

"Darlin', you're gonna get the building. Only question is the final price. Bernard will want to dicker a bit—he's a horse trader from way back—but I predict you won't need to raise your offer more than three thousand dollars. Especially if the news I spread around the Bluebonnet Café this morning gets back to Bernard's wife, Marsha. She's an avid reader. She's gonna love having a bookstore in town. Shoot, if I'd had my thinking cap on, I'd have tipped her off at church yesterday morning. If Marsha had been working on him for twenty-four hours, we probably could have lowered your initial offer five thousand."

Caroline grinned at the woebegone note in his voice, then decided to trust in his confidence. She pulled out her notebook and began a priority list. She'd made it only to number six when the agent checked his phone and let out a chortle. "Here's your counter offer, Mrs. Carruthers. He's asking for two thousand dollars more and a promise you'll have a book club that meets on Monday night for old geezers like him who still read Westerns. Tuesday and Wednesday are already full."

Delight along with a measure of real panic washed through her. "Counter the counter. I can't discriminate based on age."

The agent chuckled, typed a text, and a moment later said, "Bernard says no problem. Redemption has its share of young geezers, too. It's a deal. He's signing the paperwork. Congratulations."

"Wow. Okay." Caroline's knees went a little weak, so she crossed to the only seating available in the empty room and sank down onto one of the staircase steps. "I guess I'm really doing this."

"We're all excited to have a bookstore in town. Now, I've been in real estate long enough to know that right about now, you'd like some time to yourself here."

"Is that allowed?"

"In Redemption it is. Now, how about we meet for lunch over at the Bluebonnet in a little bit to celebrate? My treat. You can return the key then. Meet in, say"— he glanced at his watch—"forty-five minutes? We will beat the rush that way. The special today is fried chicken, and there's always a crowd."

"Lunch sounds lovely. Thank you. Though I'll probably skip the fried chicken and stick to salad."

"Now you sound like my missus. She's into rabbit food, too." He clicked his tongue and shook his head. "I tell her she doesn't know what she's missing, but she worries about keeping her girlish figure." He patted his oversized belly and said, "Luckily, I don't worry about that."

He winked at her as he handed her a key, waved goodbye, and exited the building, shutting the door softly behind him.

Caroline hugged her notebook to her chest and rose from her seat on the staircase. Again, she turned in a slow circle, picturing the shop like she'd imagined it since the first time she'd walked into the space. Shelving there and there and there and there. Revolving displays here and here. A new-releases and featured table at the front. The checkout counter there. The aroma of fresh roasted coffee perfuming the air. Classical music playing in the background accompanied by the *kaching* of a cash register ringing up sales and giggles from the Children's section during story time. Locals and tourists milling about, exchanging recommendations. Energy. Good, positive energy vibrating throughout.

Old-fashioned gold lettering spanning the picture window: The Next Chapter.

Caroline's Next Chapter. Her friends all thought she was crazy.

She laughed aloud and tried to steady her nerves. From out of nowhere, tears stung her eyes, and she blinked furiously. What were these? Tears of joy? She'd like to think so, but she couldn't be sure. It had been so long and there had been so many of the other kind. Sadness. Despair. Mourning.

It had been eight months and three weeks since she'd buried her husband.

The Next Chapter. She was still debating whether to add "Books" or "Bookstore" at the end. If she did that, would she need to add "and Coffee Shop," too? Since she planned to sell more than simply books and coffee, she leaned toward stopping at Chapter. "I'll need to decide soon," she murmured as she headed upstairs to check a window measurement. Logo design was one of her top priorities.

The building dated back to the 1880s, and previous owners had modernized the facilities. Twenty years ago or so, someone had converted the office space above the shop into an apartment. It would be a perfect space for her for now with two bedrooms and an office. A cozy nine hundred square feet—so much better suited to her than the lovely, tastefully decorated, four-thousand-square-foot mausoleum where she'd tottered around for the past decade. The house had been Robert's choice, located in the right zip code and with all the appropriate amenities to impress.

It had sold within six hours of being listed. Closing was next week.

Caroline had been tackling the downsizing process for some time now, the keepsakes chosen and stored, the rest of her things ready to be sold or donated to charity. Caroline planned to live in the apartment until she found a house she wanted to buy, and then she'd list it as a vacation rental. She'd furnish her new home from the ground up. That's what starting over was all about, wasn't it?

After determining what size blinds she needed to order, Caroline stood in the window of what would be her bedroom and gazed out upon Main Street of Redemption, Texas. "It's a nice little town, Robert. I like it here. I think I can make a home here."

She allowed herself a little cry then, mournful tears this time for sure. This wasn't what she'd wanted. Wasn't the life she'd dreamt of when she married. But this was the hand she'd been dealt. The last year, the last few years, had come close to breaking her, but she was still standing. She'd survived.

And now she'd found her way to Redemption. After a dozen visits since Robert's death, she'd returned to Redemption for good. She didn't know what it was about this little town. Didn't know why it called to her or calmed her troubled spirit, but it did just that. The coincidental meeting on her and Robert's anniversary with that sweet Celeste from Colorado had been her own personal blessing. She liked it here. She intended to make a home for herself here. In Redemption, Texas, where her troubled spirit found a measure of peace.

She lifted her finger to the windowpane and drew a heart in the dust. "I miss you, Robert. I've missed you for so long. I've loved you for so long. I will always love you."

But now, finally, it was time to move on. To move forward. "I can do this. I *will* do this. I know it's what you would want me to do."

Caroline turned away from the window and headed downstairs, to go to lunch, to buy a building, to begin building.

Toward the next chapter.

In his Airstream trailer parked beside the bucolic waterfall, the local representative of the Enchanted Canyon Family Land Trust stared at the single lonely can and sighed. Jackson needed to go into town if he wanted something more than beans for lunch today.

Definitely needed to make a grocery store run. He

was also out of paper towels and milk. Could use some eggs and avocados. Probably should run by the lumber-yard, too, and pick up another box of screws before he tackled the next item on his to-do list, the shelving proj-ect in the pantry at the house.

Plus, he hadn't left the canyon in almost two weeks. He'd always had a tendency to hermit away, but over the past year, he'd gone pro about it.

Not that he didn't speak to people almost every day. One of the first big jobs he'd tackled after setting up shop here was getting the technology issues solved. They now had Internet and cell service in the majority of the canyon, so Jackson spent most mornings in the office they'd outfitted in the saloon, much of that time making phone calls. He directed the work crews that ar-rived each weekday. Most afternoons, he touched base with Boone about the progress they'd made in their ef-forts to give the canyon property a new life.

The brothel was well on its way to becoming an inn. The saloon would reopen as a bar and restaurant. The place had the makings of a nice Hill Country destina-tion resort.

But the heart of Jackson's idea—the dream, the thing that got his strings vibrating—was the plan to reopen the dance hall. The Last Chance Hall.

He couldn't think of a more appropriate project for him at this point in his life. It was coming along on schedule and just a shade over budget. He was deter-mined to get the numbers down, however, in order to keep Boone off his ass, so he'd decided to tackle more of the finish work himself. The innkeepers his cousin had hired were due to arrive early next week, and they'd scheduled a houseful of guests for a test run the first weekend in June. He thought they'd be ready. It helped that he liked holing up by himself so much because he got a lot done.

Except for songwriting. That pretty much remained a dry hole, and after this much time had passed, he wondered if his creative muse would ever put in another appearance. Not that he hadn't tried to write. He had written a bunch of crap since moving to Texas. The only piece worth keeping was that unfinished song that Caroline Carruthers had inspired.

Caroline. Word around the Redemption water cooler was that the lady might be moving to town. Jackson's heart had gone *thud-a-thump* at that bit of news. He had this crazy hope that she might feed his muse.

A knock sounded on his trailer door. He opened it to discover his plumber wearing a frown. *Uh-oh.*

"Got a few minutes, boss? We've run into a problem."

"I don't want to hear that, Willie," Jackson said as he reached for his ball cap and his keys.

Thoughts of Caroline fled as the setting of toilets and tubs demanded his attention. It was only when he walked into the Bluebonnet Café—*three cheers for Fried Chicken Tuesday*—looking for lunch that he thought of Mrs. Carruthers again.

Because there she was, live and in person and sitting in a booth with Sam Willis, being served a slice of lemon meringue pie.

Guess the gossip had been right.

Jackson had arrived in the middle of the lunch rush. He studied Caroline as he stood in a line of folks waiting to be seated. While they'd exchanged a couple of cards during the past year, this was the first time he'd seen her. She'd cut her hair, the style now short and sassy. She'd lost weight, too, but that wasn't a surprise considering what she'd gone through.

In the fall, a thank-you card addressed to him in care of his cousin had arrived at Boone's law office. She'd written a nice note, thanking him for the kindness he'd shown her when her husband had suffered his heart attack, and informing him that the man had passed in his sleep in early summer. Jackson had sent a sympathy card to the return address listed on her note. If he'd googled Robert Carruthers' obituary the next time he had decent Wi-Fi, well . . . that was normal curiosity. Impressive man, her late husband. Long list of accomplishments.

"Just one, Jackson?" the hostess asked, interrupting him. "Or are you joining someone today?"

"I'm single."

"Too bad I'm not, handsome," the middle-aged woman fired back, giving him a wink. "Ten-minute wait for a table or you can take any open seat at the counter."

"Counter's fine." He headed for the U-shaped counter that spanned the width of the restaurant, a path that took him past Caroline and Sam's booth. When he stopped, she looked up. When she recognized him, her polite smile warmed. "Jackson. It's nice to see you again."

"Hello, Caroline."

"You two know each other?" Sam asked, extending his arm toward Jackson for a handshake.

Jackson and Caroline both nodded. He said, "We met last spring when my cousins and I made our first trip to the canyon. So, rumor has it that you might be moving to town. Any truth to it?"

She smiled. "I just bought a building on Main Street. We're here celebrating with pie."

"Fabulous pie." Sam gave his fork an enthusiastic lick. "I couldn't talk her into the fried chicken. She ordered salad."

Jackson scowled and teased, "On Fried Chicken

Tuesday? Aw, Ms. Caroline, you're going to have to work a little harder to fit in around here."

"That's what I told her."

"Congratulations on your purchase." Jackson tried to recall which Main Street properties were for sale. "Which building are we talking about?"

"The Sinclair," Sam said.

Jackson's brow wrinkled. He couldn't place it.

"It's between the bank and the quilt shop. It used to be a general store. The downstairs space suits her just fine, but the upstairs needs a little work. It was converted to a living space some time ago." Sam glanced at Caroline. "Remind me to e-mail you that list of contractors before we leave."

Jackson held up a hand. "Whoa. Whoa. Whoa. Hold on just one minute there. You're not thinking to give her the secret list, are you?"

"Of course I am." Sam's eyes twinkled as he scooted over to make room in the booth. "Take a load off, Mc-Bride. Sit down and join us."

"Thank you. I think I'd better." Jackson gave the agent a mock glare. "We need to discuss the list."

"The *secret* list?" Caroline repeated, glancing from one man to the other.

"Well, apparently not as secret as I was led to believe. Seriously, Sam. You're just giving it to her? I had to win it in a poker game!"

"She's a lot prettier than you, McBride." Sam smiled fondly at Caroline. "You'll want to schedule your contractors ASAP, honey. Good ones are worth their weight in gold. Always been scarce around here. You especially want to get your name on the plumber's list. Perhaps tomorrow he—"

"Keep your hands off my plumber," Jackson interrupted. "My electrician, I'm happy to share. You can have my framers, I'm done with them. But if you try to get near my plumber before he has all my toilets set, there will be war."

Caroline grinned at Sam. "I think he means it."

"It hasn't been smooth sailing out at the Last Chance when it comes to plumbing, I'll admit."

"And that is the understatement of the year," Jackson said.

Her eyes alight with mirth, Caroline said, "I promise to be respectful of your plumbing needs, Mr. McBride."

"Thank you. That's a relief." He tipped an imaginary hat then waved at the waitress. "I'll have the special and sweet tea, please, Janice."

His order placed, he asked, "So what are your plans for the Sinclair Building?"

She lit up. "I'm going to open an independent bookstore."

"Are you now," he observed. "Bookish, are you? Tell me about it."

She did just that, explaining about her Children's section and the Texas-focused section and the coffee shop. Jackson's questions encouraged her to supply details, and the conversation remained on the topic when Jackson's lunch was served and Sam finished his pie and said he needed to go. "Don't you rush on my account, Caroline. You still have more than half of your pie left and besides, if we both leave, Jackson here is gonna get in trouble for taking up a whole booth by himself during the lunch rush."

After Sam's departure, Caroline offered Jackson a sheepish smile. "I got carried away. I'm sorry. Enough about me. Tell me about your plans. Maisy tells me you and your cousins are opening a B and B?"

"Yep. Kinda hard for me to believe because I'm definitely not the B and B type. Not that I'll have much to

"That's not a surprise. Nobody is gonna be as good as Celeste. But Celeste trained her. Celeste thinks she'll do a fine job." After a moment's pause, Boone added, "Eventually."

"And there you have it." Boone buttoned his pants and reached for the T-shirt. "I'm a little worried. How long is Celeste scheduled to be here?"

"She said she'd give us until the Fourth of July. At this point, Angel's Rest pretty much runs itself, so she doesn't need to be here. But the Fourth is a big deal in Eternity Springs. She wants to be home for it."

"So she'll get us through our soft opening. That's a relief."

"What's the problem with Angelica?"

Jackson considered. "I don't know. It's hard to put your finger on. You know how Celeste is like the awesome grandmother? She does the whole-milk-and-cookies-warm-from-the-oven thing? She wears an apron, but she's still cool? She's everybody's favorite?"

"Whole or skim?"

"What?"

"Never mind."

Jackson rolled his eyes as he pulled on the shirt and continued. "Well, Angelica is the polar opposite of apron grandma. She dresses like a cross between a gypsy and an aging hippie. And she acts like . . . well . . . I don't know if she's Lucy from *I Love Lucy* or that grumpy cartoon old lady—the smart-ass one—"

"Maxine?"

"Yeah. That's her name."

"I see."

"Do you? Though I can tell she's trying to suppress her inner Maxine, it does escape."

"Have you discussed your concerns with her?"

"In a general way. She hasn't actually done anything

yet. I just don't know that she has the temperament to be an innkeeper. I mean, I offer the tiniest bit of criticism and she tells me to lighten up, buttercup. Boone, did you know that she's recently done time in prison?"

"More a Club Fed than prison. It's unfortunate and shouldn't have happened—basically a good intention gone south big time—and her sentence was only for two weeks to set an example. She violated parole. But she's put it behind her and promised to turn over a new leaf in Texas."

Jackson sighed.

Boone suggested. "Look, why don't you talk over your concerns with Celeste. See what she has to say."

"I've tried! She seems to be listening to me. She smiles and pats my arm and then somehow the conversation goes off track, and before I know it I'm okaying a change in wall color for the Sundance suite."

"That's our Celeste," Boone agreed.

"So what do we do about it? From everything I've read since we decided to do this thing, an innkeeper can make or break an enterprise."

"Okay, here's the deal. We need to trust Celeste. If she says that Angelica is the right person for us, then it's true."

"I dunno. Every family has their problem child. I'm afraid she might be dumping her own problem onto us."

"Look. You haven't seen Celeste in action. You can ask anyone in Eternity Springs. The woman is uncanny. You have to believe me on this one, Jackson. If Celeste says Angelica's right for us, then she's right."

"Okay. But if it goes south, don't say I didn't warn you."

They covered a couple of more issues as Jackson picked up his damp towel and hung it on the towel hook. While his cousin yammered in his ear, he stared at his reflection in the bathroom mirror. Damn five-o'clock shadow. Maybe he should shave. Should he shave?

This isn't a date.

Annoyed with himself, Jackson sat on his bed and pulled on his socks and boots. "Wrap it up, Boone," he said. "I'm losing interest."

"Bite me," his cousin fired back. Following a moment's hesitation, he asked, "You doing okay today, Jackson?"

The question hit him like a fist. He closed his eyes and clenched his teeth. He'd worked like a dog and filled every minute of the day in an effort to keep his thoughts away from the significance of the date. "I'm fine. Talk to you tomorrow, Boone."

The called ended and he stood for a long moment awash in despair. He was tempted . . . oh, so tempted . . . to call and beg for one act of mercy, one conversation, one opportunity to speak to his little girl. He ached to wish her Happy Birthday.

"Can't do it," he muttered. "Do not do it." His lawyers had assured him that even one single ding against the court order would provide ammunition to his ex for their next custody battle.

Jackson closed his eyes and sucked in a deep breath as he mentally worked to shore up his defenses. Tuck it away. Think of something else. Think about the afternoon and Caroline and her song.

See that girl.

This wasn't a date. It was a Hail Mary. Caroline Carruthers had inspired him once before. He was superstitious enough to believe that she might do it again. If the stars aligned after spending some one-on-one time with her today, maybe he'd finally be able to finish her song. What he had of it was good, but it needed another verse or two. Once he got a single good song beneath his belt, surely this mental block of his would dissipate.

He missed his music. He wanted it back. This wasn't a date, it was . . . therapy.

In a burst of optimism, Jackson slipped the harmonica into his pocket, and then took one last look around the trailer. He spotted a paper towel on the floor, scooped it up, and arced a perfect throw into the trash can. He checked the fridge. Steaks and salad ready. Potatoes washed and wrapped in foil. Everything was good to—oh, wait. The dishwasher. He'd meant to unload the dishwasher in order to facilitate cleanup.

He tackled the task and five minutes later, exited the trailer and climbed into his truck. He took the new road they'd had built out of the canyon. It wasn't as scenic as the original one, but it was wider and safer with half as many switchbacks. It cut the time of the trip into town by a third, and he rolled in five minutes before the hour.

A parking spot opened up in front of her building right as he approached. Jackson whipped into the space, shifted into park, and turned off his engine. He wasn't the sort of man who bothered glancing into a mirror after he finished his morning shave. Nevertheless before reaching for the door latch, he flipped down the sun visor and checked his reflection.

Then Jackson climbed down from his truck and headed for the door where a new sign hung. "The Next Chapter," he read aloud. "I like it."

Moments later, Caroline Carruthers answered his rap on the door wearing snake boots and a smile. And so began the date that wasn't a date.

Chapter Eight

"Good afternoon, Jackson. Come on in."

He stepped into the building and took a curious look around. A half-dozen pieces of sheetrock stood against one wall with lumber stacked beside sawhorses and power tools. A pile of PVC pipe and plumbing parts filled one corner, and the acrid scent of paint thinner hung in the air. Considering how he'd spent much of the past year, Jackson felt right at home.

He turned in a slow circle. "This is a good space."

"It will be." Caroline braced her hands on her hips and mimicked his motion. "We still have a lot of work to do. I had hoped to be a little further along by now, but unfortunately"—her eyes twinkled as she gave an exaggerated sigh—"my plumber is running behind. Apparently he had a callback to a previous job."

Jackson's grin was unabashed. "Hey, it's not my fault that he screwed up his parts order."

"But the job I need him to do is tiny compared to yours! If you'd loan him to me . . ."

"Can't do it. It's a dog-eat-dog world in the Texas Hill Country, Mrs. Carruthers. When it comes to contractors, it's every man for himself."

She shrugged. "Can't blame a girl for trying."

"Never. Those Bambi eyes of yours might have worked, too, if I didn't have our soft opening coming at me like a freight train."

She gave him a look of surprise. "Bambi eyes?"

"Big, beautiful, and soulful. Surely you've heard that before."

"No. No, I haven't."

She tilted her head and studied him, and Jackson began to feel like a bug on a microscope slide. In an effort to change the subject, he made a sweeping gesture around the room. "Will you show me your vision of your shop, Caroline? I'm interested."

"Sure. I love to talk about The Next Chapter."

"Great name, by the way."

"Thank you. It feels appropriate." She led the way toward a desk at the back of the space. "I have a 3-D rendering on my computer. Let me pull it up."

They spent the next few minutes discussing her plans, and she asked his advice about a couple of ideas she'd been debating. "I know it's not original to this building, but I don't think I really care."

"Don't let our new friend Henry the historian hear you say that," Jackson cautioned.

"I know. He's a stickler for historical accuracy, but I think a tin ceiling like the one in your saloon would add a lot of character and atmosphere. Besides, I like them. I don't need a reason beyond that, do I? This will be a bookstore, not a museum."

"Go for it. You don't need a reason. That's one of the nice things about being a boss. It's your shop. You get to decide."

"Unfortunately, I'm a ditherer. Decision making has never been my strong suit. I can whittle it down to two or three options, but when it comes time to make the final choice, I waffle. I've always needed a sounding board, someone to give me a kick in the pants when I need one." Her smile turned reflective and a little sad. "I still have trouble believing I actually pulled the trigger on this move and career change, and that I did it all by my little lonesome."

Her little lonesome. Jackson studied her and wished he knew her better. The elephant in the bookstore was taking up half the space. Should he bring it up or leave it . . . well . . . buried? Was Caroline the sort of person who would like to talk about her husband or did she want to put the past behind her and move on? Jackson was the move-on type, but women were different.

Very different. *Might as well just ask.* "I take it your husband served as the pants kicker?"

"Yes. Well, actually, I take that back. Usually, he made the choice for me." Her gaze flicked up to meet his. "He was a take-charge kind of guy. He liked to take care of me."

Huh. Caroline didn't strike Jackson as being the little-woman type who needed a man to take care of her. He wondered if he gave his thoughts away when her next words addressed exactly that.

"Not very modern of me, I admit, but I was young when we got together, and he was older and experienced and smart. Robert was an extremely intelligent man." She hesitated a moment and added, "Alzheimer's was a brutal diagnosis for him. He tried so hard to be strong for me, but on days when he was feeling low . . . more than once I heard him say maybe he'd get lucky and get run over by a bus. Well, he got lucky."

She gave her head a shake and said, "I'm sorry. I shouldn't yammer on about that."

"Hey, feel free to yammer. It's not healthy to bottle stuff up inside."

"It's been almost a year."

"So what? Nobody gets to decide how long somebody else gets to grieve. If you need to talk, I want to listen. That's what friends do."

"Not all friends," she replied with a wry note to her voice. "I have it on good authority that too much wallowing in the past is boring."

Jackson frowned. "You need better friends, Caroline."

"Yes. Yes, I do."

The woeful expression on her face tugged at his heart. He reached out, took hold of her hand, and gave it a supportive squeeze. "Don't let anyone tell you how to mourn. That's about as personal a thing as we have to deal with in life."

"Thank you," she said softly. Then she drew a deep breath, lifted her chin, and changed the topic. "I'm excited to see the ghost town. I'm coming prepared." She lifted a foot and pointed toward her obviously new snake boots.

Jackson grinned. "Good girl. So, are you ready for Ruin?"

"I am. Mind if I bring my camera bag along?"

"Not at all."

In Jackson's pickup during the drive to the canyon, she asked about his cousins. "Boone is doing fine for someone who is burrowed away in a Rocky Mountain snowdrift. Don't get me wrong. I like Eternity Springs a lot. But they had an unusually long winter this year, and I'm just not much of a snowbird. Give me heat over the white fluffy stuff any day."

"I'm with you. Austin gets a trace of snow once or twice a year, and that suits me just fine. And Tucker? What is he up to?"

Jackson pursed his lips. "We don't hear from him

much. I figure that's a good thing, considering that he's active duty military. No news is good news."

"I'm glad to hear it." She waited until he navigated a sharp turn on the narrow road they traveled before asking, "Do you have other cousins? Any siblings? Are your parents and grandparents still around?"

He gave her a recap of his family—no siblings and he'd lost both his parents within the past three years. He had various aunts and uncles and one surviving grandmother.

He remembered that she'd denied having any family beyond the sister-in-law during that drive to Austin, so he asked about another sort of family. "What about pets? Are you a cat lady? Dog person? Fish aficionado?"

"No, no pets. Yet. I've been thinking about getting a dog, but I want to get settled first."

"Oh, yeah? What kind of dog to you want?"

"I'm not sure. Something small. What about you? Do you have a pet?"

"No, I don't, although I've been thinking about getting a dog, myself. Not a little ankle-biter type though. I want a real dog, something with some size like a bird dog or a boxer or a Lab. A friend of mine has a chocolate Lab who's a great dog."

Caroline wrinkled her nose. "Little dogs *are* real dogs."

They talked dog breeds for a bit before the conversation waned, and a comfortable silence fell between them that lasted until they passed a lump of roadkill that reminded him of a story he'd heard from one of the painters at the saloon.

"Did you hear about that skunk that came calling at the house behind your shop last night?"

"What do mean 'came calling'?"

"You've met Denise Sears? She owns the candy shop catercorner to you." Caroline shook her head, and Jackson continued. "Anyway, Denise has an old hound dog named Barney who has taken to waking her to go out in the middle of the night. Last night she put the dog out and a few minutes later saw him hauling tail toward the door. She opened it, Barney darted past her, and before the stink made it to her nose, the skunk actually chased the hound inside. Barney knocked over a lamp and broke it, then threw up on her carpet. The skunk ended up under her bed."

Caroline covered her mouth with her hand and groaned. "That's horrible. Although, now that you mention it, I did notice a skunky smell when I went for my run this morning."

"It gets worse," Jackson said as they approached the canyon turnoff. "Denise has sense, so she hurried to open the sliding glass door in her bedroom in order to give the skunk a path of escape. Then she went out the front door to wait him out, but all the noise woke her brother-in-law who was asleep in the guest room— wearing only his tighty-whities. He's about five ten, weighs at least two fifty, and doesn't have the sense God gave a goat. He grabbed a broom and went down on his hands and knees and tried to shoo the skunk out from beneath the bed."

"He didn't!"

Jackson smirked. "The skunk unloaded everything he had before he finally wandered out of the house half an hour later. Denise is gonna have to replace most everything she owns."

"That's terrible. I wonder if her homeowner's insurance would cover something like that?"

"Haven't a clue," Jackson replied.

They rode for a few moments in silence until a giggle escaped her. "I'm sorry. I do feel so sorry for the woman. It's just that the visual you painted . . ." Caroline gave her head a shake. "You are an excellent storyteller, Jackson."

"I used to be." *Time for another change in subject.* "Look off to the right. The sunflowers and lavender fields are in bloom."

"Oh, wow. That's so gorgeous. What a fabulous backdrop for your B and B. Except, this isn't the same road that Maisy and I took, is it?"

"No." He told her about their decision to build a private road into the canyon.

"Whoa. Let me try to make sense of this. You built a road in Texas. And, finished it in less than five years? In Texas?"

"Well, I didn't do it personally . . ." Jackson laughed when she gave him a chiding look. "Although, I did run the Bobcat a lot because it's fun. Boone and I had a bet, and I wasn't going to lose. Actually brought the job in two days ahead of deadline."

"Congratulations. It's a nice smooth road."

"Thank you. I will own up to a handful of potholes, however."

"Are you in charge of the flowers, too?" she asked, nodding toward the sunflower field.

"The sunflowers, yes. We planted them with dove season in mind. The lavender fields were established by one of the farmers who owned land in the canyon years ago. A little TLC has done those plants a world of good."

"I hope you've had someone out to take photographs."

"We have. Boone has a friend who owns and operates a resort in Colorado, and she's here helping us get ready to open. She brought in a photographer earlier this week. If you want, after we finish at Ruin we could stop by the inn and dance hall, and you can see the changes we've made."

"I'd like that."

Caroline gazed around with interest as they traveled the canyon road. She laughed softly when she spied the first of the signposts they'd installed: Beware, You Are Traveling the Road to Ruin.

"The next one says Drive Friendly on the Road to Ruin," Jackson said.

"Cute."

"It was Tucker's idea. Our families often vacationed together when we were kids—usually in Colorado. The drive between Fort Worth and the mountains is never-ending, the stretch between Wichita Falls and Amarillo boring as dry white toast. You're probably too young to remember, but these were the days before cars had video on demand."

"Too young? I don't know whether to be flattered or insulted."

He took his gaze off the road long enough to flash her a roguish grin. She rolled her eyes and asked, "What do your signposts have to do with a boring drive across Texas?"

"Between Childress and Clarendon there were a series of billboards that advertised a roadside convenience store. One sign would dangle pecan logs, another frozen slushes, the next one clean restrooms—you get the drift. One year we counted twenty-five of them. By the time you got to the one-thousand-yards sign, then the one-hundred-yards sign, no way was a parent gonna get past it without stopping. Getting out without buying some sort of souvenir was next to impossible, too." He paused, and then wistfully recounted, "I really liked those pecan rolls. I still have my plastic squeaking alligator. Remind me to show it to you later."

"A squeaking alligator?"

"I think it was probably a dog toy, but I loved it. Was great for scaring my mom and aunts and the girl cousins. Good times."

She laughed freely and the sound made Jackson grin all the way to Ruin.

As Caroline stepped down out of Jackson's truck and onto the road at Ruin, she said, "How cool is this? I feel like I should be wearing a prairie dress and a bonnet."

"I know. It's all I can do not to strap on a gun belt and a six-shooter every time I come here."

"Do you own a six-shooter?"

"I might have purchased a non-firing replica Colt. And a holster and gun belt. And a black hat."

The gleam in his eyes amused her. "A black hat?"

"Ruin *was* an outlaw hideout. I'm talking stagecoach and train and bank robbers. Murderers, cutthroats, cattle rustlers. Black hats. No white hats allowed. Although, in a spirit of transparency, Boone's mother did send me a sheriff's badge."

"So there's a new sheriff in town," she said as she gazed around at Ruin. "Wow, this really is straight out of a movie, isn't it?"

The dilapidated buildings that backed up to the tall canyon wall had the false façades, tin-roof overhangs, and hitching posts typical of structures in the Old West. A barn and the remains of a corral stood apart from the rest of the structures at one end of the town. A building made of stone anchored the opposite end.

"So what were these buildings used for?"

Jackson began pointing from the left. "Bunkhouse,

there's a stove in that one so we figure it was probably a cook shack and saloon, another bunkhouse, a store of sorts, a smithy, and the stone building was a jail."

"A jail! In an outlaw town?"

"Well, it has bars on the window and door, so that's what we think it must have been. Imagine what a bad hombre you had to be to end up in a jail in Ruin."

"That's just scary. Or, maybe it was for bounty hunters or Texas Rangers who tracked them down."

"Could be. Except I imagine they'd just shoot those guys. But who knows? Ruin could have had its own lawman and trials, judge, juries. We don't know. We've found very little historical information on the place. I keep hoping that we will discover that Butch Cassidy or Billy the Kid holed up here."

"That would be cool."

"A great tourist hook, most definitely. However, reality is probably a lot more boring. Remember that this place had two lives, the first being when the original settlers attempted to establish a town and the second when outlaws took it over and renamed it Ruin. So, are you ready to go exploring?"

"Lead the way, sheriff. However, I have to ask. What are the chances I'll be glad I'm wearing these boots?"

"Ah, don't worry. I haven't seen a snake all month."

"All month?" she repeated with a bit of a squeak in her voice. "Jackson, it's only the third."

"Oh, really? I thought it was the fourth." He laughed and grabbed hold of her hand and pulled her toward the smithy. "Let's start at the smithy. I think it's the coolest thing out here."

Caroline was taken aback by the handholding. The last time anyone had held her hand was . . . well . . . longer than she could recall. Unless . . . had he held her hand during that god-awful drive from Redemption to

Austin last spring? She thought she had a vague memory of it, but she couldn't be sure. That day had become a blur.

But that was then and this was now, and now felt a little . . . personal. He'd squeezed her hand on the way out here, too. Yet, neither one of the instances had struck her as being a come-on. Maybe the man was just a toucher.

"Careful," Jackson warned as he guided her around a low-growing cactus and then safely over the sharp edges of a rusted iron bar.

Okay, so maybe he wasn't acting too personal. Maybe he was simply being a gentleman. Old-fashioned manners. Maybe this was no different from a gentleman offering his arm to a lady in escort. Some men still did that. Robert used to do that. Why was she even questioning it?

Because she noticed, that's why. Because his actions made her feel . . . something.

Something.

Sexual awareness.

She looked up at him and found him staring back at her. Their gazes met and held, and that something sizzled between them.

Whoa. She hadn't felt "something" in a very, very long time, and she didn't know how she felt about feeling it now. Caroline moved to tug her hand free just as Jackson dropped it. "Oops, I forgot to grab my camera bag. Be right back."

Technically, she didn't run away from him, although she didn't drag her feet on the way to the truck, either. Her cheeks were warm with the flush of her embarrassment and if there'd been a crack in the earth between her and his truck she'd gladly have run straight into it.

Why now? Why had her hormones picked now to flicker back to life? Why now and why with Jackson McBride? Sure the man was drop-dead gorgeous with shoulders that stretched from Dallas to El Paso and a voice as smooth as angel tears, but he'd never flirted with her, never said or done a single suggestive thing.

Until now.

No. Hold on. Be fair. He hadn't done anything suggestive. If anything, the suggestive shoe was on her own foot. Or at least they had on simultaneous suggestive shoes. Maybe her hormone flare had emitted a scent that attracted his attention.

Or, maybe she'd imagined it. Maybe she'd seen something that wasn't even there. Surely that was it. She'd been so overwhelmed by her own pheromones that she'd imagined the heat sizzling between the two of them.

Okay, then. Reassured by her conclusion, Caroline relaxed as she reached the truck, opened the passenger door, and grabbed her camera bag from the floorboard. She slipped the strap over her shoulder, pasted a pleasant smile on her face, turned, and headed back toward the buildings of Ruin where Jackson waited. *Please, let me pull this off. Please let things remain natural between us.*

Jackson was hunkered down beside a bench made of two stumps and a board, staring at the edge. Oh, good. She had something she could say to him. Brightly, she inquired, "What do you see?"

"Initials carved into the wood. Haven't noticed this before."

"Not BTK, are they?"

"For Billy the Kid?" Jackson flashed a grin as he rose to his feet. "Unfortunately, no. Not BC for Butch Cassidy, either. They're a T and an M. I'm trying to recall if Tucker hung around here when he visited. When we were kids, he was always carving his initials in something."

Nothing in his manner suggested that they'd so recently exchanged a sexually heated look. She must have imagined it or else it had been all one sided. Good. That was good. Things wouldn't be awkward between them the rest of the afternoon.

"Come see this, Caroline," he said, waving her inside.

As she stepped into a twelve-foot-by-twelve-foot room with windows on each wall and a chunk of the roof fallen in, a large black buzzard fluttered his wings and lifted off from a rafter, disappearing through the hole in the roof. Near the center of the structure, a huge iron anvil sat on a stump. Next to it something that looked like a birdbath on four legs with a wheel attached lay on its side, green weeds growing up around it. Half a dozen tools hung on pegs in the wall, including various sizes of pliers and tongs, a mallet, and something with an iron point on it, the name of which or purpose for it Caroline didn't know.

"That's a portable forge," Jackson explained, gesturing toward the item on its side. "At one time it had a wooden handle that the smithy would use to pump air to keep the coals glowing."

"That's cool. Imagine how hot it must have been in here during the summertime when the fire was burning."

"I've always wondered how anyone managed to live in Texas before air-conditioning."

"Pioneers were a hardy stock."

After exploring the blacksmith's shop, they wandered through the rest of the ghost town. Caroline was beyond grateful that the only wildlife they encountered was a jackrabbit they stirred from beneath a bed frame in one of the bunkhouses. She took dozens of photographs and even managed to cajole Jackson into posing for two of them, though he refused to allow her to shoot his face. Quintessential cowboy, she thought, as she framed him in her viewfinder. So sexy.

Whoa. There they go again. Down hormones, down!

"Well, that's about it," Jackson said. "The grand tour of Ruin."

"I'm happy I got to see it. Thank you so much, Jackson."

"You're very welcome. So, what next? Do you still want to stop by the inn or are you ready for that steak I promised you?"

"I'd like to see the inn."

"Sounds like a plan."

On the ride along the road to Redemption, she spied another series of signposts advertising Fallen Angel Inn and the Last Chance Saloon and Dance Hall. "Why Fallen Angel?" Caroline asked.

"Cheesy, I know. But it was a brothel once upon a time, and the innkeeper who is helping us get the place up and running has a thing for angels. I voted for Angel Falls because when we have a hard rain, there's a waterfall on the canyon wall behind the house. Tucker and Boone sided with Celeste. She's the innkeeper I mentioned."

"Well, I like it and the logo is cute. The bent halo is memorable."

"That's what Boone says. Like I mentioned before, I'm along for the ride where decision making for the inn is concerned."

"So when do you open your dance hall?"

"We'll have our first show the weekend of the inn's soft opening. That's in six weeks."

"That's awesome. I'll be there. Did you know I won the Chamber of Commerce Enchanted Weekend drawing?"

"No, I didn't know that. Well, good. I'm glad to hear that there will be someone there I know. I think almost all our other visitors are friends of Boone's from Colorado."

"I was excited to win. The certificate I received promises pampering, and I'm a sucker for that."

"Well, fair warning. They're still working some of the kinks out. Pampering may be the goal, but I'm not positive they'll pull it off."

"That's the purpose of a soft opening, isn't it? To be a practice run for the grand opening and identify problems that need to be addressed before the big event? When is your grand opening?"

"Fourth of July weekend. And you're right. We do need at least one dry run. We're doing a big benefit show for a veterans charity Tucker supports to kick things off. We'll have some high-profile guests for that weekend who will bring in a crowd."

"Who is your headliner?"

He glanced over at her. "Can you keep a secret?"

"Absolutely!"

"We haven't announced it yet or put tickets on sale because we're waiting for our star to get home and sign the contract. He's been in Nepal climbing mountains on vacation. We hope to have everything wrapped up by Friday, though."

He told her the name. Caroline wasn't well versed in the Texas country music scene, but even she recognized the singer. "Wow. That's exciting. You'll have a huge crowd for that show even with the short notice. You'll let me know when I can buy tickets?"

"I sure will. We'll be working with Maisy and the Chamber, too, to set up some things in town to piggyback onto our event. We're hoping to raise some serious jack for Tucker's cause."

They drove in comfortable silence for the next few minutes. Caroline began to wonder if she'd imagined the charged moment between them earlier. Nothing he'd said or done since suggested anything suggestive. Maybe she'd dreamed the whole thing up.

Well, except for her own hormone flare. *That* she definitely had not imagined. The after-bursts she continued to experience proved that.

He smelled good. Something he wore had an appealing woodsy, masculine scent, and she'd noticed it. When was the last time she'd noticed the scent of a man? She hadn't a clue.

Caroline glanced at him. He noticed and returned the glance, adding a smile. That action drew her gaze to his mouth. Wonder what he'd taste . . . whoa. She jerked her head around and stared straight ahead. *Down hormones. Down!*

Moments later, he took a curve in the road that provided her the perfect distraction. "Oh, wow. The flower fields are even more spectacular from this direction. What a gorgeous setting for the inn. Would you mind stopping? I'd like to snap a few shots."

"Glad to."

He pulled onto the shoulder, and Caroline hopped out with her camera. "Don't get out with me. I'll just be a moment."

"No rush." Jackson switched off the ignition.

She took a dozen or so shots, and then switched out her lens in an effort to get a closer shot of the Fallen Angel Inn. As she peered through the viewfinder, she saw two figures step from inside the house onto the wide front porch. One of them carried a glass pitcher filled with what appeared to be lemonade and looked familiar. Caroline tried to place her. She'd met so many people since moving to Redemption.

She shifted her attention to the other woman, who held a tray filled with four glasses and a plate of cookies. She appeared to be close in age to the first, somewhere north of seventy, Caroline guessed. Both women were slender. Both were smiling, but that's where the similarity ended. The one who seemed familiar to Caroline wore her silver hair short and bobbed. The other's hair was waist long and fire-engine red. The silver-haired woman was dressed in a simple and stylish yellow sheath with matching flats. Her companion sported a bohemian look in a flowing ankle-length patterned skirt in shades of purple and gold, a white peasant blouse with embroidery on the trim, and gypsy sandals.

Caroline focused her lens and studied them more closely. What interesting faces. They were related somehow, she'd guess. Same high defined cheekbones and brilliant blue eyes. Caroline saw the classy woman say something. The bohemian gave an exaggerated roll of her eyes and responded. Classy set her mouth into a stern line.

Yes, probably sisters. Caroline snapped a few more pictures, and then returned to the truck. "Someone is waiting on the porch with cookies."

"I warned Celeste that we might stop by. She's our innkeeper guru. You'll love her."

"Celeste!" Caroline snapped her fingers. "I remember now. Is her name Celeste Blessing?"

"You know her?"

"She's the reason I visited Redemption the first time." Caroline told him about meeting Celeste outside of Robert's memory care facility. "That's how I came to be writing that travel article when I met you."

"That was Celeste? Seriously?"

"Yes. Her twisted ankle changed my life."

"Whoa. That's sort of spooky. Although . . ." Jackson shrugged. "Boone says that's how she is."

"There's another woman with her. A sister?"

Jackson gave a small sigh and his expression grew pained. "No. A cousin. Angelica. Celeste is training her. She'll be the Fallen Angel innkeeper."

"You don't look pleased about that."

"I'm sure she'll be fine," Jackson said, sounding as if he was trying to convince himself. "She just needs a little practice." Following a moment's pause, he added, "She does bake the best bread I've ever tasted. Cookies, too."

"That's a good skill for an innkeeper to have, I'd think."

"True. That's true. We're going to serve fresh cookies every afternoon in the parlor, so cookies are important." He twisted the key and restarted the engine. "Well, let's go see what the Fallen Angel has in store for us today, shall we?"

Chapter Nine

As Jackson pulled into the drive, Celeste and Angelica both rose from their white wicker rockers and descended the front steps. Angelica opened the gate of the gleaming white picket fence, and then stood next to Celeste along the stone path that led to the front porch steps. Celeste's greeting rang out in her melodious voice, "Welcome to the Fallen Angel Inn!"

When Angelica failed to speak, Celeste gave her a prodding look. "Oh, yeah." Angelica mimicked her cousin's smile. "Where chunks of your heart are mended."

"Angelica!" Celeste scolded.

She grimaced. "Where pieces of your heart . . . um . . ."

Celeste sighed. "Where wounded hearts find peace. It's not that difficult, cousin!"

Angelica sniffed with disdain. "Maybe not difficult, but it is stupid. I don't know why we need a motto, anyway. Not everyone who stays with us is going to have a wounded heart. Happy people do exist in this world, you know."

She rolled her eyes at Caroline and added, "Come on up to the porch and have a cookie and lemonade, sweetheart. They'll make you happier than any old slogan. I make cookies so good they make your toes curl. Now, they're not as good as sex, but they're pretty darned close."

Celeste closed her eyes. "Angelica! Don't say something like that."

"Okay, you're right." She winked at Caroline. "They are better than *bad* sex."

Jackson muttered, "I really don't know if this is going to work."

Celeste ignored both her cousin and Jackson and focused on Caroline. "Why, you and I have met before, haven't we? You're Caroline Carruthers. You wrote that fabulous article about Redemption and you did it while your poor husband was in the hospital. Such a kind thing you did for me."

"It turned out to be a kindness for me," Caroline replied. "The note you sent when it was published touched my heart. You have a way with words."

Jackson observed, "Celeste has a way with just about everything."

Angelica slipped her arm through Caroline's and began walking her toward the house. "What he means is that Celeste has a way of sticking her nose into everything. So, you're a writer? I thought you might be the stained-glass artist here to repair the window after my little accident."

"Little!" Celeste protested. "I'd hate to see what you call big."

Jackson spoke up. "Caroline is opening a bookstore in Redemption. Caroline, meet our innkeeper, Angelica Blessing."

"A bookstore!" Celeste swooped up beside Caroline and took hold of her free arm. "Oh, I heard about this. You're calling it The Next Chapter, correct? I just love that name for a bookstore. So clever. Please do join us for refreshments. My cousin's questionable humor aside, she does bake heavenly cookies."

"Lemonade and cookies sound lovely. Thank you."

Jackson knew from recent experience that cookie breaks with the Blessing cousins could be a gauntlet of questions. Probably wouldn't hurt to give Caroline a word of warning first. "Caroline was with Maisy on the day we first visited the property. We stopped so I could show her all the improvements we've made. How about we do that first, and then sit a spell with y'all?"

"Want me to show you around?" Angelica asked.

"Now Angelica," Celeste chided. "Don't be a buttin-sky. Can't you see they are on a date?"

"No!" said Caroline.

Simultaneously, Jackson said, "No we're not." He added, "We're friends."

"I'm a widow. I don't date."

"I'm divorced. I *really don't* date."

Celeste and Angelica shared a look that Jackson couldn't read, and then Celeste said lightly, "Our mistake. You two go on and enjoy your tour. Angelica and I were just about to sit and discuss activities for our soft open-ing. A number of my friends from Eternity Springs are coming in for it, and we're planning some special events."

"I'll be one of your guests," Caroline shared. "I won the Chamber of Commerce drawing."

Celeste smiled widely and clapped her hands. "I am delighted. I think we're going to have a wonderful weekend."

Jackson said, "Boone told me he'll be here for it."

"Yes. It's such a shame that Tucker won't be able to join us. I do so hope I get the opportunity to meet him soon."

"So do I, Celeste," Jackson replied with fierce sincerity. That would mean his cousin had made it home, at least temporarily, safe and sound. "Now, if you ladies will excuse us, I'll show Caroline around."

"Show her the suites upstairs," Angelica suggested. "I believe the Chamber contest winner is assigned to the Edna Milton Suite."

"Angelica! This has been settled." Celeste smoothed away the scowl she'd directed toward her cousin and smiled serenely toward Caroline. "It's the Bluebonnet Suite. You'll be in the Bluebonnet Suite."

"It's right next door to the Etta Place Suite," Angelica called with a sharp edge to her voice.

"The Indian Paintbrush Suite!"

As Jackson led Caroline inside, the sound of the women's bickering followed them. "We are not naming our suites after infamous Texan prostitutes and that's final," Celeste declared.

"Well, neither are we using Texas wildflower names," Angelica fired back. "That's boring and mundane."

"And easily decorated!"

"I agreed to put angels all around the place, didn't I?" Angelica continued.

"After you broke their wings!"

"Wing. Singular."

"That's a step too far. The dented halo on our logo is enough!"

Caroline and Jackson's amused gazes met. His mouth twisted with a rueful grin as he said, "Why do the words 'cat fight' come to mind?"

She laughed aloud, and the sound vibrated through Jackson like the strum of a perfectly tuned guitar. Caroline asked, "What do *you* want to call the Fallen Angel suites?"

"Like I said, the dance hall is my baby. I'm staying

far, far away from this one. However, they need to come to a consensus PDQ. The decorator is chomping at the bit to order window treatments and knickknacks, and the opening is right around the corner."

Jackson decided to conduct his tour from the top down, so he led her to the suites on the attic level first. Caroline oohed over the size of each of the suites and aahed over all the bathrooms. "I covet those soaker tubs. I may need to call my contractor. Do you know how much lead time would be required for me to get my hands on one of them for my apartment?"

"It's possible . . . for the right price . . . I might just have a connection," he told her as he led her downstairs to tour the guest room on the second floor.

"Oh, yeah?" she asked with suspicion in her tone. "What price?"

"I am bribable with brownies."

"Oh, really?"

"Angelica doesn't make them." Jackson watched with contented pleasure as she inspected the suites, opening drawers and wardrobes and verandah doors. In the third suite, she shot him a knowing look. "Has Angelica not taken a good look at the fireplace mantles?"

"Noticed the wildflower carvings, did you? I don't know her well, but Boone tells me that it's useless to attempt to resist Celeste once she makes up her mind about something."

A grin flickered on Caroline's lips. "I doubt that Angelica agrees with that viewpoint. Have you taken a good look at the blades on the ceiling fan?"

Jackson glanced upward. He saw tulip-shaped frosted glass globes and gold scrollwork on dark wooden blades. "I don't . . . oh. Well now." The scrollwork wasn't a free-form decoration like he'd previously believed. He chuckled softly. "Broken angel wings. I hadn't noticed."

"The design is very pretty. It's subtle."

"I thought the mantles were sneaky, but the fan blades top those. I've been told never to bet against Celeste, but now I don't know. I'm beginning to think I may have been wrong about Angelica. I suspect there's more to her than we think."

"You do appear to be a man in the middle."

"Tell me about it," he groaned. "I think it'd be a good idea for me to make myself scarce around the Fallen Angel for the next week or so."

He led her downstairs to the ground floor, where they toured the large chef's kitchen, the dining room, and the enlarged parlor. Caroline was obviously impressed. "You've done a fabulous job, Jackson. It's as enchanting as the canyon."

"I agree it's a great place, but I take no credit for the house or the cottages in back."

"Cottages?"

Jackson nodded. "Celeste convinced us we should have a private honeymoon cottage. We decided we'd build it and three other freestanding suites that offer a little more privacy. That gives us an even dozen rooms. Want to see them?"

"I'd love to."

He led her out the back door and along the garden walk to an area made private by clever landscaping. Each of the three freestanding structures had a gabled tin roof, rough wood siding, and a covered front and back porch.

"How cute!" Caroline said when she spied the first.

"These three cottages are all two-bedrooms to make the Fallen Angel a little more family friendly," Jackson explained.

Each of the cottages had a fireplace, a king-sized bed, a small kitchenette with a sink and a small refrigerator, and a pair of fabulous rockers on both porches. The honeymoon cottage was a dream. When she walked inside she gasped aloud with delight. "Oh, wow. It's like stepping into a suite at the Four Seasons."

"I know. Celeste had very definite ideas about this place. Angelica nipped at her heels the entire time, too." He gave a little chuckle and added, "Once or twice the argument drifted to which of them had superior expertise when it came to honeymoon sex, and I had to cover my ears."

Caroline laughed. "I do believe I adore both Celeste and Angelica."

"They are a trip," he ruefully responded as he led her onto the back porch, pulling the door shut behind them. "A fun, interesting trip, but definitely a trip."

She marveled over the small in-ground pool and hot tub, the pots of flowers, burbling fountain, and double hammock. "What a romantic oasis!"

"That was the plan." He gestured toward an unobtrusive gate in the back corner of the fenced-in yard. "Ready to wander on over to the saloon?"

"Absolutely."

He guided her through the gate and along the stone path that meandered through what Celeste called a meditation garden—Angelica referred to the area as the pollen factory—before taking her into the saloon through traditional saloon front doors.

"Fabulous!" Caroline said. "You've added swinging doors."

"The building cried out for them," Jackson replied, preening a bit. He'd had more to do with the saloon remodel than he had with the inn.

Her brow furrowed. "I love them, but . . . how do you lock the building?"

"Pocket doors," he said, pointing them out.

"Ah." She moved farther into the building and made a slow circle, a faint smile on her face. "It's really nice, Jackson. You've kept all the charm and atmosphere, but made it warm and inviting and fun. Is that a player piano?"

"Yes. Want to hear?"

"I'd love that."

He crossed to where the piano stood against the north wall, explaining as he loaded a music roll and prepared it to play. "We'll serve breakfast and tea in the dining room next door, but this will be our restaurant for lunch and dinner and if Boone has his way, eventually our backup wedding venue for when the weather is bad."

"You're planning to host weddings?"

"Eventually. Boone and the Blessings think we should do it. Celeste says she does a bang-up bridal business at Angel's Rest, and we have a perfect spot beside the river for ceremonies. Boone believes the dance hall is a good place for a reception, but I don't agree. I say we put up another building to use for weddings and meetings and the like. We're still discussing it. It'll certainly be a Phase Two or Three type of thing."

"Hmm." Caroline replied noncommittally.

He closed his eyes. "I know. I know. I'll probably lose the battle. At least in the near term. But I have a vision for the dance hall, and I'm going to stick to my guns."

"I think you should. I also think I'd like to see your dance hall."

Jackson discovered he wanted to show it to her rather desperately. He'd imagined having Caroline Carruthers back in the dance hall again for months now.

They exited the saloon a few minutes later, and approached the Last Chance Hall. "After seeing the renovations of the other two buildings, this might not be what you're expecting," he warned as he climbed the front steps. He opened the hall's screen door, held it, and motioned for her to precede him. As she stepped past him, he caught a whiff of her perfume. Spicy and exotic. Sexy. A surprise. Not what he would have expected from her.

He would have pegged her for a floral, friendly, girl-next-door type of fragrance. Well, sure as hell wasn't the first time he'd been wrong where women were concerned.

She walked to the middle of the hall, stopped, and made a slow, full-circle turn. Once she'd finished, she shot him a look of confusion, then made another turn. Finally, she said, "Okay, I admit it. You've confounded me. Except for clean shiny windows and the absence of cobwebs, I don't see any changes."

"Excellent. That means I've succeeded." He launched into an explanation about updated wiring and various safety measures taken to bring the building up to code. "We stayed true to the history and heritage of the hall. For example, we didn't install air-conditioning."

"What?" Caroline gazed at him in shock. "Seriously?"

"Seriously."

"But . . . but . . . this is Texas! You *must* have air-conditioning. People will expect it. They need it! Shoot, there've been plenty of February days when I ran my air-conditioner."

"No air-conditioning at the Last Chance Hall. Not in its heyday and not now."

"But people *dance* at a dance hall. They sweat!"

"That's why they built the side-wall flaps. Besides, dancing yourself sweaty is all part of the fun."

"You have a peculiar concept of fun, Mr. McBride."

"You know you've just issued a challenge to me, don't you? I'm going to have to show you just how much fun you can have getting sweaty in a dance hall."

Just like that, the atmosphere in the building changed. It grew heavy, hot, and electrified, like the air in advance of a violent thunderstorm. Without making a conscious decision to do so, Jackson dropped his gaze to the fullness of her lips. He took an inadvertent step toward her. Caroline went still, her chin up, her spine straight, like a rabbit in a field upon sensing a predator.

Jackson wanted to kiss her. He wanted to close the distance between them and bury his fingers in that sassy, silky hair of hers and capture her lips with his. He wanted to explore her mouth with his tongue and discover the taste of her, the essence of her. He wanted . . . *Whoa. Whoa! Stop right there. What the hell is wrong with you?*

He tore his gaze away from her and focused on the stage, breaking the spell. To give his hands something to do rather than reach for her, he shoved them into his pockets, and his right hand found the harmonica. He grabbed hold of it like a lifeline, tugged it from his pocket, and said, "Look at this. We found it along with a gold watch and a journal in a box in the house next door that first time we visited. I kept the harmonica, Tucker went for the watch, and Boone snagged the journal. This thing is pretty darned old. I took it apart and cleaned everything. This was the first instrument I learned to play. My great-grandfather played. He was really good."

Then, because he was babbling and needed to stop, he brought the harmonica up to his mouth and blew a bluesy rift.

Caroline reached for the rescue line herself by observing, "An antique harmonica. How cool is that? Will you play something for me?"

Gladly. Anything for a distraction.

He launched into the first song that came to mind, "Isn't She Lovely," and played it through to the end. With the final notes still hanging in the air, he lowered the harp from his mouth and gave a beaming Caroline a sheepish smile.

"That was fabulous, Jackson," she said. "Simply fabulous. And not what I expected. I thought I'd hear 'Turkey in the Straw' or something like that."

The admiration in her gaze made him want to show off. "I can do 'Turkey in the Straw.'" He proved it by playing the chorus, then saying, "And then there's this."

He watched her closely as she identified the next song he played as a classical piece, and her delight made him feel ten feet tall. "That is the most beautiful song," she said. "I admit I don't know my composers. Is that Mozart? Schubert?"

"Bach. 'Jesu Joy of Man's Desiring.'"

"I've never heard classical music played on a harmonica. You're very talented, Jackson."

"Thank you." As he tucked the instrument back into his pocket, he realized just how much he'd enjoyed performing for her. It felt good. Really good. Better than it had in ages. Maybe tonight after dinner, he'd drag out his guitar.

The fact that he'd even considered it filled him with joy, and Jackson acted on instinct. This time, he actually did it.

He leaned down and kissed her.

Chapter Ten

Caroline's heart leapt as his lips touched hers. Her eyes closed. A part of her wanted to melt into him, to lose herself in the pleasure of a man's mouth . . . in this man's mouth . . . to sink into the heat and scent and sensation. The taste of him. She *liked* Jackson McBride. She liked his boyish grin and the wicked glint in his eyes. His kindness touched her, as did his obvious love for his cousins. His in-your-face masculinity attracted her like a spring-fed creek on a hot summer day. *It's been so long.*

Simultaneously, she experienced a stabbing sense of grief. Lonely. Alone. Hollow and aching and empty. Single. Widowed. Lonely. So lonely for so long.

His tongue slid across her lips and they parted. Shivers skidded along her nerves and she began to tremble. Began to respond. Caroline kissed him back. She kissed him back and the emptiness receded. *Jackson. Jackson.* He stepped closer. His arms stole around her waist and drew her against him. Drew her out of the loneliness. Her head fell back. She lifted her hands to his shoulders. Those broad, muscular shoulders.

Tears stung her eyes. So long. So long. She'd missed this. Oh, how she'd missed this.

She made a sound. A moan? A sob? She wasn't sure. But it was enough to catch Jackson's attention. His arms fell away from her and he lifted his head and stepped back. For a long, breathless moment, their gazes locked. His green eyes burned into hers.

She blinked. Once. Twice. She sensed the tear pool at the corner of her eye, swell, and spill.

Jackson winced as if it pained him. He lifted his hand and used the pad of his thumb to wipe away the wetness. His voice barely above a whisper, he said, "Caroline. Ah, Caroline. You break my heart. Don't cry. I'm sorry."

Don't be sorry. She wasn't sorry. "Sorry" wasn't the right word. "Sorrowful," perhaps.

He closed his eyes, gave his head the slightest of shakes, and took another step backward. "That was way out of line. Really. I apologize. I should explain, try to explain, anyway. It's the music."

The desire still humming through her veins made her thoughts sluggish. She licked her lips, tasted him, and then cleared her throat. "The music?"

"Yeah." He raked his fingers through his hair. "See . . . the way it has always worked for me—or, used to work for me, anyway—is that the music lived inside me. It was part of me. But when all the crap happened with my daughter, I had my 'American Pie' moment."

It was the first time he'd mentioned his daughter since the day they'd met. Hearing the continued pain in his voice cooled her blood. American pie? What did pie have to do with this?

Oh, wait. The fog finally cleared from her brain. He was a songwriter, and he was talking about music. A particular song. That old seventies ballad "American Pie." Caroline recalled the lyrics and finally made the connection. "Your music died."

He nodded. "Flatlined. Vaporized. Went silent as a

stone-cold grave. But you . . ." He hesitated. Looked away and shoved his hands into his pockets. "Playing for you just now was the first time in forever that I not only heard it, but I felt it again. It felt good, Caroline. Really, really good. And that revved me up, and so I, well, I got carried away."

Oh. Hmm. She wasn't sure whether she felt hurt or happy for him.

"I didn't intend . . . this wasn't what I . . . ah, well, I know this isn't a date."

The slight note of panic in his voice settled the question. Hurt. Was the idea of going on a date with her that awful?

Jackson continued to dig his hole deeper. "I'm really sorry. It's a line I shouldn't have crossed. A mixed message I shouldn't have sent. I'm not looking for a relationship, Caroline. At all. Well, except for friendship. I could use a friend. Actually, I'd very much like for you to be my friend, but I can't . . . I'm not . . ." He shut his eyes and murmured a curse beneath his breath. "I totally screwed this up, didn't I?"

Uh, yeah. Before she could formulate a response, a piano riff ringtone sounded from the back pocket of his jeans. He repeated the curse and reached for his phone, adding, "And I totally compound the screw-up. Sorry, Caroline. I meant to mute this before I picked you up. Actually, I meant to turn it off completely. The weeks before we brought cell service to Enchanted Canyon were awesome. I seriously considered keeping the canyon unplugged."

Caroline waved his apology away, glad to have a moment to collect herself. However, her moment lasted only seconds due to his reaction upon reading his screen.

Every drop of color drained from Jackson's complexion.

He looked as if he were carved from granite as he thumbed the green dot and lifted the phone to his ear and shot his words like bullets. "Is she okay?"

Caroline read the response he received in the visible relaxation of his body. Obviously, whoever "she" was meant the world to him.

"Hell, yes, I want to talk to her," he said into the phone after listening for a long moment. "Except for seeing her, there's nothing I'd like better. You know that. But why would you take the risk? If Sharon finds out, my ass will be grass and yours won't be in great shape, either."

The person on the other end of the phone responded and Jackson listened, rubbing the back of his neck with his free hand as he did so. Finally, he said, "Damn, Mary. I'd owe you big time."

Whatever she said in response had him closing his eyes. When he spoke, his tone was gruff. "Thank you. I appreciate that. It means a lot to me."

Caroline could pick up the sound of a feminine voice—Mary, she guessed—though she could not make out the words. Then, ignoring her curiosity and thinking to allow him privacy for his call, she stepped away, headed for the dance hall's front door. She'd taken only half a dozen steps before his hand snagged hers and held on, stopping her in her tracks.

"That's so sneaky that it just might work," Jackson said into his phone. "If Sharon hears about it, I guess I can follow her example and lie like a rug. What's good for the goose and all that." He paused another moment, listening, and then added, "Absolutely. Right now is great. Yes. Sure. Mary, thank you."

He disconnected the call, but didn't release Caroline's hand. If anything, his grip tightened. "That was Haley's nanny. They're going to call me. I'm going to talk to her.

My daughter. I haven't seen her since February. Talked to her since April fifth. But today is her birthday. She's in Europe and—" Jackson broke off abruptly when his phone rang again. His grip on Caroline's hand tightened like a vise when he connected the call and said, "Hello? Lovebug? Are you there?"

Raw pain etched across his face and his bittersweet smile bloomed. He closed his eyes. "Yes, Haley. It's Daddy. It's so good to hear your voice. I've missed you so much. Happy birthday, baby. Happy birthday."

The phone call lasted a little over six minutes. His grip on her hand never once loosened. Her heart ached when she heard him ask about Haley's lost teeth and her pet goldfish and her imaginary friend, Pickle Kumquat. It melted when she heard him softly sing a vaguely familiar tune about Daddy's little lovebug.

When one lonely tear spilled from the corner of his eye and trailed slowly down his cheek oblivious to his notice, Caroline's heart broke.

"'Lovebug' is my song," Haley said to Jackson. "You wrote it just for me."

"That's true. I did."

"It's a really pretty song. I love it. I never get to hear it anymore unless I sing it to myself. Mommy took it off my playlist."

Jackson's jaw tightened with about a million pounds of torque at that but he managed to keep his voice gentle as he asked, "Do you like to sing, Haley?"

"I do. Mommy says I'm a natural. Will you write another song for me, Daddy?"

"I would love to do that." He envisioned the mounds of crumpled balls of paper he'd created during the past year when he'd attempted to do exactly that.

In the way of six—no, now seven-year-olds—Haley

switched gears and started talking about a recent visit to an interactive children's museum. Jackson didn't interrupt the recital with questions. He was content to listen to her voice. The sound of it had matured during the past year, the timber wasn't pitched as high and she'd lost that childish lisp. She definitely sounded older.

". . . and the robot cow made burping sounds and it even tooted! But it didn't smell bad. I was glad it didn't smell bad. There was a big fly there, too, Daddy. And it talked about vomit."

She sounded so prissy and prim and disgusted about it that he couldn't help but laugh. "You didn't like learning about cow digestion and fly vomit?"

She paused and Jackson mentally pictured her little brow wrinkling in thoughtful consideration. After a long moment, she said, "Well, the cow was kind of funny, but I didn't like the fly. He was gross! There were these boys there, too, and they liked the fly. One of them pretended he was a fly and he ran around flapping his arms and pretending to vomit. He pretended to vomit on me, and Poppins got after him for it."

"Good for Poppins."

"I don't like boys. Are you going to give me a birthday present, Daddy?"

With that one innocent question, she cut him off at the knees. As he fumbled for an answer, Mary swooped in and saved the day. Even as she ruined it. "Coco is home."

The call disconnected abruptly. The silence was a knife to Jackson's heart.

He closed his eyes and sucked in a deep breath, fighting hard to cool the rage that had ignited inside him. He held his phone in a crushing grip and came within a hairsbreadth of throwing the damn thing against the wall. Only Caroline's quiet presence prevented him from surrendering to his temper. *Damn Sharon. Damn her to hell.*

"Jackson?" Caroline asked softly. "Is there anything I can do?"

He laughed bitterly. "Depends. Do you know a hit man?" When she widened her eyes, he added, "Just kidding."

He covered his eyes with his hand and wiped away the wetness pooling at the corners under the guise of massaging his temples. If he didn't get hold of himself, he was liable to start bawling like a baby. Like Haley used to do. Only Haley wasn't a baby anymore. She was seven years old. Seven! A first-grader. Homeschooled, or as Jackson thought of it, hotel-schooled, because Sharon continued to drag the child along on her tours.

That had been one of their fiercest arguments during the separation. The day they'd learned that Haley was on the way, Coco had promised him that they'd quit touring when their baby started kindergarten. Jackson had wanted a childhood like his own for their child. In the small town just west of Fort Worth where he'd grown up, neighbors had known one another and watched out for one another. It had been safe for Jackson and his friends to walk to school and ride bikes all over town without adult supervision. He'd had a happy, healthy, idyllic, normal childhood and he wanted that for his child.

A touring musician's lifestyle was anything but normal. Hayley's life was anything but normal. She spent months on end on the road and away from home. Her only playmates where ones somehow attached to people who were in one way or another were indebted to her mother, which created an abnormal balance of power in the playgroup. The only reason Haley wasn't already a spoiled princess brat was because she had a fabulous nanny, and she'd been born with a gentle heart. Kindness appeared to be hardwired into Haley. She'd need both of those qualities to survive being "Coco's Little Precious" with her character intact.

Cocoa's Little Precious. The tabloid name that her mother had encouraged made Jackson physically ill.

He was so angry. So consumed with rage. Without intentionally planning to do so, he voiced the question that continued to plague him to this day—despite the fact that he knew the answer. "How could the woman I fell for change so much?"

Though he didn't open his eyes, he sensed Caroline stepping toward him. Her arms slid around his waist. "Don't take this wrong. I'm a hugger. Is that okay?"

He smiled and embraced her, burying his face against her hair when she pillowed her head against his chest and began to croon soothing sounds. They stood that way for the better part of a minute and ever so softly, words whispered through his mind. *See that girl. Sweet heart. Learned to fight and now she's sharing what she knows.*

Then she spoke, and the tune in his head went *poof.*

"Do you want to talk about it?"

"No. Maybe. In a minute. Let me . . ." His voice trailed off. The word that came to mind was "wallow" but he wasn't going to say that to Caroline. It was one thing to have a pity party. Something else entirely to admit it. Bad enough that he was pretty sure she'd caught him in his dust-in-the-eyes moment.

Holding her . . . being held by her . . . felt good. It was a slather of aloe vera over the rawness in his soul, but her hugger observation aside, this moment probably came too soon after that inflammatory kiss for him to allow it to continue.

He sucked in a deep breath, drawing in the heady

scent of her, and he allowed himself a moment, just one moment, of indulgence. Then he exhaled heavily, dropped his arms, and stepped back. "Obviously, the call was from was my daughter, and today is her birthday. It's always hard to be away from her, but on a day like today it's the hardest damn thing."

"I'm so sorry, Jackson. I know what it's like to lose a loved one, but to be separated from your child in this way." She shook her head. "It's just horrible."

"It sucks. It's like I've lost one of my limbs and the phantom pain never leaves." He raked his fingers through his hair and added, "And, I feel like a heel for having whined about this to you. Your husband passed away. Compared to you, I'm lucky. Haley is celebrating a birthday today."

"Don't compare," she chided. "My situation doesn't diminish your loss. She's your child and today's her birthday and you aren't with her. It's okay to grieve, Jackson."

"'Grieve' isn't the right word. You're grieving. I'm . . ." His voice trailed off as he searched for the right word.

"Devastated? Shattered?"

"Pissed as hell. I'm pissed and I'm embarrassed and I'm ashamed that I was stupid enough to ignore the red flags where Sharon was concerned. There were plenty of them. Boone never liked her. Tucker cooled on her before I ever popped the question. She never got along with my mother. Never tried. I turned a blind eye to all of that because . . ." He didn't finish the sentence. He didn't want to admit how easily he'd been seduced.

Caroline waited for him to finish, and when he didn't, she observed. "She's a beautiful woman."

He gave his head a dismissive shake. Even before Sharon's words and actions revealed her inner ugliness,

Jackson had never considered her beautiful. She was attractive, yes, but her looks weren't what made him notice her. That voice of hers had been what drew him into the outdoor patio bar in the Fort Worth Stockyards the Sunday afternoon they'd met.

She'd been a hairdresser who moonlighted on weekends playing acoustic guitar and singing for tips. He'd been on the hunt for breakfast burritos, having just rolled out of bed following a late night at Billy Bob's Texas as a member of the band who'd opened for Jerry Jeff Walker, a man whom Jackson considered to be one of the greatest Texas songwriters of all time. Sharon had been crooning a Patsy Cline song when he'd followed the sound of her voice. That's what had seduced him. Her voice.

"She's had a lot of enhancements since we met. Not much of anything about her these days is original equipment, and even with all the work, she's not nearly as beautiful as you are, Caroline. It's that voice. I fell for her voice. It's honey with a touch of smoke that lingers in the air like morning dew. As much as I despise the woman today, when she sings, it's magical."

In a lighter tone of voice, Caroline said, "I don't believe you intended the compliment you gave me. Nevertheless, I thank you. It's been a long time since a man told me I was beautiful."

He turned a keen look her direction. Caroline's observation was just what he'd needed to drag his mind away from the ugly to the lovely. He suspected that had been her intention. "I like to think that I've always been an honest person, but the events of the past five years have made me a stickler about it. I don't lie, Caroline. You *are* beautiful, and I'm happy to tell you so whenever you'd care to hear it." Following a moment's pause, he added, "If you promise not to consider it a come-on."

"I promise. Now, tell me more about your little girl, Jackson. Do you have a picture of her?"

"Only about a million. Want to see?"

Her eyes twinkled. "Maybe not a million, but I'm up for a couple of hundred."

"Let's find a place to sit." He glanced around. He hadn't brought in any chairs yet, so the stage provided the only place to sit. "No chairs in here. How about we adjourn to one of the porch swings next door? That lemonade Celeste mentioned is starting to call my name."

"Lead the way."

He escorted her through the backstage door and took the long way around, which took her past the pool. Upon seeing it, Caroline stopped in her tracks. "How gorgeous! The pool looks so inviting. I can't believe y'all have accomplished so much in such a short amount of time. My experience with the construction industry is that things seldom get finished on time. You've pulled off a miracle."

"Things just came together. We only lost a handful of days to weather, and the suppliers came through. Our contractor said he's never had a job go so smoothly. The pool company even finished ahead of schedule, which is unheard of in this part of the world."

"It's a fantastic pool. Such a creative design. If I didn't know better, I'd think it was natural. You recreated the swimming hole, didn't you? Complete with a waterfall."

"Yep. We decided to keep the section of land that the waterfall is on private. It was Tucker's idea to recreate it here."

"There's nothing more inviting than a swimming hole on a hot summer day in Texas."

"That's the truth."

They climbed onto the porch by way of the side steps

and walked around to the front only to halt abruptly. Celeste and Angelica stood faced off and arguing in fierce whispers, Celeste with her hands braced on her hips, Angelica with her arms folded and her chin lifted mulishly.

For a long moment, the two women's angry gazes remained locked. Angelica slowly arched a challenging brow. "Fine!" Celeste flung up her hands and turned on her heels in a huff. "It's your funeral."

"It certainly is!" Angelica fired back.

Celeste spied Jackson and Caroline, and her cheeks flushed with embarrassment. "Oh, dear. I apologize that you had to see that."

"See what?" Jackson asked, as innocent as an angel. "Did you see anything, Caroline?"

"Not a thing."

He winked at Celeste and continued, "May we take you up on that lemonade offer now?"

"Certainly."

"I'll bring cookies," Angelica added.

"I'm counting on it. We're going to sit in the west side swing for a spell."

It was Jackson's favorite spot at the inn due to its fabulous view of the sunset. Painted a creamy white and hanging by metal chains, the wooden porch swing sported a thick yellow cushion. Jackson gestured for Caroline to take a seat, and then pulled his phone from his pocket before taking a seat beside her. "Want to start with baby pictures or how she looks today?"

"They send you pictures?" Caroline asked, her surprise obvious.

"Not hardly. But I was married to a woman who used to call her favorite paparazzi to tip them off about when she was going to the gym. Haley is a pretty little girl so Sharon likes being photographed with her. I can find a new shot somewhere online almost every day. I don't like it, to be honest. It scares me to think of all the predators and pervs out there who might be looking at her, but I have no ability to change it, so I find the good in the bad and keep up with how she's growing and changing every day. Some days it breaks my heart, but I try to keep those days to a minimum."

"Why don't you start with the baby pictures," Caroline suggested as Celeste appeared with two glasses of lemonade. Angelica followed on her cousin's heels carrying a plate piled high with cookies. "Let me watch her grow up, too."

For the next ten minutes, Jackson chowed down on Snickerdoodles as he played proud father scrolling through photos and videos of his daughter. Caroline acted genuinely interested in Haley, and he appreciated the opportunity to share stories about his baby girl now on her birthday more than he could have imagined.

When he judged he'd whipped Caroline enough with kid pics, he put away his phone. "Thank you. I needed that."

"I enjoyed it," Caroline replied. "I love children."

The wistfulness in her voice had him looking hard at her. He recalled that she'd told him she didn't have any. Had she wanted them? Should he ask? It was such a personal question. He wasn't sure what to do.

She took the decision out of his hands. "I badly wanted children. We couldn't have them."

"I'm sorry."

She paused a moment and sipped her lemonade. "Me too."

Now the wistful note took on a hard edge. Jackson's already keen glance sharpened. There was a story here. He wanted to hear it, and something in her expression conveyed the idea that she wanted to tell it. "Caroline—"

The swing swayed as she abruptly stood. "I need to move. Too much sugar between the cookies and lemonade. What else do you have to show me, Jackson?"

He could take a hint. He filed away the question for another time. Climbing to his feet, he glanced down at hers. Her boots were Ropers. That would do. "Do you ride?"

Warily, she asked, "Ride what?"

"Well, your choice. There's an animal trail I've found that winds from the canyon floor up to the rim. Some pretty views along the way. Hiking it takes a couple of hours. An ATV can do it in a quarter of that. The best way to go, in my opinion, is on horseback."

Her expression lit up like a sparkler. "Horseback? You'll take me horseback riding?"

"If you'd like."

"Oh, Jackson." Impulsively, she threw her arms around him and gave him a hug. "I haven't been riding in years. I'd love that. I'd just love that."

A hugger. Definitely, a hugger. And it felt so damn good. "Then let's go."

Go. Quick, before he kissed her again.

Chapter Eleven

Caroline had flipped her desk calendar to over to June when she heard a rap against The Next Chapter's plate glass window. She glanced up to see Angelica Blessing finger-waving a hello. Caroline smiled, waved back, then rose and crossed to the front of the shop. She flicked the lock and opened the door. "Good morning, Angelica. This is a pleasant surprise. Please, come in."

The older woman swept into the bookstore wearing a green gauze tunic over a patterned gypsy skirt. A coin belt cinched her waist. "I'm sorry to barge in on you dear, but at least I don't come empty-handed. Lemon cookies."

She handed Caroline a white bakery box and continued. "I realize you aren't open for business yet, but I am desperate for professional advice, if not an outright solution. I ran into Maisy Baldwin at the post office this morning, and she mentioned that your inventory has been arriving for the past week or so. Is that true?"

"Well, yes."

"Do you have a selection of children's books?"

"Yes, but why—"

"What about bereavement titles?" Angelica interrupted.

That stopped Caroline. "Bereavement?"

"Yes. You know, self-help and inspirational stuff. Now, I know lots of that stuff is claptrap. I don't want claptrap, which is why I need your professional help."

Caroline wouldn't begin to claim that she'd read every book she intended to inventory, but she did have a good handle on self-help books dealing with grief. She'd read them all. But why would Angelica be in here looking for bereavement books? Had she recently suffered a loss?

Caroline was searching for the perfect, gentle words to sensitively ask the question when the older woman added to her request.

"Sex books. I need sex books, too. Although I probably know which titles I want there."

Caroline almost dropped the bakery box. "Okay. Hmm. . . . I think I need a little more information in order to suggest appropriate titles. Are these to be gifts?"

"No. They're for the Fallen Angel. I've just accepted delivery for the most magnificent antique bookcase, and I want to stock it with books that my guests might find useful during their stay. I think some books about the canyon flora and fauna might be helpful, too. And if you have anything on the history of this area, that would be fabulous. I'd wait until you are open to place this order, but I have all these people from Eternity Springs coming in this weekend, and I do so want to put my best foot forward. Ms. Perfect is expecting me to trip and fall, you know."

"Ms. Perfect?"

"My cousin. She can be a real"—Angelica gave her long red hair a toss—"angel . . . at times, I'm telling you. Our mothers were sisters. Twins. Identical twins. I take after my father."

"I see." Caroline smothered a smile.

"Can you help me, dear? I'm happy to pay you for the books right now in cash if that will make any this any easier. I know it's an imposition."

"I'm happy to help. That's what owning a business in a small town is all about. We will just make note of what you choose, and I'll bill you. The Fallen Angel will be my first sale!"

"That's a change, isn't it?" Angelica observed with a wicked glint in her striking blue eyes. "Usually fallen angels are the ones doing the selling."

Caroline laughed and opened the drawer of her desk to remove a pad of paper and a pen, and then she headed toward her storeroom, gesturing for Angelica to follow. "Don't let all the boxes scare you. This won't be as much trouble as you might fear. I have everything opened and organized. Books would be on the shelves already if my painter hadn't instructed me to give the varnish on my bookshelves until Friday to thoroughly dry."

"You've made fabulous progress, Caroline. I love that beige you've chosen for your walls. It sets the bookshelves off nicely. I don't often wear neutrals, but I do find them pleasing."

"Thank you."

"When do you plan to have your grand opening?"

"I'm hoping to open one week before Jackson opens his dance hall. That will give me a chance to work out any kinks before Redemption becomes packed with visitors." Caroline picked up an order pad as she passed her desk. "Maisy Baldwin tells me every hotel room within a hundred miles is booked."

"It's true. The campground is at capacity and of course the inn is sold out. I'm not nearly as nervous about that weekend as I am this one, though."

"Why is that?"

"It's all of Celeste's friends. The pressure is enormous. That's one reason why I'm so glad you're going to be there. I need someone on my side!"

Caroline wasn't sure why Angelica thought guests would take "sides." Nevertheless, she attempted to be reassuring. "I'm sure Jackson supports you. Boone and Tucker, too."

Angelica's expression turned woebegone. "I don't know. Jackson was terribly upset about the broken mirrors."

Mirrors? Plural? "I thought you broke a window."

"That, too. I'm a bit of a klutz. I can't blame Jackson for being upset with me. I deserve it." Angelica's eyes grew watery.

If Jackson had been there at that moment, Caroline would have kicked him rather than kiss him. "Was he mean to you?"

"Oh, no. Jackson is stoically nice. If he was mean I could tell him to take a flying leap, but he just winces and tries to hide it or whispers beneath his breath—but I have the acute hearing of a snowy owl, so he doesn't sneak anything past me. He's just as sweet as can be when I mess up. That, of course, only makes me feel terrible. It would be so much easier if he'd just yell at me."

Caroline gave Angelica an understanding smile. "Jackson McBride may be a gentleman, but he isn't perfect. I'm sure he's broken a thing or two in his life. Now, let's talk books. How big is your bookcase? Do you want to fill it up? Do you want one topic weighted more heavily than others?"

Angelica gave Caroline a tremulous smile. "You do make me feel better. I knew you would, of course. Ms.

Perfect isn't the only one who knows things. Maybe let's start with the books for the little ones?"

Choosing the children's books were easy, and Caroline had everything she thought the inn needed already in stock. With that task finished, Angelica rattled off the twelve "sex books" titles she wanted, only five of which Caroline had in inventory for her Relationships section. It was a wide-ranging selection, everything from Kama Sutra to Dr. Ruth to some advice books written for men and others for women. After reading online reviews, Caroline decided to add the seven new titles to her stock.

Angelica obviously knew what she was talking about when it came to books about human sexuality. What an intriguing woman. She was a fascinating mix of worldly and innocent, of exotic free spirit and little old lady next door. While her cousin Celeste fairly radiated confidence and—well, power was the best-fitting word— Angelica seemed just a little bit injured. If Celeste was a tranquil dove of peace, Angelica was a brightly colored songbird with a damaged wing. Caroline liked both women very much, but she found she was rooting for Angelica.

"So, tell me a bit about the people I'll meet at the Fallen Angel this weekend. Is everyone from Colorado?"

"No, not everyone. Boone's parents are coming from Fort Worth, and two of the four Callahan couples who are joining us live in Texas." Angelica ticked the names off on her fingers. "The Colorado Callahans are Gabe and Nic and Brick and Lili. Luke and Maddie, and Matt and Torie are from Brazos Bend, a little town west of Fort Worth. Our other Coloradoans are Sarah and Cam Murphy. They have a new baby they are bringing along. Apparently, Cam isn't ready to leave his daughter yet. Something about old history. They also have a daughter who won't be joining them and a son who will. Devin Murphy and his wife." Angelica's brow furrowed in thought. "What is her name? She's a doctor, I remember that. Hmm."

Suddenly, she snapped her fingers. "Jenna. Devin and Jenna. They have a son who is around the same age as Cam and Sarah's younger son, but those two boys will be staying with other family at the Callahan ranch outside of Brazos Bend."

Caroline was a little lost. Lots of information there that she wasn't certain she needed, but Angelica was intent. The finger snap had lost her so she started over silently. "Six. That's six couples. So who am I missing? Oh, I know. Artist. Sage and the six-shooter."

"Who?"

Angelica laughed. "It's a way I help myself remember names. A six-shooter is a Colt revolver. His name is Colt. They're Sage and Colt Rafferty. We'll also have Ali and Mac Timberlake. And you, of course. Thank heavens."

"So I'm the only single?" Caroline asked, her anticipation dimming. She'd grown accustomed to her status, and most times she was okay going places by herself, but in a situation like this with an inn full of a close-knit group, she expected the reminder of what she was missing to be sharp.

"No. We had a late cancellation. I received word last night. The Tarkington couple. He was a child movie star! Isn't that exciting? She runs a daycare in Eternity Springs and apparently her facility had a water leak yesterday that did significant damage. She's working furiously to get repairs done and didn't feel like she could afford time away under the circumstances. I offered their room to Maisy this morning. She jumped at the chance to join us."

Caroline's anticipation brightened once more. "That's nice. Really nice."

Since Caroline's first visit to Redemption, she and Maisy had developed a friendship that meant a lot to her. She and Robert had enjoyed a large circle of friends, but in hindsight, they'd been first and foremost *his* friends. As a rule they'd been closer to his age than to hers, people who'd entered their lives as a result of his business contacts or family social set. In Robert's defense, he'd never discouraged Caroline from making her own friends. She simply hadn't done so. She'd liked their friends. Frankly, between her work and their busy lives, she hadn't had time to expand her social life any further. She'd made casual friends at yoga and with some of the nurses at the hospital where she volunteered rocking babies in the NICU. She'd even gone to lunch with a couple of the nurses after Robert's death, but she hadn't made any effort beyond that. She stopped going to yoga and neglected to get her hospital security clearance renewed, so in time, those tenuous bonds melted away.

In contrast, since the weekend they'd met, Maisy had been a regular leaky faucet with a drip . . . drip . . . drip of phone calls, e-mails, invitations, and text messages. A good will ambassador extraordinaire for Redemption, she'd been the first person to suggest the idea to Caroline of moving there. When Caroline had not immediately rejected the notion, Maisy took that as a sign and launched her determined campaign.

In the beginning, Caroline believed that Maisy acted on behalf of the Chamber of Commerce, but she soon came to realize that the kind, energetic, enthusiastic woman was sincere. After they'd met for dinner one evening when Maisy was in Austin on a shopping trip, and she'd shared a recent vivid dream she'd had that convinced her she and Caroline were destined to be fast friends, Caroline also came to believe that Maisy might just need a friend as much as she herself did. Caroline sensed a wound inside her new friend, something Maisy kept well hidden beneath friendly smiles, a happy disposition, and an outgoing personality. Sometimes Caroline had to fight back her instincts to mother and offer comfort for an injury that Maisy had never hinted at, much less admitted to suffering. She sensed her new friend wouldn't appreciate the gesture. It fact, it might damage their fledgling friendship.

No, not fledgling. The friendship had moved beyond fledgling to fast. Caroline and Maisy touched base almost every day. Maisy Baldwin was important to Caroline, and she wouldn't do anything to cause harm to their relationship.

And once Maisy finally confided in her—and she would—Caroline intended to return the favor and be the friend to Maisy that Maisy had been to her since that first visit to Redemption.

Maybe they'd make some progress along those lines this weekend at the Fallen Angel. Perhaps they could sit beside that fabulous pool sipping mimosas Saturday morning and share secrets. Or do it after a late swim over a nightcap. "I can't wait for Friday evening, Angelica," Caroline said. "I have a feeling this might just be a life-changing weekend."

"Oh, honey!" Angelica declared in an amazingly realistic Texas drawl for someone so recently arrived in the state. "If you only knew."

* * *

A scowl creased Boone McBride's brow as he braced his hands on his hips and muttered to Brick Callahan, "Herding cats."

Brick nodded sagely in agreement. "Easier to turn a tornado than get these women out of a store when they're busy shopping."

"You should have warned me. I would have taken a different route through town."

Brick shrugged. "You've lived in Eternity Springs long enough at this point. This shouldn't have surprised you. Our women are strong women."

"I know they're strong. I just didn't know they go gaga over trinkets. Seriously. Your wife bought a scorpion in a glass paperweight."

"She got up to go to the bathroom in the middle of the night last night and almost stepped on one. It's a souvenir."

"Didn't she grow up in Oklahoma? That can't have been the first scorpion she's ever seen."

"She's jealous because I have my snakeskin to show off to kids who are guests at our campground. She wanted something of her own. The way the glass curves makes that little scorpion look a lot bigger than it actually is."

"Sorta like that snakeskin you've stretched."

Brick grinned and nodded toward the doorway of the shop. "Incoming."

"Finally!" Boone exclaimed. He levered away from door of the Suburban upon which he'd been leaning and sauntered back toward the second of the three-Suburban caravan carrying the group the roughly two hundred fifty miles south from the Callahan ranch in Brazos Bend west of Fort Worth to Enchanted Canyon. Halfway there, he watched in alarm as the leader of the pack, Nic Callahan, caught sight of the pet shop two doors down from their current position. He shot a pleading look toward her husband Gabe, who threw an arm around his wife and steered her toward the SUV.

Despite the assist, Maddie Callahan and Sarah Murphy got away, and Boone had to play cow dog and herd them back. "Herding cats!" he repeated loudly with exasperation.

"Turning tornados!" Brick called back, grinning.

Finally, everybody found his or her spot in his vehicle, and Boone climbed into the driver's seat. He watched through his rearview mirror and drummed his fingers on the steering wheel as he waited for the other vehicles to fill.

Boone was nervous and he didn't know why. Okay, maybe he did know. Twenty-four hours of parental pestering loomed on the horizon like a locust cloud. He loved his parents. He truly did. But they'd taken his decision to move to Colorado like a stake through the heart. They didn't understand his decision, and he couldn't explain the real reason why he'd done so.

It would kill them.

Maddie Callahan did him the blessing of interrupting his dark thoughts from the shotgun seat by asking, "Boone, the girls and I were talking while we were shopping . . ."

"Imagine that," he drawled.

"Ha ha. Seriously, though, we thought we should ask before we arrive at your inn. After you accidentally name-dropped your cousin's ex last week to Sage, one or two of us might have gone googling."

Boone smothered a groan. Jackson was going to kill him. "Maddie—"

"Don't worry," she interrupted. "None of us intend to march up to him and demand to know the dirty deets of his breakup. That's why I'm bringing it up now. There is some curiosity bubbling amongst the women. Is the subject of Coco off-limits with him? If so, I'll do my best to keep the ladies in line."

"Thank you. That would be good. Jackson can be real touchy about Sharon."

"Sharon?"

"That's her real name. I think it would be best if y'all will avoid any reference to Coco. Feel free to ask about his daughter, though. Jackson loves to talk about Haley."

"Great. I'm glad I asked."

Movement in the side mirror caught Boone's notice, and he spied Torie Callahan approaching the SUV. *Now what?* He smothered a sigh as the front passenger door opened. Torie said, "Luke? Will you switch cars and join us, please? April sent Matt a text asking for a group call. Apparently Branch is up to his old tricks."

Branch Callahan was Matt and Luke's father, the elderly patriarch of the Callahan family. April, Boone knew, was Branch's caretaker.

Luke groaned, but reached for his car door. "We are not canceling this weekend for anything short of a legit and serious medical emergency."

"I hear you, brother," Torie commented. Glancing toward Boone, she said, "And if you'll wait just a few more minutes, Maisy is locking up her shop, and she's going to ride to the canyon with us so she can have her mechanic look at her car over the weekend. She'll ride shotgun with you."

Boone remembered Maisy Baldwin very well. A pretty firecracker of a package with eyes as big and blue as the West Texas sky. His anxiousness to hit the trail hit the road.

"Sounds good. We're not on any schedule."

He glanced at his reflection in the rearview mirror and finger-combed his hair. Dang it. He never did get that haircut he'd meant to get. His mother wouldn't let him hear the end of it.

He spied Maisy exit the door of her shop with a backpack slung over one shoulder. She carried a straw tote that advertised her flower shop. A woman who traveled light. His kind of girl.

Not that he was looking for a girl. Not in any permanent sense of the word, anyway. He was still a long way from being ready for that. When . . . if . . . Boone ever settled down, he intended to follow his parents' example and build a marriage, a partnership, on a bedrock of love, trust, and respect. He could meet a woman and fall in love today. He had no problem respecting the women in his life. Those he didn't respect didn't remain in his life for long. But trust? Trust was the bugaboo.

Boone had been burned by betrayal, and his trust well was a dry hole.

A dry hole, but maybe no longer bone dry and covered with dust. Eternity Springs was said to be the place where broken hearts go to heal, and Boone was beginning to think it might be starting to work its magic on him. He detected just a faint touch of humidity in the well.

But that didn't mean he was ready for a relationship. A flirtation, however, was right in his wheelhouse. So he quickly opened his door, hopped down from the SUV, and hurried to offer Maisy his assistance. "My oh my, Miss Maisy. Don't you look pretty as a Parker County peach."

She rolled her eyes, but the way they had brightened told him his compliment had scored a point. She said, "You are showing your Fort Worth roots."

"There's no place like home. No women like Texas women. Let me help you with your bags." In a move smooth enough to earn his father's approval and gentlemanly enough make his mother proud, Boone took possession of her bags and escorted her to the SUV.

After stowing her things in back, he gave a "ready" wave to the two cars behind him, climbed into the driver's seat, and started the engine. He winked at Maisy. "Enchanted Canyon, here we come!"

Chapter Twelve

Waiting for the guests to arrive, Jackson was nervous as a virgin, which was stupid because most of the people coming this weekend were family and all of them knew it was a practice event. Besides, this was Celeste and Angelica's deal, and the inn and restaurants had lots of moving parts to sync. He had a stage to set up for a band—something he'd done a million times.

He admitted to being excited about the band he'd invited to perform—mainly because the band members were beyond excited themselves. He'd heard them play three weeks ago during an open-mic afternoon at an outdoor café in Kerrville when he'd stopped to buy a burger for lunch. They had a sweet sound that played to their strengths. The drummer was their writer. Couldn't hold a tune worth beans, but the man had a way with words. This would be their first paid gig and an expected crowd of two dozen, their largest audience.

Okay, maybe Jackson did understand why he was nervous, after all. He was nervous on the band's behalf. They called themselves the Backroads Hazards. He wanted them to do well.

They would have a receptive audience, for sure. The Callahan men were big music lovers, and their ladies truly did love to dance. He wondered if the other women from Eternity Springs would take a turn at two-stepping. He wondered if Caroline Carruthers liked to dance.

Despite spending the majority of time in places with music and wood floors, Jackson seldom took a turn around one. In fact, he couldn't recall the last time he'd had a chance to do so. He had every intention of taking a spin or two around the dance floor tonight with Maddie and Torie and anyone else with a tingle in their toes.

Caroline liked show tunes. He remembered that. Maybe she didn't two-step, but surely she waltzed. Her husband had been a society guy. A waltz was a waltz was a waltz. Maybe he'd ask her to waltz. The Backroads Hazards would have a waltz to play. Every Texas country band had a waltz or twelve on their playlist. He'd be sure to suggest that they include a few tonight.

In fact, he needed to add that to his list for every act that came to the Last Chance. Because unless he had a marquee act booked in, he wanted every night at the hall to include dancing. Bands playing the Last Chance needed to provide a mix of music that made the audience want to sit and listen for bit, and then get up and dance for a while—rinse and repeat. As an artist, he didn't particularly like it when someone told him what to play, but he'd always understood that venue managers understood their patrons. Good venue managers, anyway. He intended to be a good venue manager, and since he'd be building the Last Chance patronage from scratch, he could surround himself with the sort of people he wanted to hang with, couldn't he?

Life might get in the way of music, but music never got in the way of life. Music was meant to be lived, to be celebrated.

He wanted to celebrate music with Caroline Carruthers.

"You are so screwed, McBride," he muttered.

"You forgot about that second-floor light bulb that my cousin asked you to change, didn't you?" Angelica said.

"What? Oh." Jackson winced. "Dadgummit."

"You'd better hurry. They'll be here in seven minutes. Celeste will have a hissy fit if you're not here to greet your cousin when he arrives."

Right that. "Seven? You're sure?"

She gave him a don't-be-silly look over the top of her sunglasses. Angelica might be clumsy upon occasion— okay, many occasions. She might end up at loggerheads with Celeste on a daily—okay, hourly—basis, but the woman had an uncanny way of being right in her predictions.

He hauled butt for the supply closet, made one of the fastest light-bulb changes in history, and arrived on the porch to stand with the Blessings as three SUVs pulled into the parking lot beside the Fallen Angel Inn.

Jackson didn't see Caroline's car. The depth of his disappointment disturbed him. *Yep, definitely screwed.*

As if on cue, doors opened and people poured from the vehicles. Boone. Maisy Baldwin. The Callahan cousins from Brazos Bend—Matt and Torie, Luke and Maddie, Gabe and Nic, Brick and his wife, Liliana. Jackson didn't recognize anyone else.

They all recognized Celeste. Her name went up on the afternoon air like a cheer. The women in the first car who Jackson didn't recognize were a little faster than everyone else, and they made a beeline to meet her. Celeste descended the Fallen Angel's front steps regal as a queen, floating forward with the peace and goodwill of an angel.

Beside Jackson, Angelica shifted restlessly during the group hug.

Then they all started talking at once. "Oh, Celeste, I've missed you!"

"I've missed all of you, too."

"How gorgeous is this place?"

"I love canyons! They're such surprises. And this one . . . we were traveling along a flat, boring, arid spot then BOOM . . . the floor drops away and it's Eden."

"Doesn't this house look inviting. It's your signature yellow. Why am I not surprised?"

Angelica leaned closer to Jackson and murmured, "Yellow has always been *my* favorite color. Hers was always blue. Still is."

Jackson slung his arm around Angelica's shoulder and gave her a squeeze. "I think the broken-wing design on the fan blades is pretty darned awesome." After she gave him a grateful smile, he slipped his arm through hers to escort her down the steps. "Let's go meet our guests."

Jackson was pleased to see the bellboys, aka "luggage wranglers," wheeling their carts toward the parking lot where the men of the party were unloading bags. "Off to a good start," he murmured to Angelica, giving a nod to the wranglers as he and his innkeeper approached the Fallen Angel's first guests.

Being a Texan and a gentleman, Jackson tipped his hat. "Ladies, welcome to the Fallen Angel Inn."

Angelica beamed a smile. "I hope you have a fabulous time at our whorehouse."

"Angelica!" Celeste snapped.

"*Former* whorehouse."

"Bordello! We agreed to use the word bordello!"

Angelica shrugged. "Bordello. Brothel. Cathouse.

House of ill repute. Everybody knows what we're talking about."

"Nevertheless—"

"I'm Jackson McBride," he said, interrupting the potential squabble by thrusting his hand out toward the nearest female, a perky, petite brunette.

"I'm Sarah Murphy. It's so nice to finally meet you, Jackson. I feel as if we already know you. Boone has talked a lot about you and Tucker."

Jackson ticked through the guest list. Sarah Murphy owned a bakery in Eternity Springs and was a very close friend of the Callahan clan. Of course, all these people seemed to be close friends. He gave Sarah an easy grin and replied, "I can't say I find that comforting. Boone has always been free with the facts."

Then gesturing to Angelica, he said, "Allow me to introduce our innkeeper, Angelica Blessing."

To a woman, they lit up like Christmas trees. Also to a woman, they failed to completely hide their surprise at the contrast between the cousins. A classy blonde stepped forward and said, "Celeste's cousin! I'm Ali Timberlake. What fabulous hair you have! I always wanted to be a redhead."

"Thank you." Angelica raised her chin. "My cousin believes it's a fitting color for someone who runs a—"

"Angelica!" Celeste snapped.

"Inn. The Fallen Angel Inn. Ali, I believe you are the restaurateur, correct? Thank you so much for the recipes you shared with our chef. That was so kind of you to do."

"I'm thrilled to help." Ali linked her arm through Celeste's. "Celeste has always been so generous. It's been nice to do something to help her in return."

"Yes," Angelica replied, thick syrup in her tone. "She's such an angel, isn't she?"

The other women introduced themselves in turn:

Sage Rafferty—another gorgeous redhead, the artist, Jackson recalled; and Jenna Murphy, a physician and Sarah's new daughter-in-law. The rest of the party caught up them at that point, and Jackson greeted all his female Texas cousins with a kiss on the cheek and the males with a handshake. He was introduced to Mac Timber-lake, Cam Murphy, Colt Rafferty and finally, Devin Murphy.

"Devin Murphy!" In addition to the handshake, Jackson gave Devin a slap on the back. "You don't know how anxious I've been to meet you. I want to buy you a beer!"

"Oh yeah?" Devin said, the lilt of Australia in his tone. "I never turn down free beer. But, why?"

"You broke Boone's nose!"

An expression of righteous indignation crossed Devin's face. "He deserved it. He kissed my woman."

"He's deserved a broken nose many times, but you're the first person to give him one. For that, I salute you."

"Bite me," Boone said. He greeted first Angelica and then Celeste with a kiss on the cheek. "Hello, angels. Are you ready to get this party started?"

"That we are," Celeste said. "Angelica?"

She cast a nervous glance toward Jackson, who gave her a reassuring wink. Drawing a deep breath, she offered them a brilliant smile. "Ladies and gentlemen, please, follow me."

Jackson and Boone waited behind as the Blessings led their guests inside. "Buy you a beer?"

"Absolutely. Next door?"

"Best saloon in town."

Five minutes later, they were seated in the rustic pine porch rockers holding frosty bottles of beer imported from Shiner, Texas, about a hundred miles away. They discussed a few pesky management issues and the schedule for the weekend, and then Boone asked oh-so-casually, "So, about Maisy Baldwin."

Jackson knew that tone. He took a sip of his beer in order to stall and give himself a moment to think it through. Did he want to give his cousin grief just for the hell of it? Ordinarily, he wouldn't think twice about doing exactly that. But today, honestly, he just wasn't in the mood.

Well, maybe he was in the mood a little bit. He lowered his bottle from his lips and said, "Dibs."

Boone muttered a curse, and Jackson laughed. "I'm kidding. Just kidding. Just don't lead her on. Maisy is really nice. I wouldn't want to see her hurt."

Boone scowled at him. "I don't hurt women."

Jackson held up a hand. "I know. I know. My apologies."

Boone was a flirt, but he was an honest flirt. And being a lawyer and a man with baggage, he hardly kissed a woman without getting a permission slip beforehand, signed in triplicate and notarized, prior to lips touching lips.

"Remember that dog that Tucker's next-door neighbor had when we were growing up? The bird dog? Her name was Shine?"

"The springer? Yeah."

"Sweet dog. She'd sit at your feet look up at you still as a statue and I swear, she'd even nod her head as if in agreement with what you said. 'Don't jump, Shine.' 'Go get the ball, Shine.' You'd think she was the best-trained dog in the world."

"Yeah, I remember. She'd listen to you, then do whatever the hell she wanted to do."

Jackson lifted his beer in toast. "I present to you Maisy Baldwin."

Boone laughed. "Nothing wrong with a headstrong girl. She sure is pretty."

"That she is."

Boone gave him a sidelong glance. "You've never considered looking that direction?"

"No. I'm not looking, period. The last thing I need is another woman in my life." Jackson's thoughts turned to Caroline, and he knew he hadn't told the complete truth.

Quietly and sincerely, Boone said, "I get that after the hell Sharon put you through, that you are gun shy, but if you let that stop you from living a full life, all you're doing is giving her power."

"Pot. Kettle."

"I know. I know. I'm climbing that mountain."

"Gonna stop by home on your way back to Eternity Springs?"

Boone rolled his tongue around the inside of his mouth. "Still have a way to go before I reach the summit."

Jackson took a pull on his beer, considered, and then shook his head. "We are a pair of head cases."

"Yep. Lucky for us Tucker isn't around much. He'd kick our asses if he realized how wussified we've become."

"True that." Jackson stretched out his long legs and crossed them at the ankles. "Have you heard anything from him recently?"

"Actually, he called me yesterday. He was in an airport somewhere. Connection was crap and the call dropped pretty quickly, but I made out that he was healthy and had some sort of news to share."

"That's interesting. I think the last time Tucker shared news, the Rangers were playing in the World Series."

"I know. I kept hoping he'd call back, but it didn't happen."

"He probably got promoted to general or something. Skipped right over a rank or two."

"I doubt the Army has enough sense to do that."

Movement on the road distracted Jackson from the conversation. He pulled his legs in and sat up as he recognized the little BMW convertible heading toward them. Caroline.

"Sweet little ride," Boone observed.

"That's Caroline."

"The Caroline who lost her husband? She'll be here this weekend?"

Jackson nodded. "Celeste sponsored some sort of Chamber of Commerce drawing, and she won. She's bringing a friend who'll be sharing a room with Maisy. Total smoke show. A brunette named Gillian."

"Oh yeah?" Boone asked with interest. Flirting with two ladies simultaneously was no problem for someone with his deft abilities.

"She's taken. Engaged to some guy who plays a lot of golf."

Boone grimaced. "I hope that doesn't mean that this weekend is gonna be twenty-four/seven wedding talk. Since Devin and Jenna's wedding, we're finally getting a tulle-and-lace breather in Eternity Springs. It's a beatdown, I'm telling you. Just brutal."

"If it gets too bad, I suggest you catch up on your reading. Angelica has brought in some interesting titles." Jackson finished the remainder of his beer, rose to his feet, and tossed the bottle into a nearby trash can. He headed down the walk, but when he turned back toward the inn rather than toward the dance hall, Boone called after him, "Hey, I thought you were going to show me the Last Chance?"

"I'm the manager, not the tour guide. Go see it yourself. I've got to go say hello to a beautiful woman."

Boone's interested voice trailed after him. "You're sniffing after the widow? Well now, isn't this interesting?"

"Maybe. Could be. I don't know." He glanced over his shoulder. "I don't think I'm any nearer to the summit than you are, cuz. But I'm beginning to think that maybe we gotta keep climbing, you know?"

"Maybe." Boone hurried to catch up with him. "That's a big step for you, Jackson. Sounds like you've come a long way since you put Nashville in your rearview mirror."

"Considering I still have a great big hole in my heart because of the situation with Haley, yeah, I guess I have. Maybe Celeste wasn't just blowing smoke when she came up with Enchanted Canyon's marketing tagline. My 'troubled soul' seems to be finding some peace."

"Celeste is nails, I'm telling you."

Jackson spared his cousin a glance. "Is your broken heart healing in Eternity Springs, Boot?"

"Jeez, we'd better stop," Boone said with a grimace. "We're starting to sound like a couple of women. If we don't want to lose our man cards, we'd better either scratch our asses and belch our beer really loud or go flirt with the pretty ladies over at the Fallen Angel."

"Sexist pig." Jackson picked up his pace. "Last one to the parlor has to put on a skirt."

Chapter Thirteen

Caroline pulled into the parking space, shifted into park, switched off the ignition, then turned to smile at her passenger. "Are you ready?"

"You know what? I am." Gillian Thacker tore her gaze away from the inn, saloon and dance hall long enough to smile at Caroline and say, "All of a sudden, I think maybe I'm happy about Jeremy's last-minute golf weekend, after all. Isn't this a welcoming place?"

"Wait until you see what they've done inside," Caroline said as she opened her door and climbed from the car. "It's really fabulous."

Gillian unfolded her long, shapely legs from the passenger seat, grabbed her purse, and then shut the door. She turned in a slow circle. "How cool is this? I've seen their advertising flyers, and they're great, but now that I'm here, I see that the photos don't do it justice. And I don't know why."

"I know. I've thought the same thing myself. Honestly, I think it's the canyon. There is something about the canyon itself that simply doesn't transfer into pictures."

"Enchantment," Gillian mused. "It's Enchanted Canyon. Maybe there's something to it."

"Maybe so."

"How is it I've lived in the Hill Country all my life and never known this place existed?"

"Well, it's private property off the beaten track with no public road."

"And, guarded over by Enchanted Rock." Both women turned to look at the pink-granite dome rising above the canyon in the distance, and Gillian continued, "Why is it I imagine an eye staring down at me?"

"Now that you mention it," Caroline said with a wry smile. "I've recently read quite a bit of local history. Supposedly archeologists have found evidence of human sacrifices at the base of Enchanted Rock dating back thousands of years."

"Ick."

"The Comanche and Tonkawa people both considered it a spiritual place, and it's been revered and feared at different times throughout history."

Gillian glanced from the Fallen Angel to Enchanted Rock and then back to the inn, saloon, and dance hall. "I imagine traveling the road to Ruin in the eighteen hundreds took some cajones."

From behind them came a familiar voice. "Oh, honey-child. If you only knew."

"The road to Redemption is not without its challenges, either," declared a second familiar voice.

Caroline turned to see Angelica and Celeste Blessing standing side by side at the end of the front sidewalk, a study in contrast but for the smiles on their faces. Celeste's crisp, white linen shirt was tucked neatly into her pleated khaki slacks. Her sparkle came from the twinkle in her eyes and the glitter of rhinestones on the buckles on her loafers.

Angelica presented an earthier picture by showcasing her hourglass figure in her gauzy, sunshine yellow peasant blouse tucked into a flowing azure skirt. The white feathers embroidered along the scoop of her neckline and hem were repeated in threads of yellow and blue across the wide white belt she wore cinched at her waist. Her red hair hung loose in a riot of curls hanging halfway down her back. It occurred to Caroline that were she dressed in a corset and fishnet stockings, Angelica would look right at home in the Fallen Angel in its prior life. *Bet she'd have been really popular, too.*

"Hello, Celeste. Hello, Angelica."

"Good afternoon." Angelica stepped ahead of her cousin, smiling warmly at both women as she nodded first at Caroline, and then offered her hand to Gillian. "You must be Gillian. Yes?"

"Yes."

"I'm Angelica Blessing, the innkeeper here at the Fallen Angel. It's lovely to finally meet you."

On Angelica's heels, Celeste greeted Caroline with a hug while Angelica continued to Gillian, "My cousin and I stopped by your store the last time I was in town and met your mother, but you were out with your beau."

"Yes. Mom said that the two of you stopped by. I'm sorry I missed you."

"I'm so glad you both could join us this weekend," Celeste interjected. "I hope you had a pleasant drive out from town?"

"It was lovely," Caroline said. "Traffic was light for a Friday afternoon."

"Excellent." Celeste waved to catch the attention of a pair of teenagers wearing jeans, pearl-snap shirts, and name tags who hovered nearby awaiting her signal. "Will our luggage wranglers need carts?"

"No. We both packed light." Caroline popped the trunk, and after sorting out their luggage, Gillian followed Celeste toward the cottage that she and Maisy would share for the weekend, while Angelica escorted Caroline upstairs to her lovely second-floor suite. "Oh, wow," Caroline said as she stepped into the room that was dominated by a king-sized four-poster bed. "That smells like fresh bread."

"It is." Beaming, Angelica showed her the bread machine concealed in the built-in cabinet along one wall that also contained a dorm-sized refrigerator stocked with bottles of water, soda, and juice. "We are going to make a loaf of fresh bread each day for our guests. It's going to be our signature. Nothing smells more heavenly than fresh-baked yeast bread."

"What a fabulous idea. Fresh-baked bread is one of the best aromas on Earth."

"The Fallen Angel is all about delicious scents. Wait until you get a sniff of the soaps and lotions in the bathroom. We didn't have those last time you were here, did we?"

"No."

"They're fabulous, a custom fragrance created for us by a soap maker in Eternity Springs. Savannah Turner. She makes Heavenscents Soaps. She's very talented."

"I know those soaps. Celeste had some with her the day we met." Caroline had forgotten all about the bag of samples from the innkeepers show that Celeste had been taking to Easterwood that day. "Is Savannah Turner one of the visitors here this weekend?"

"No, I'm afraid not. Her husband is the Eternity Springs sheriff and can't get away this time of year. Savannah and Zach are scheduled to visit later this summer once the tourist season is over in Eternity Springs." Angelica pointed out a couple of more amenities of the room, and then said, "Now, I'll let you settle in. If you need anything at all, please don't hesitate to ask."

"Thank you, Angelica."

Caroline spent the next few minutes unpacking. When she placed her makeup bag in the bathroom, she unscrewed the cap from the small bottle of body lotion, took a sniff, and smiled. Appealing and unique. Faintly citrusy. Maybe a little lavender? She liked it. She'd need to not forget this time. She wanted to carry a few fragrant items at The Next Chapter—candles and such— but she had yet to find a vendor she wanted to work with.

As she hung the dresses she'd brought to wear to dinner in the suite's antique chifforobe, she wondered if the Fallen Angel planned to sell their fragrances in a gift shop. Maybe they'd be interested in selling them through the bookstore, too. A little cross-promotion wouldn't hurt. They were already doing that on her behalf, what with all those books Angelica had bought. Caroline hadn't missed the tent card advertising The Next Chapter that Angelica had placed prominently next to them. She'd have to remember to ask Celeste or Angelica about their plans for retail. Maybe tonight—

"No," she said aloud as she closed the chifforobe door and stared at her reflection in its mirror. No business tonight. She was officially off the clock. The weekend had begun. It was not to be a working weekend. Period. She was going to hold herself to that vow.

It had been a crazy week at the shop, and she'd been working like a dog arriving early and staying late into the night. Everything was coming together, though, and she was on track for her own grand opening. This past week she'd completed hiring what she hoped would be a competent, dependable staff. She'd put the finishing touches on her decor, and next week they would begin stocking the shelves. That's why she'd given herself permission to take the weekend off. She'd decided to take this opportunity to pause and rest and relax and store up energy for the busy weeks to come. This weekend would be the calm before the storm, and she intended to enjoy herself. Freely, wholly, in a way she hadn't done so in a very long time.

This weekend, Caroline was going to be a girl. She was going to flirt with Jackson McBride.

Somewhere between shelving the Cookbooks and the Local History sections, Caroline had figured out that this was the logical next step. The necessary next step. Because in order to live the next chapter of her life, she needed to turn some pages. One of those pages was beginning to date again. But in order to begin dating, she needed to shake the feeling of still being married whenever she talked to a man. She'd need to start feeling single again.

How was it that she could feel so alone, but not feel single?

In the months since Robert's death, only one man had broken through her married shell—Jackson McBride.

She'd been bummed that he hadn't stopped by the bookstore since her visit to Enchanted Canyon. Not because she was ready to leap into anything hot and heavy and serious, but because she'd managed to read a few paragraphs down her page and she wanted to get to the bottom of it. She wanted to turn it and flirt a little. Jackson made her want to flirt.

She'd put quite a bit of thought into understanding why he did it for her when others didn't, and she'd finally figured it out. Jackson was a nice guy. He was kind and thoughtful, and he was definitely hot. And she could tell that he genuinely liked her.

Most importantly, he was safe.

Jackson toted around more baggage than she did on those broad, sexy shoulders of his, so he wasn't in the market for anything more than she was ready to give. He'd been upfront about that. She could test her wings with him, grow her wings with him without leading him on. And vice versa. She was safe for him because she wasn't looking for anything beyond help moving on. She and Jackson were both on the same page, both were at points in their lives when they were attempting to turn that page and begin their next chapters, which made them perfect for each other. For this weekend.

Which was why she saw a sparkle of excitement and anticipation in her eyes. She was ready to kick this thing off.

She touched up her lipstick, ran a brush through her hair, and glanced at her wristwatch. Perfect timing. Guests had been asked to gather downstairs in the parlor five minutes from now to discuss the schedule for the weekend's activities.

She nodded at her reflection, then turned and left the room. Downstairs, she discovered a parlor filled with good friends who appeared ready to expand their circle. Jackson approached her as soon as she crossed the threshold. "Hey there. Glad to see you made it."

"Hello, Jackson. I wouldn't have missed this for the world. I've been dreaming about soaking in your hot tub all week. I've lost count of how many cartons of books I've shelved."

"We'll have to make sure you fit that into your schedule this evening." He lowered his voice and added, "Word of warning: Angelica is being a little obsessive about her sign-up sheet. One of our bartenders didn't show up for tonight's shift, and she's in a bit of a scheduling tizzy now."

"Poor Angelica. Surely she knows that staffing issues are part of the business."

"She does. I think once she gets this first weekend

behind her she'll be fine. At least, I hope that will be the case." He waved over a waiter who was carrying a tray of champagne. "Something to drink?"

"Yes, thank you."

Taking two, he offered one to Caroline and then clinked their glasses. "Here's to successful openings. To next chapters."

"To next chapters," she repeated.

He gestured to the crowd beginning to gather. "Have you had a chance to meet everyone?"

"No."

The family resemblance between the Callahan men and the McBride men was obvious and made it relatively easy to tell the Eternity Springs crowd apart from the Brazos Bend gang. They were a friendly, welcoming group that teased and traded jibes and immediately made Caroline feel like a longtime friend. She enjoyed the cocktail hour immensely. It didn't hurt that Jackson barely left her side.

Not that he was flirting with her, because he wasn't. What he was doing was giving an amusing play-by-play commentary of his cousin Boone's blatant flirtation with every female in the room, which somehow, despite being so broad, was obviously focused on Maisy. Maisy didn't seem to mind Boone's attention at all. For her part, Caroline felt like she was blooming under Jackson's.

She wasn't the only person to benefit from his consideration, Caroline noted when the Callahan wives and husbands began bickering amongst themselves about their Saturday afternoon activity. She watched as Jackson cut an anxious Angelica from the herd, easing her out of the parlor and into the entry hall where he attempted to soothe her as he would a skittish horse. Caroline moved closer, not hesitating to eavesdrop.

". . . put a ride to the south rim on the schedule? That's a steep, challenging trail."

"Our guests are all accomplished riders."

"But . . . but . . . but what about the bicycles? The ATVs. The croquet course."

"I'm still not at all sure about the croquet—I told you that—but the bikes and ATVs will get plenty of use. Just not this weekend. They can do that at home."

"Exactly. The Callahans can ride horses at home. They're ranchers for heaven's sake! Why do they want to ride horses here?"

"They want to see the canyon."

"But we're supposed to practice *everything*. How can we practice everything if—"

Jackson gave his innkeeper's shoulders a gentle squeeze. "Deep breaths, Angelica. You have this. You've trained your people well. Everything will be okay."

Caroline watched his gentle smile and listened to his encouraging words as he detailed the many preparations Angelica had overseen the past weeks and months. "Everything will be okay," he repeated, and Caroline closed her eyes and let the echo of his whiskey-timbered voice skid along her nerves.

She told herself, *"Yes, yes it will."*

In the parlor, the Callahans apparently came to an agreement, because Gabe threw out his hands and declared, "Finally! Okay. Does that work for everyone?"

"Yes!" came a chorus of female voices.

Gabe glanced around the parlor, spied Jackson and Angelica in the hallway, and walked toward them. "Angelica?"

She gave Jackson a wobbly smile and met Gabe just inside the parlor, clipboard in hand. "Yes?"

"Change in plans. The ladies are going to hang by the pool in the morning instead of joining us for the canyon ride. Boone says the trail is accessible by Jeep. He suggested that the women come up that way and bring a picnic lunch. Said you have a couple of drivers who know the way. Then tomorrow afternoon, we'll all go together to tour your ghost town."

Angelica turned an uncertain and faintly accusing look toward Boone, who was too busy chatting up Maisy to notice. "Boone suggested that?"

"Yeah. Weather is supposed to be great."

Frowning, she nibbled at her lower lip and flipped the pages of on her clipboard. "It's a problem. A picnic at the canyon rim is not on the schedule."

From her seat in the corner, Celeste gave an exasperated sigh then spoke with a bit of bark in her tone. "Oh, for heaven's sake. You cannot be a good innkeeper if you are not adaptive. The schedule is not written in stone, Angelica. Change it!"

Angelica's insecurity evaporated at her cousin's words. Temper flamed to life in her eyes. Her spine snapped straight. She smiled with more teeth than the great white in *Jaws*. "Cousin dear, would you please step with me into the other room?"

Uh-oh, Caroline thought as once again, Angelica exited the parlor. This time she sailed out like a three-masted warship under full sail. Celeste's expression remained serene. However, Caroline didn't miss the fact that she'd clasped her fingers tightly. Really tightly.

Having moved to stand in the threshold between the entry hall and parlor, Jackson scowled at Boone, whose arched brow wordlessly asked, *What?*

Then the Blessing cousins' whispered conversation began to carry. Caroline clearly heard Angelica say, "If you will recall, Celeste, you were the one who suggested I draw up a schedule."

"I haven't forgotten anything, especially the guidance I've attempted to give you based on my long experience."

"Guidance? Guidance?! Honey, you don't guide. You dictate. You decree. You've been Miss Bossy Butt all our lives!"

At that, Caroline lost track of the conversation taking place in the entry hall because she was so captivated by the reactions of the Fallen Angel's guests. To a person, their chins dropped. Nic Callahan covered her mouth with her hands in shock. Sarah Murphy silently repeated the words "Miss Bossy Butt"? Brick Callahan's eyes bugged out, and Devin Murphy sank onto a chair as if his knees had given out.

Jackson closed his eyes and massaged his temples with his fingertips. Caroline barely stifled a laugh as Boone groaned aloud. He set down his drink and prepared to referee.

However, he'd taken only one step toward the door when suddenly, the Blessings returned to the parlor and stood side by side. Caroline didn't know what had happened in the past thirty seconds or so, but the pair now presented an apparently calm and united front and spoke like a team.

Angelica said, "Gabe, we're able to make this little adjustment with no problem at all."

Celeste added, "Because we expected a full house, my dear cousin made sure to have a full complement of staff for the weekend. One word of caution, though: we will be sticklers to our schedule and make a concentrated effort to run on time. We'll ask riders to meet at the stables no later than seven o'clock for a seven fifteen departure."

Angelica nodded in agreement. "I understand you are all experienced riders, so that shouldn't be a problem. If you have any special requests regarding mounts or tack, please stop by the stables tonight or call extension twelve and leave a message for Ben. He'll take care of you. For the picnic, the Jeeps will be in front of the inn at eleven thirty."

Celeste held up her hand with her index finger extended. "If you have any special menu requests, please call extension five before you retire this evening."

Pencil in hand, Angelica glanced down at her clipboard. "We have the horseback ride to the rim, the Jeep tour and picnic, and let me double-check the list for the hike to the hidden waterfalls. I have Caroline, Maisy, Gillian, Liliana, Brick, Jackson, and Boone. Anyone else?"

Gillian raised her hand. "Actually, if you have a spot for one more in the Jeeps, I'd like I'd like to do the canyon tour. I wasn't up to a morning on horseback, but I'd love to see Enchanted Rock from the viewpoint Boone described."

"We absolutely have room. Consider yourself added to the picnic list, Gillian." Angelica made a note, then smiled to the guests. "So, any other requests?"

"Cookies for the picnic dessert?" called out Luke Callahan.

"You've got it," Angelica replied.

Celeste offered, "She makes excellent cookies."

During the exchange, Jackson had drifted back to stand beside Caroline. She glanced up toward him now and offered, "They appear to have worked out their differences."

"For now. I'm too experienced at this point to believe it will last. I don't what it is about those two. Boone says that the Eternity Springs Celeste is a real angel. Here with Angelica . . . well . . . we see another side of her."

Caroline's lips twitched. "Maybe it's the cathouse influence."

"Maybe. Maybe our angel hears the voices of the fallen ones while she's here, and they rub off on her."

"Or maybe it's a cousin version of sibling rivalry."

"I don't know. Tucker and Boone and I have our share of disagreements, but we don't snipe at each other like that."

"What do you do?"

"We throw punches." He paused, considered, and then added, "If Celeste and Angelica start throwing punches, I'm moving to Manhattan. Or Miami. Or Marfa."

Amused, Caroline couldn't help but laugh. "I've always wanted to visit Marfa. Have you been to see the lights?"

Marfa was Marfa, Texas, a small, southwest Texas town so isolated that it made Redemption look urban. The lights to which she referred were a strange, unexplained phenomena that could be observed in the surrounding desert on clear nights. Recorded in historical accounts now one hundred and forty years old, the colored balls of lights could still be seen today dancing on the horizon in no predictable pattern. Tourists and townspeople alike gather in the public viewing areas after sunset to watch the lights and speculate about their origins.

"Never been to Marfa. Takes some commitment to go there. Thought about paying a visit once when Boone and Tucker and I went camping in Big Bend, but we went to Terlingua instead. It was Chili Cook-off time."

"I've heard the Terlingua Chili Cook-off is a serious party."

"Serious doesn't begin to describe it. That was a weekend I'll never remember."

"You don't mean never forget?"

At his rueful look, she laughed. Then Angelica spoke up and recaptured their attention. "All right then. I believe we are all set for tomorrow. Jackson, you are leading the hike to the waterfall. When and where would you like your group to meet?"

"Let's try the parking lot at seven."

"All right then. I hope you all enjoy yourselves tomorrow, and I'm going to ask you to please take care. Celeste has warned me that in the general course of business I can expect accidents. We'll have scrapes and falls and bites and breaks. It's something we simply can't avoid when people are out enjoying the great outdoors, which is something we want them to do. I want to assure you that we're prepared with trained first responders on staff, and we'll be ready for any boo-boos large or small.

"That said, I know that you are all adults who are experienced being outdoors. Why, you're probably the outdoorsiest group of visitors we'll ever have because almost all of you are either ranchers or mountaineers. And Gillian, you own a bridal salon. I can't think of many more dangerous occupations than that!"

"Hear! Hear!" Sarah Murphy called.

"So my point is that you are all intelligent, capable people so I probably don't to lecture you but I'm going to do it anyway because it is our opening weekend and I need to practice and sometimes smart people do stupid things. Right, Boone?"

"Use your commas, Angelica," Celeste urged in a stage whisper.

"Me?" Boone asked, slapping his hand against his chest. "She picks me out of *this* group to ask that question?"

"Tomorrow as you are out and about stomping around

our wilderness, I beg you to take care. Enchanted Canyon is a beautiful place, a wild place. It is not an amusement park. Any animals you might happen to see will not be young adults in costume ready to entertain. Neither are you in Yellowstone National Park with its hot spots, where a wrong step might land you in an acidic, skin-eating pool. We don't have grizzly bears or bison here, but we do have wild hogs and mountain lions. Not to mention rattlesnakes and copperheads and cottonmouths, and frankly we are close to the southern border so I'm sorry to say, that upon occasion I'm told, we have had some coyotes invade our land—the evil, two-legged variety."

"Two-legged coyotes?" Sage Rafferty asked.

"Smugglers," Boone explained. "Human traffickers. The damn cartels."

She rounded her mouth in a silent O.

"Ordinarily they avoid Enchanted Canyon. Their routes usually take them west of here, but when the border patrol is active, we have had some visitors. I don't mean to scare you. It's no more dangerous here than on your ordinary city street, but if you want to go for a sunrise run on one of the trails, take a running buddy with you."

"Like I'm getting up at sunrise," Maddie Callahan said with a snort.

"Only place I'm running while I'm here is to the bread machine when it signals it's ready," her sister-in-law Torie added.

"I knew the bread would be a hit." Angelica clasped her hands and beamed with delight. "Now, I have one more caution before I run next door and visit with Chef Paul to make sure that all is well in the kitchen in advance of dinner. As part of my take-care request, I must urge you to remain selfie-aware."

Gillian gave an embarrassed smile and asked, "I'm sorry. What?"

"Selfie-aware," she repeated. "Do you know how dangerous selfies can be? The statistics will amaze you. Why, more people die from taking selfies than from shark attacks each year. It's tragic!"

"It's stupid," Gabe Callahan observed.

"And *rude*!" Angelica declared. "I wanted to make the entire canyon an unplugged zone, but *some people*"—she cast an accusing glare toward Boone and Jackson—"didn't agree with my vision. My goodness, it seems like everywhere you go these days people are too busy taking pictures of themselves to stop and actually look at what they're touring. It's criminal. Life is meant to be experienced, not witnessed through a screen. And don't even get me started about view hogs."

Caroline cleared her throat. "View hogs?"

Angelica gave a disdainful sniff. "It's self-descriptive. Try visiting Yellowstone and viewing Lower Yellowstone Falls on a summer afternoon. Or go to Rome to St. Peter's to see the *Pieta*. I take no pleasure in photobombing, but at some point, a girl simply must use her elbows. Otherwise, you'll never make it past the view hoggers taking their selfies!"

In the silence following her pronouncement, the Fallen Angel guests shared looks with one another. Matt Callahan shrugged and summed up the general response. "She does have a point."

With an echo of his native Australia in his voice and a twinkle in his eye, Devin Murphy drawled, "I'll admit to wanting to help a charter customer overboard a time or two as his selfies got in the way of my doin' my job."

Celeste gave her cousin a reassuring pat. "I don't think we need to worry about this group being photographic hogs, cousin, but a caution on self-awareness will not be inappropriate for regular guest of the Fallen Angel Inn. Perhaps we can add a little printed something in our guest rooms."

"That's a good idea, Celeste."

"Now, shall we make our way to the Saloon? I imagine Chef Paul is ready to go over that final checklist."

As the two women swanned from the parlor, Boone nudged up against Maisy, who stood next to Caroline, who stood beside Jackson. "You know what this means, don't you?"

Maisy shook her head. "What?"

Boone reached into his pocket and pulled out his phone. "Everybody smile for a selfie!"

Chapter Fourteen

See that girl. She's moving on. She's holding strong and she's taking on the world.

The blare of the alarm pierced Jackson's dream, and the song began escaping his grasp like air through a pinprick of a balloon. Damn. Damn. Damn. It was there. So close. *She's close. Just down the road.*

Jackson's eyes flew open. Red numerals on the bed-side clock read 6:15. Ordinarily, he would have groaned. Jackson had never been a morning person. Considering the way he'd made his living, being a night owl was a good thing. Haley's birth had complicated his sleep schedule—but that was the normal way of things for all new parents, wasn't it? He'd started getting up in the mornings to spend time with her, and that's when he'd rediscovered the joy of afternoon naps.

He'd adapted to a more ordinary schedule during the renovations of the canyon properties, but ordinary to him still didn't mean waking up before eight o'clock. *See that girl. Sleepy smile. Roll her over and start the day right.*

"I wish," he muttered.

Twenty minutes later with hair still damp from his shower, he climbed into his truck for the short drive to the inn with a smile on his face, softly singing Houston-native Johnny Nash's 1970s hit, "I Can See Clearly Now."

He had a feeling it just might be a sunshiny day.

After parking, he ambled to the saloon in search of coffee and something to eat. He greeted the kitchen staff, poured himself a cup of coffee, snagged a breakfast burrito, and sauntered into the main body of the restaurant.

Boone sat perched on one of the stools at the bar, and upon seeing Jackson, made a show of checking his watch. "Whoa! Seven minutes before the hour? We might have to rechristen this place Miracle Canyon."

"Hardy-har." Jackson took a seat beside his cousin. "I suppose you've already been for a five-mile run, milked the cows and slopped the hogs, and discovered a cure for lumbago?"

"Lumbago? Does a cure for lumbago not already exist?"

"I'm not sure what lumbago actually is." He savored a sip of coffee, and then began unwrapping his burrito. "So, was there any more activity around the inn after I cashed in my chips at the poker game last night?"

"Nah. Nothing of interest to you and me, anyway. Based on the lights shining in the cottage windows, the hen party in the cottage was still going strong when I turned in."

The "hen party" was the continuation of a discussion about Gillian's wedding plans that had begun over dessert in the parlor after dinner. Gillian, Maisy, Caroline, Lori Timberlake, and Liliana Callahan had all traipsed out to the cottage that Gillian and Maisy were sharing in order to look at Gillian's computer, surf her Pinterest wedding boards, and continue the all-things-wedding talk. Boone chose to play dominoes while Jackson had played cards until the Callahan brothers cleaned him out, then he'd gone home to his trailer.

"I hope they got all that wedding talk out of their systems last night," Boone continued. "Of course, that would almost be better than listening to Brick go on and on about his twins. I swear, you'd think he's the first man to ever have a kid. They are cute—don't get me wrong—but he'll wear you out talking about them. Honestly, I'm surprised Liliana actually got him to leave the little squirts in Brazos Bend with the grandparents."

"I heard this is the first time they've left them."

"Heard that, did you? I think he only mentioned it one hundred and twelve times last night."

"Maybe one hundred and thirteen." Jackson finished off his burrito and licked his fingers. "He's no different than any of the Callahans. They're family people."

"True. Matt was saying last night that Branch isn't doing well. They decided on the trip down here that they're not going to make their usual trip to Eternity Springs for the Fourth of July this year. They're going to ask the family—extended family included—to go to the ranch. They're afraid he's not going to make it much longer."

"I hate to hear that, but I'm not surprised. He's getting up there."

"Way up there. I know you have the dance hall grand opening concert on the holiday weekend, but if the Callahans have a party—"

"I'll do my best to be there." Jackson wadded up his burrito wrap and shot for two into the trash can behind the bar. "Ready for a walk, cuz?"

Boone slid off the barstool. "I am. Gotta get in my shine time before the 'rents arrive. It'll be hard to make time with Miss Maisy with my Mama lookin' on."

Jackson snorted. "Somehow I don't doubt that you'll make it work."

Outside they found Caroline, Gillian, and Maisy waiting along with Angelica. The older woman walked toward them with her hands clasped at her waist. "I'm afraid I have some disappointing news. Brick and Lili won't be joining you. They got a call in the middle of the night, and they've had to cut the weekend short."

"Oh no," Caroline said.

"Did something happen to one of the twins?" Jackson asked.

"No, thank heavens. It's a problem of a different sort. Liliana's mother suffered a fall. She hurt her hip. Brick and Lili have gone to Oklahoma City to be with her during her surgery."

"That's a shame," Boone said. "I hate to hear that."

"The good thing is the doctors have assured the family that she should make a full recovery. Anyway the group hike is two people smaller and"—she gestured to the ladies—"you're all here."

"All right then." Jackson's smile encompassed all three women, though it lingered a bit on Caroline. "Good morning. I guess we can all fit in my truck, so why don't—"

"No sense cramming," Boone interrupted. "I planned on taking my truck, too. Somebody can ride with me. Maisy?"

"Sure. I'll ride with you."

"Meet you at the trailhead, cuz," Boone said, tipping his hat. He and Maisy had climbed into the cab of his truck and pulled out of the inn's parking lot almost before Jackson managed to complete another sentence. He glanced at Gillian and Caroline and shrugged. Both women were smiling. Caroline said, "That was rather obvious, wasn't it."

Jackson debated with himself for about half a moment. "You might want to give Maisy a heads-up that Boone isn't . . . well . . . he doesn't want . . . um . . ."

"That's perfect," Gillian said, giving his arm a reassuring pat. "Neither does she."

Jackson nodded. "Good. That's good." He paused a moment and added, "Does she know that his parents are arriving this afternoon?"

"Well, I don't know." Then Gillian softly laughed. "I guess the course of true love doesn't run smoothly, does it?"

"Amen!" Jackson and Caroline said simultaneously and with fervor. Then Jackson shook his head and motioned to the pair of backpacks on the walk. "That's your gear?"

At their nods, he stowed them in the back, then loaded up and headed after Boone and Maisy. Jackson knew his cousin wouldn't get too far ahead of them because he didn't know exactly where they were going. They weren't going to the waterfall that Maisy had shown them on that very first trip to Enchanted Canyon. These were actually three spring-fed waterfalls, smaller, more remote, and something Jackson had happened on quite by accident when he'd climbed the northeastern slope of the canyon in an attempt to recreate an old photograph of the dance hall that he'd discovered in some of the historical records in town. When he'd shared news of his discovery with Boone who'd mentioned it to Celeste, she'd suggested that it'd make a nice day-hike destination.

Soon after, their construction crews had been put to work cutting a moderately challenging three-mile trail that began at a parking area constructed at the opposite end of the canyon from Ruin. From there, hikers took a scenic path to the waterfall that stair-stepped three levels from just below the canyon rim.

It was a beautiful morning for a hike: sunny, with temperatures in the mid-seventies and just enough breeze to keep things cool. On the first half of the trail, they were content to let the squirrels and mockingbirds do the chattering. By the second half of the walk though, Boone had turned his flirt on. Jackson had forgotten just how annoying his cousin could be.

The man was good at it, for sure. Smooth and witty, oh so subtle—except when he was being blatant about it. They ate it up, because of course he was an equal-opportunity flirt, giving all three women his attention. And he loved to take potshots at Jackson.

How could he have forgotten how irritating Boone could be?

"This is beautiful, Jackson," Caroline said. "I thought I wouldn't like anything as much as the falls and swimming hole by your place, but this is pretty awesome."

"I know. There's an even better spot, too. " He pointed off to the right at about three o'clock. "You can see all three falls and Enchanted Rock. It sorta peeks up over the canyon rim and watches over things."

"The trail doesn't go up that far?"

"No. We didn't take it up there because, well, honestly"—he lowered his voice—"I didn't tell the others about it. It's tough climbing in a few spots, and I decided we didn't need the liability issues."

"Oh, I want to see. You'll show me, won't you?"

Jackson glanced over to where the lower falls pooled and Boone, Gillian, and Maisy were embroiled in a rock-skipping contest. "Sure. Just promise you won't sue me if you fall."

"You have my word."

He motioned for her to follow him. They headed off without giving notice to the others, though just before they disappeared into the woods, Jackson glanced over his shoulders and met his cousin's gaze. Boone grinned, nodded, then stooped to pick up another stone and asked, "Who'll bet me five bucks that I get it to skip five times?"

"I'll take that wager," Maisy said.

The sound of their voices faded as Jackson and Caroline moved away from the trio and farther into the trees. "It seems like you're taking me away from the falls," she observed.

"I am. We have to go the long way around to get there unless you brought belay devices in your pack."

"No. Rock climbing is not my sport."

"It's not that far, and we won't need ropes and pulleys going this way." Jackson took her hand and helped her up an incline slippery with gravel, but dropped it once she'd successfully navigated the slope. They maintained a comfortable silence during the hike that took a little less than ten minutes. As they neared the viewing spot that was their destination, the wash of the falls began to drown out the chatter of the squirrels and the mockingbird's squawks. Jackson wouldn't call the sound a roar. These falls weren't big enough to roar.

"I love that sound," Caroline said. "The falling water."

"What's a step down from a roar?" he asked her.

"A rush? A rumble? A whoosh? It's beautiful. I don't see Enchanted Rock, though."

"We're not there yet." He tightened his hold on her hand and gave her another tug. "Come along around this bend, and then we actually go downhill."

"Lead on, Magellan."

As he led her along a path that wasn't much of one, he was vaguely aware of his anxiousness to share this unique spot in Enchanted Canyon. It was small, hardly bigger than a closet, and if he hadn't happened to glance just the right way when he'd been walking past, he would have missed it. And yet every time he found himself in this quadrant of the canyon, he found himself wandering this way. Something about the spot called to him.

Caroline yanked her hand from his grasp and froze. "Is that a snake?"

He followed the path of her gaze and spied the four-foot-long black snake wrapped around a tree limb at eye level. "Yep. Bullsnake. Perfectly harmless."

"Perfectly don't care. Perfectly can't stand snakes."

"But you have such stylish snake boots."

"I'm not wearing snake earmuffs." She hesitated a moment, then asked, "Can you get him to move?"

He chided her with a look. "It's *his* living room, not ours. Look at him, gal. He's wrapped around that limb like a lace of licorice."

"I don't like licorice any better than snakes," she grumbled.

Jackson rolled his eyes and walked beneath the branch into the clear, and then he turned and waved her through. Caroline drew a deep breath, and then dashed forward and into Jackson's arms. Once there, she squealed and he laughed.

She was sweet as corn fresh off the stalk, and she melted against him like ice cream on a summer day. "Why am I thinking about Eve and the Garden of Eden right at this moment?"

"I'm not sure if that's a compliment or an insult."

"Compliment. Definitely a compliment."

"Are you the Devil, Jackson McBride?"

"Me? Ha. You are the one who is pure temptation, Caroline Carruthers." She smiled slowly and so sweetly that it was all he could do not to take her mouth with his here and now. He'd back her against the tree and grind his body against hers and scratch this blasted itch—except the damn snake was still curled around the branch.

Her tongue slithered out from her mouth and circled her lips. "Maybe you should show me Enchanted Rock."

Temptation. Pure temptation.

See that girl.

"Maybe I'd better." He took her hand and led her down the final few yards to the blink-and-you'll-miss-it spot framed between two boulders that revealed all three horsetail falls and Enchanted Rock. He watched in quiet pleasure as her eyes widened and her mouth circled in a silent O.

"It's magical. It's like something right off of a post-card."

"I know."

She smiled at Jackson with delight. "Enchanted Canyon is spectacularly cool. It's like we've stepped back in time. Everything is unspoiled and undeveloped. Nature at its most raw and real and powerful. It makes me feel small and insignificant."

He saw her eyeing the flat-topped boulder to his right and surmised that she was considering a climb. "Here. Let me help."

He put his hands around her narrow waist and lifted her. She scooted over, making room for him, and soon they sat side by side staring out at the waterfalls and the giant rock rising behind them. Though they were closer to the spring-fed falls than they'd been before, the canyon walls deflected the sound so the spot was eerily quiet. The upper and middle falls were above them, the lower one slightly below. They sat without speaking maybe fifty feet above the canyon floor where the river, narrow at this point, snaked its way south.

Almost five minutes passed before either of them spoke. "This is so peaceful. Thank you for sharing it with me, Jackson."

"I like having you here."

She smiled up at him again, and this time he couldn't resist. He leaned over and kissed her. It was a steamy kiss, a thorough kiss, but ultimately, a safe kiss because he couldn't exactly lay her back on the rock and have his wicked way with her. One wrong roll would send them plunging to the canyon floor.

With a sigh, he ended it, taking one last taste, and then murmuring against her mouth, "You taste like butterscotch."

"Maisy gave me candy."

"I like butterscotch. I'll have to hit her up."

"Good luck with that," Caroline said with a chuckle. "I don't know that Boone will give you a chance. She said he's been hitting on her since the second the weekend started."

"Yeah." Jackson grimaced and added, "I hope she's not taking him seriously. He's just having some fun. I think he's being obvious about it. *He* thinks he's being obvious about it, but sometimes men can read women wrong. Boone has a lot of baggage."

"No worries. It's perfectly clear and besides, this is right up Maisy's alley. She has plenty of baggage herself."

"Oh yeah?" Jackson couldn't help but be curious, but he wasn't nosey enough to ask. Was he? Before he'd quite decided, a sound that was definitely out of place caught his notice.

"Did you hear that?" He turned his head and listened intently.

After a moment, Caroline softly asked, "What am I listening for?"

"I'm not sure. Something's crying."

"Someone is hurt? Maisy? Gillian?"

"No. No. Not human. Not that direction, either. I know the wildlife in the canyon pretty well by now, but this one is different." He closed his eyes and leaned forward.

Faintly, ever so faintly. *Mewl mewl whimper mew mewl.*

"I hear it!" she said. "It sounds like—oh, Jackson— it sounds like a baby. What if someone is down there?"

Not a baby. "That's not human. That's an animal. One that's hurt. Probably a coyote. It's below us." He leaned as far forward as he was able without falling off the damn rock and studied the ground below.

"Can you see him?"

He shook his head. "View of the ground is limited."

"We have to go down. We have to find him."

Jackson hesitated. An injured animal wasn't anything to play around with. Not only were they dangerous themselves, they attracted predators ready to take advantage of the weak.

"We could at least try to spot him, couldn't we?" Caroline asked. "We wouldn't have to get close. If it's dangerous, you could put it out of its misery."

Jackson couldn't stand to hear animals of any type suffering, but still, he hesitated. "I'm not sure how we'll get down to the canyon floor from here, Caroline. It's not exactly a marked trail."

And yet, even as he said it he knew he was going to try. The animal's cries were no longer haunting him, but now he heard whispers. It was as if the canyon itself was talking to him. Telling him to go . . . to look . . . to seek . . . something.

He heard Angelica Blessing's voice echo through

his mind, "Enchanted Canyon is where troubled souls come to find peace."

He shivered and slid down from the boulder. "But I guess it won't hurt anything to try."

Jackson helped Caroline down from her perch, and taking her hand firmly in his, he scanned the area for a possible path down. He thought of the old saying about not seeing the forest for the trees even as a pathway became obvious to him. "This way," he said, to himself as much as to her.

A switchback slope brought them to the canyon floor more quickly and with less effort than he ever would have guessed, bringing them a short distance downstream from the lower waterfall. Jackson motioned for Caroline to stay safely in the cover of the trees as he stepped out onto a flat, narrow riverbank clear of trees and shrubs. About five yards ahead of him the river stretched probably fifteen yards wide with a sheer cliff wall on the far side. From this position the waterfalls *did* roar. No way would they be able to hear the animal's cries. If they didn't see him, they'd never be able to find him.

He looked up, trying to coordinate their current position with that of the boulder where they'd been sitting.

Caroline moved from the trees to stand beside him and raised her voice, the note of sadness obvious. "The water is so loud here. How did we hear anything before?"

"Maybe we didn't," Jackson suggested. "Maybe it was the wind whistling through the rocks and playing tricks on us."

And yet, he didn't believe that. The wind whistling through the rocks was telling him to keep looking, that it was important to keep looking, that he had something important to find in Enchanted Canyon. He turned his head and looked at Caroline and was struck by a sensation so intense that it was as if the ground beneath his feet had shifted.

She stood in a beam of sunshine surrounded by a rainbow mist. Her eyes were wide and luminous with emotion. Her lips still swollen from his kiss. The waterfalls roared.

A dog barked.

Music flowed into his head and his heart and back into his soul.

See that girl, she's your last chance to dance.

"I hear it! Do you hear it, Jackson?"

He laughed aloud. He heard it all right. Not an acoustic guitar. Not a trio of strings and a drum. Not an effing orchestra. What he was hearing was a three-hundred-member marching band.

"Where is it coming from, Jackson?"

He looked up at the canyon walls surrounding them. "Here. It's coming from here." He looked back down at Caroline Carruthers. "You. The music's coming from you."

"Music! What music? I hear barking!"

Arf. Arf. Arf. Arf.

Jackson grabbed Caroline around the waist, picked her up, twirled her around once, twice, then kissed her hard and fast before setting her back down.

"Jackson! What in the world!"

"It's Enchanted Canyon. We have to go with it. Now, look!" He gestured across the river to where just above the waterline he could just make out the golden snout and big brown eyes of an animal that definitely wasn't a coyote and just might be a golden Lab.

"Oh wow. It *is* a dog! How did he get there?"

"No telling, but he appears to be stuck."

"Poor thing. How do we help him? We swim across, I guess?"

"*I* swim across. Just because he's a dog doesn't mean he isn't seriously injured and seriously mean. He could have tangled with a boar or a bobcat or a rabid raccoon for all we know. Besides, I might need you to rescue me."

Arrf. Arrf. Arrf.

Jackson eyed the river as he slipped his backpack off and lowered it to the ground. Hard to gauge the water depth up against the canyon wall, but it was certainly over his head. He leaned against a nearby boulder for balance, and then bent over to unlace his boots. He pulled them and his socks off, grabbed his T-shirt by the hem, and yanked it up and over his head. It was only when he reached for his belt that he hesitated and glanced up.

Caroline was looking at him with avid interest. He arched a brow. Color stained her cheeks, but she shrugged before she turned around. "Can you blame me?"

He shucked out of his jeans, left on his drawers, and waded into the refreshingly cool, gently flowing water, wincing when his feel caught the sharp end of stones a time or two on the rocky river bottom.

Arf arf arf arf arf arf arf!

Jackson lifted his legs and began to swim. A dozen strong strokes took him a few feet away from the cliff face. He pulled up to get his bearings. He couldn't see the Lab.

"The current carried you a little below him!" Caroline called. "He's behind the rock at your ten o'clock."

Jackson corrected course and moments later, approached the dog.

He'd been right. It was a golden Lab, full grown, but on the small side. At first glance, it appeared that he'd had somehow managed to get both hind legs wedged between a rock and the canyon wall.

Arf arf arf.

"Hey, boy. Poor fella." Jackson saw raw, bloody skin. "How the hell did you end up in the middle of nowhere stuck between a rock and a hard place?" And how the hell was he going to get him loose?

Arf. Arf. Arf. Arf. Arf.

"I'll bet you are tired. Looks like you've been fighting this for a while." He swam closer, took a better look. Adding an extra bit of soothe to his voice, he asked, "Gonna let me get near you, big guy?"

Propping one foot on the rock, one against the cliff wall, he slowly reached for the Lab and hoped he wouldn't get bitten for the effort. Couldn't budge him one bit.

Arr . . . arr . . . arr. The dog whimpered.

Jackson swallowed a sigh. The dog's legs were already wet, so slicking them down with water wouldn't solve the problem. They'd managed to get in, so they should come out, but all the tugging had made the Lab's flesh swell. Crap. "We're gonna need to move that rock just a little bit, fella. Too bad I don't have a Caterpillar in my pocket."

Under other circumstances, he'd get a tree branch and use it as a lever, but the angle here made that impossible. There wasn't enough purchase for leverage. He was going to have to do it with his legs. At least give it the old college try. If he could nudge it even the slightest little bit and the dog had any sense, he'd wiggle loose.

Well, the rock probably weighs a ton, and if the dog has any sense he wouldn't be trapped between a rock and a hard place in a river in the middle of nowhere.

Whimper . . . whimper . . . whimper.

"Sorry. I'll try to think positive, fella."

Maybe they'd both be lucky, and the rock would be easily shifted. Maybe that's how old river dog got trapped in the first place. "Okay, buddy. Here's what we're going to do. I'm going to get my Hercules on and when the boulder budges, you skedaddle."

Jackson got into position with his back against the wall and his feet against the rock and his knees pretty close to his chest. Three times, he filled his lungs and exhaled. Then he took a deep, bracing breath and pushed.

Movement. The boulder moved. Didn't it? It did. He knew it did.

The dog didn't move. Dammit. "When the rock moves, you've gotta go, fella."

"Wait!"

Caroline's voice sounded close because she was close. Just when she had decided to jump into the river, Jackson hadn't noticed, but here she was. "Dammit, Caroline. What are you doing?"

"What do you think I'm doing? This is a two-person job."

He couldn't argue with her logic. "If he starts to snap at you—seriously—he could be sick. Be careful."

"I will."

It took them four tries, but when he pushed the boulder that fourth time, Caroline was able to free the dog. Jackson breathed a sigh of relief at the same time he held his breath and prepared to dive into the water ready to assist Caroline if the Lab reacted poorly or started to sink. Thankfully, he took off swimming across the river and emerged onto the bank beside their backpacks and piles of clothes where he limped out and plopped down.

Piles of clothes. Huh. Caroline had stripped down to her bra and panties before jumping into the river. He must really have been distracted to let that salient fact escape him.

Well now. Jackson let his feet drift to the riverbed when the water was about waist deep, and he watched with undisguised interest as Caroline approached the shore. Hot pink bra straps. The lady liked color in her lingerie, did she? He grinned in appreciation.

She looked at him and slowly shook her head in disgust that he was pretty sure was feigned. "Perv," she said, loud enough to be sure that he could hear over the sound of the waterfall.

"Hey," he called back. "I caught you looking earlier. What's good for the goose and all."

"Fair enough. However, why don't we both keep our eyes to ourselves in this instance?"

"I don't mind if—"

"Jackson, quit teasing me," she interrupted. "Be a gentleman and promise to keep your eyes to yourself. We need to get dry and dressed and see about getting our new friend to someone who can doctor his legs."

"All right. I promise." Keeping his gaze averted, yet very aware of the figure moving beside him nevertheless, he waded from the river and stepped toward his clothes. He peeled off his wet drawers—hey, if she cheated, let her get an eyeful—and used his T-shirt to dry himself before pulling on his jeans commando-style. He sat in order to dry his feet. "Be sure to dry your feet thoroughly. The hike back won't be any fun if you rub blisters."

"True, but luckily I came prepared. I have extra socks and blister bandages in my pack."

"Good girl."

"I try to be," she said with a sigh. "I don't always succeed, I'm afraid."

A guilty note in her voice had him shooting her a look. She had her jeans and T-shirt on, and she was petting the dog that'd rested his head on her thigh.

Lucky dog. "Did you peek?" he asked with aggrieved accusation in his tone.

She went for an innocent look, but she didn't quite pull it off. Jackson scowled, rolled to his feet, and met the dog's brown-eyed gaze. "Word of warning, river dog. You have to watch out for this one." Addressing Caroline, he said, "Have you been able to get a good look at his legs?"

"Not really. He scooted over here, instead of walking, and I haven't tried to touch more than his head."

The way the dog was lying, Jackson couldn't see anything, either. It was impossible to judge how badly injured he was.

"What are we going do with him?" Caroline asked.

Jackson extended a hand toward Caroline. "Go ahead and stand up. Let's see if he attempts to follow. I'll carry him if I have to, but I'd just as soon avoid that if possible."

She placed her hand in Jackson's, and he pulled her to her feet. The dog rose. His tail started to wag. Caroline said, "That's a good sign."

"Yep. It is." Jackson pulled on his backpack and watched as Caroline donned hers. "You ready to make the climb?"

"I am. Boone and the girls are probably wondering what happened to us. I thought about calling them, but when I checked my cell I saw that we have no service."

"Yeah. We're in a hole here. Once we're up out of it, I'll give him a ring. We haven't been gone long enough to worry him." Jackson knew that Boone would think he'd led Caroline off for a little alone time.

He led the way up the hill, keeping watch on the woman and the dog following behind. Halfway to the spot where they'd looked down from and spotted the dog, it became clear that the Lab wasn't able to make the climb. Luckily, the dog didn't snap at Jackson when he attempted to pick him up. However, hiking mostly up-hill with probably fifty pounds of dog wasn't a heckuva lot of fun. Jackson was glad when they rendezvoused with Boone and the others because he figured to share the burden with his cousin. He figured wrong. The dog was having none of it, snarling and snapping when Jackson tried to hand him over.

Jackson was one whipped puppy by the time they hiked all the way back to the truck, the one redeeming factor that he got to preen in front of the ladies and in front of his cousin. Boone reached out to the Eternity Springs group, and by the time Jackson made it back to the inn, Nic Callahan, a veterinarian by profession, was standing by to examine the yellow Lab in a makeshift exam room set up in the inn's laundry room.

"He's one lucky dog," Nic said after her exam. "All I see is bruising, cuts, and abrasion from his efforts to free himself. No crushing injury and no apparent fracture."

"That's good," Jackson said, relief rolling through him. "Really good. Can you tell how long he might have been trapped?"

"With any certainty? No. If I had to guess, I'd say since yesterday sometime. Angelica said you had a heavy rain yesterday morning. Perhaps he got washed into the river then."

"That occurred to me, too. Thanks, Doc. I really appreciate the help. Sorry you had to work on your holiday."

"Glad I was here to help. To be honest, I raced Lori to the stethoscope. We've been discussing the possibility of my rejoining the Eternity Springs Animal Clinic now that my children are older and Lori has her little girl. I think this pretty boy here might have been just what I needed to help me make my decision." She scratched the yellow Lab behind his ears and cooed at him a bit. "Brave boy. Gotta be a fighter." Nic glanced up, her friendly blue eyes meeting Jackson's gaze. "So, what are you going to name him?"

Jackson didn't even hesitate. He understood that some things were meant to be. "He's the river dog. River. His name is River."

"That's a good name for a dog," Nic said.

"A great name," Caroline agreed. "A *really* great name. It'll remind me of a special morning every time I hear it."

Surprised by her arrival, Jackson looked over his shoulder to see her standing in the doorway holding a ten-pound bag of dog food. "Where'd you get that?"

"Celeste."

"Celeste? Why does Celeste have dog food? She doesn't have a dog."

Caroline shrugged, Nic Callahan laughed, and Angelica swept into the room and declared, "She's stealing my thunder, that's why. *I'm* the one who said we needed dog food."

"But why—" Caroline began.

Jackson had been down this road more than once before. "Let it go. You are not going to make any sense of anything. Only thing we need to know is that in a battle of the Blessings, we all come out winners.

Chapter Fifteen

Caroline straightened the beverage napkins for perhaps the sixty-seventh time and gave the punch another stir. Maybe she'd made a mistake with the punch. She should have stuck with tea and coffee. "Too late now," she muttered as she carefully rested the ladle against the side of the crystal punchbowl.

The Next Chapter bookstore in Redemption, Texas, would officially open its doors for business in nineteen minutes. She was as nervous as a long-tailed cat on a porch full of rockers. She had three Texas authors coming in later tonight to sign their books during this evening's grand-opening events. One was a botanist who'd published a book about Texas wildflowers through Texas A&M University Press. Another was a celebrity in the quilting world with a new book out, and the last was a superstar romance author whose fans had preordered more than three cases of books through the bookstore's website—and the link had gone live only yesterday!

She heard the back-door buzzer, and frowned. What in the world? She wasn't expecting any deliveries this time of night.

"Want me to get that, Caroline?" one of tonight's counter clerks asked.

"No thanks, Allison. I'll see to it." She was honestly glad to have something to do rather than rearrange cookies on a plate. Once in the storeroom, she pushed aside the curtain that shielded the window in her back door and saw flowers. Nothing but a huge bouquet of yellow roses. Someone had sent her flowers. One of the vendors she'd worked with perhaps?

Delight filled her and she hurried to open the door only to discover that the person behind the bouquet was no vendor, but a friend. "Jackson!"

"Happy grand opening," he said, handing her the flowers.

"Oh, Jackson. They're gorgeous. Just gorgeous." She stepped back and motioned for him to enter the building.

"Well, so are you." Jackson took off his hat and hung it on the hat rack beside the door.

She smiled up at him with pleasure and delight. "Thank you. And thank you for coming tonight. You could have come through the front door though."

"I didn't want to stand in line."

"A line?" Her head jerked up. "What line?"

"There's a line forming out there." He hesitated a moment and added, "Some of them are wearing lime green capes."

"Aww." Caroline's delight only grew. "My romance author's fairy heroine wears a lime green cape. But the signings don't start for two more hours."

"I don't know what to tell you. There's a line, and they're wearing lime green capes."

"Wow."

"Yeah. I guess I'll have to buy one of those books for

Boone's sister. She loves romances with the weird stuff. But right now I'm here to buy something for myself. I want you to ring me up as The Next Chapter's first official sale."

"Aww," Caroline repeated, touched by his gesture. She decided she wouldn't mention the books Angelica bought to serve as the "first official sale." Or, those that Maisy bought. Or the ones Gillian ordered. The fact was that Jackson was here to buy at the opening, well . . . "You'd better get out there and pick something out, in that case. The doors open in"—she checked her watch—"less than fifteen minutes."

"Yikes. I'm running later than I anticipated. Maisy was awfully chatty while she was putting together the flowers. Took way longer than I figured it would."

Caroline made a shooing motion toward the sales floor. "Do you know what you want?"

"No."

"Do you want some suggestions?"

"Well—"

"Caroline?" Allison called. "We have someone on the phone with a question about Naomi Parker backlist titles?"

"I'll be right there," Caroline called. To Jackson, she said, "Let me—"

He cut her off. "No. Thanks. I'm happy to browse. That's what bookstores are all about, right?" He headed for the front of the store, and she made a spot for the flowers on her refreshment table before tending to the phone call. After that she dealt with another issue and then another and before she knew it, Tiffany, who was her author liaison for the evening said, "Five minutes, Caroline."

"Oh." Caroline patted her hand over her fluttering heart, and she looked around for Jackson. Their gazes met as he hastily shelved a book. Later she would be amused that he'd found his way to the section of the store which she privately thought of as Angelica's department, though was discreetly labeled Relationships in her small-town bookstore, but right now she was too busy becoming a nervous wreck.

Jackson must have judged her mood, because he gave her a reassuring wink. He tucked a coffee table–sized title with a photo of a golden Labrador retriever on its jacket beneath his arm and ambled toward her. Leaning down, he kissed her on the cheek. "You've got this, hon. It's time to open the doors of your Next Chapter. It's gonna be great. You're gonna hit a home run, and I'm gonna be sitting behind home plate watching."

The evening passed in a whirl of laughter and activity and gratifyingly constant lines at the registers. The authors were pleased, the customers complimentary, and Caroline closed the door at the end of the night with euphoria humming through her. She flipped the lock and took a bittersweet moment to think of Robert. What would he say if he could see her tonight? He'd be proud of her, surely. Happy for her. Robert hadn't encouraged her to be independent, but that was because he liked to take care of her, not because he tried to hold her back. Had she gone to him and professed a dream of opening a bookstore, he may well have supported her in that dream. He'd loved her, and her happiness had been important to him.

She rested her forehead against the door, closed her eyes, and fought back a moment of tears. *It still is. Be happy, Caro. Write the next page.*

Her heart stuttered. She was engulfed in warmth, in a sense of love, so real that it took her breath away. *Robert?*

It was gone as quickly as it came, but before she could

absorb the loss, cheering and applause drew her back to herself and to this moment. She turned to accept her employees' congratulations and met Jackson McBride's proud gaze.

Her next page?

She didn't question why he hung around during the process and procedures required in order to close the shop at the end of the first day of business, and when she closed the door behind the last of her employees to leave, she wasn't the least bit surprised that he took her into his arms.

"Look at you," he said. "Just look at you."

"It was a great night, wasn't it?"

"I was wrong. You didn't just hit a home run. You hit a grand slam."

"I did, didn't I?" Then she did something out of character for the Caroline of the previous chapter. She reached up and pulled his face down to hers and kissed him with all of the joy and euphoria and passion running through her blood.

The kiss went from hot to molten in seconds, and in the recesses of her mind where rational thought remained possible, Caroline recognized that she teetered on the edge of the volcano. *Am I ready to dive in? Is this what comes next?*

Jackson ended the kiss and lifted his head, breathing heavily. "Wow. That's um . . . wow. You pack a punch, Caroline Carruthers."

"So do you." She licked her lips, filled her lungs with air, and dove. "Jackson, would you like to come home with me?"

He didn't even pause to think about it. "More than I want to breathe my next breath."

Okay, then.

"But honey, that's a pretty big step. I know this is your

next chapter and all, but are you sure this is the right time?"

She stiffened ever so slightly. "I'm not trying to use you."

Well, actually, maybe she was.

"Use me. Please." He showed her a crooked grin, then lifted her hands to his mouth, one at a time, and kissed them. "It's been an exciting night for you, and I know you're riding high. I'd feel horrible if I took you up on your most-tempting offer, and you regretted it in the morning."

"I think that's insulting, Jackson. To both of us."

"Well, better to roll out an insult or two than to ruin a friendship I value. Since we're talking frank here, I suspect you haven't been with anyone since Robert. Going to bed with me will be a big deal."

Attempting to lighten the mood, she pulled away from him, folded her arms, and snapped, "Braggart."

He laughed and pulled her close. "Ah, Caroline, you are a delight."

He kissed her again, then stared down into her eyes and made a promise. "When we go to bed, Caroline, it will matter. I don't sleep around."

"I don't either."

"But I'm not ready for a relationship. I'm certainly not looking to fall in love."

She put her hands against his chest and gave him a shove. "I'm not, either!"

Jackson took a step backward. For a long moment, they stood staring at each other. In that instant, Caroline wasn't sure whether she wanted to kiss him or hit him. Finally, he said, "So, maybe we can enjoy each other. Have fun with each other."

"Yes," she said. "I'd like that. That's what I want."

He lifted his hand, trailed his thumb down her cheek.

"Starting tonight? Are you sure? This isn't an I-conquered-the-retail-world high?"

She shuddered at his touch. "Maybe a little of that. I do feel like I've achieved world domination."

She considered the state of her home. Dishes were done. No underwear lying around. She'd changed the sheets yesterday. "Yes. I'm sure. Come home with me, Jackson."

"Do I need to make a drugstore run on the way?"

Oh, no! She hadn't even thought about condoms. She was so out of practice with this sort of thing. "I'm afraid I don't . . . oh. Wait." She snapped her fingers and smiled. "Angelica!"

"Angelica?"

"We're good to go. One of the books in the Relationship section comes with a kit."

"A kit, huh? What does Angelica—no, never mind."

"I'll grab one on our way out."

"I'm really intrigued. So, what else needs to be done here before we can go? What can I do to help?"

"Nothing. We can go. There's nothing that needs doing that can't wait until tomorrow."

"All right then. Get your kit, Caroline, and take me home." He snagged a bottle of champagne from a bucket that she hadn't brought into the store, and she went gooey over his thoughtfulness. For a man who hadn't set out to seduce her, he'd sure done a right fine job of it.

It was a beautiful summer night, a lingering hint of color fading in the west while stars began to burst like popcorn with increasing frequency in the darkening sky. They didn't speak as they walked hand in hand toward the Craftsman bungalow Caroline had bought the day it went on the market and moved into earlier this month. Actually, Caroline wasn't sure she was walking. She felt more like she was floating.

Having her feet off the ground was a good place to be. She wasn't ready to come down to Earth yet. Tonight had been a fabulous success. She'd had fun. She was happy. She was about to get laid by the hottest guy in town. She wanted it to happen. She needed it to happen. It was time, the right time, and Jackson McBride was the right man.

The porch step creaked as he stepped up onto it. Caroline reached into her purse for her keys. The gentle evening breeze carried the sound of cheers and the aroma of funnel cakes from the baseball fields a short distance away.

She opened the door and he followed her inside. She set down her bag in its usual spot on a desk near the door, and as she turned toward him, her toes brushed the ground. Nerves fluttered. "Jackson, I'm a little—a lot—out of practice. Would you take it from here?"

"Honey, it'll be my honor. Show me the way to your bedroom."

She did that much. He did the rest, and he did it with such slow, sweet, focused attention that he all but drove her mad. Jackson McBride wouldn't be rushed. His love-making was a ballad of many verses. Her body, his guitar. He played her like the master musician he was, knowing just how to use his talented fingers, mouth, and tongue to make her vibrate, make her hum, make her weep, make her sing. Finally . . . finally . . . he rose above her, the thick, hard heat of him poised at her entrance until she met his gaze.

Jackson wrote a bridge for his song. "This is special to me, Caroline."

"To me, too."

He played a pulsing, pounding chorus that sent them both soaring, and as the final notes faded on this magical summer night, Caroline knew that Jackson

McBride's melody would linger in her mind for a very long time.

Over the Fourth of July weekend the Last Chance Hall opened—or reopened, to be precise—to excellent reviews from musicians and patrons alike and raised a significant amount of money for Tucker's favorite veteran's charity. The weather was hot, the beer cold, and the music would have rocked the walls except Jackson kept them winged up so that the breeze blew through.

Next door at the inn, Angelica made it through the grand opening and the first-of-month operations without any major disasters. Celeste returned to Colorado, and her cousin was managing on her own passably well. July ended with only one minor fire and three broken windows. All in all, Jackson thought, things were going pretty darn good.

His vision for the Last Chance Hall was coming to life. The place had a good vibe. He'd heard some seriously fine music played here in just a few short weeks. And people came to dance.

On the personal front, he and Caroline were clicking along together just fine. They saw each other almost every day and slept together almost every night. Beyond agreeing that they were to see each other exclusively, neither one of them tried to define what was between them. Neither had taken this step lightly, and both were content to explore the possibilities, to see where time would take them. Caroline said she tended to write lengthy chapters. Jackson had no problem with that.

Neither one of them was about to float the "L" word, but if it had begun to drift through Jackson's mind like a haunting melody just beyond reach, then . . . well . . .

Sitting on Caroline's front porch on a Tuesday night with River lying at his feet as he waited for her to come home from the bookstore, he pulled the harmonica from his pocket and played . . . something. River lifted his head and looked at him. Jackson looked back. This something wasn't awful. It was something that might just become something someday.

"Huh," he muttered aloud.

"Rrarf."

When Caroline arrived home twenty minutes later, River lay asleep on the dog bed she kept for him in her living room while Jackson sat at her kitchen table writing on the back of a brown paper grocery sack. "Are you making a grocery list?"

"Something like that." He gave her a wicked grin. "Red meat. Need some red meat around here. Rib eyes. T-bones. Porterhouse steaks. A man needs to keep up his strength, you know." Then he was out of the chair, and he scooped her up and threw her over his shoulder in a fireman's carry and hauled her off to bed.

Caroline laughed until his attentions had her moaning instead.

The weeks passed and Jackson began to think there might something to Celeste Blessing's Enchanted Canyon tagline. His troubled heart was certainly finding peace.

That changed on August fifteenth when he received the first of a series of text messages from Beelzebub, aka Ray-Walker Parks, Sharon's manager, changing the arrangements for Jackson's next scheduled visit with Haley.

Seeing that number on his phone sent Jackson's temper into volcanic eruption–land every damn time. The slimy, slick, manipulative old bastard might not have caused the divorce, but he'd damn sure contributed to it. He wasn't a musician and he couldn't sing a lick, but he'd been the most powerful voice in the band from the moment Sharon hired him. Ray-Walker's power lay in his keen ability to recognize talent, his ruthless willingness to use it and abuse it. He possessed the devil's own tongue when it came to saying what said talent wanted and needed to hear in order to get them to do exactly what he wanted them to do.

He'd even fooled Jackson for a time. Young and green back in the day, he'd let his head be turned by Ray-Walker's extensive industry history and list of contacts. And face it, his instincts about creating "Coco" had been spot on. He'd fulfilled Sharon's dream. Created a superstar. That's what she'd really wanted in the end, wasn't it?

She'd certainly wanted it more than she'd wanted Jackson, that's for damn sure. Jackson had been convinced that she wanted to be Coco more than she wanted to be Haley's mother, too. That's why in the beginning, he'd actually believed she'd agree for him to be the custodial parent. That's why he never believed he'd actually lose his daughter—until he lost.

Haley. Her absence in his life, his need to be with her was constantly with him, a wound that never healed. As time for a visit approached, the scab that covered the wound and helped him to get by between visits started flaking off.

It was the weirdest damn thing. He was so excited about seeing her. So anxious to see her. A five-year-old waiting for Christmas morning. He couldn't wait. But the closer he came to seeing her again, the more not seeing her hurt.

Over the next ten days, he heard from Ray-Walker seven different times changing the meeting time, the meeting place, and the travel schedule, and that made him pissy as a junkyard dog. He ached for Haley. He was constantly reminded of the abject failure that been his custody fight with Sharon, how angry he was at his ex and the people in her sphere of influence, and how her army of attorneys and bottomless bank account had left him completely and totally defcated on the custody battlefield.

On August twenty-eighth, three days before he was due to leave for California to meet up with Coco's month-long West Coast tour, Jackson awoke at dawn, alone and in an extraordinarily foul mood. Sharon herself had condescended to call him yesterday afternoon with a time change, and as a result, had totally tanked his mood. He'd been unable to drag himself out of his funk and had cut last night's date with Caroline short. He sat up, scowled at River who once again had sneaked onto the foot of his bed, and all but barked at his dog. "You don't listen for beans, do you?"

River perked one ear, opened one eye, and snarled at him. Jackson snarled back, then embarrassed by his actions, said, "Sorry, boy. I'm going for a swim. You're welcome to join me or sleep in if you'd like."

The dog turned his head and went back to sleep. "Don't blame you one bit," Jackson murmured as he rolled out of bed. He grabbed a towel and headed outside into the hot August sunshine. With any luck, the exercise and refreshing waters of the swimming hole might restore his humor. At least he wouldn't have to worry about getting text messages or phone calls during a swim.

He gave it a good effort, spending the better part of an hour in the water, trying his hardest to keep his thoughts in the present, but for the most part, failing.

In three days, he'd have five days to spend with his

little girl. Five days that had to last him until January. It was better than the schedule she'd won in court almost a year and a half ago now, so he shouldn't complain, but damn, she jerked him around like a puppet on a string, and he resented the hell out of it.

But, bottom line, he got to see Haley more often. Every five months instead of six. For five days at a time.

The reason behind the change was idiotic. Flat-out crazy. Apparently Coco had decided that in order to channel her inner songwriter, she needed let the Circle of Fifths guide her life.

Music theory! She was basing their visitation schedule—in fact, rescheduling her entire life—around some crazy-ass idea she had about chords and keys. As if music were a religion! The woman had lost her ever-loving mind.

He wondered if this was something that Ray-Walker had cooked up or if it had come from that California cowboy she'd started sleeping with recently. Un-freaking-believable.

"It's a G-major month, Jackson," she'd said when she'd interrupted his phone conversation with Haley last month with the news. "That won't do. I'm feeling F-sharp. You'll need to see Haley in September rather than in August."

F sharp my ass.

He was a little worried she'd started doing drugs. He was even more worried that she'd find another weird religion and tell him he couldn't see his daughter again until October of next year.

Damn. What had happened to that sweet young woman with the angel's voice who he'd married? Ambition, that's what. Ambition, fame, and fortune, and a slick, sonofabitch manager and high-powered lawyers and bottomless bank accounts.

He despised all of it.

Jackson filled his lungs with air then dove beneath the surface, kicked hard, pulled hard, went down . . . down . . . down until he touched the bottom. He tucked, planted his feet, then used all his roaring inner rage to flex his muscles and shoot upward.

Chasing celebrity.

He pulled toward the surface. He'd never wanted celebrity. All he'd ever wanted was the music. He'd let her, let them, take it from him.

It was time to take it back. Past time.

His head broke the surface. He gave it a shake, slinging droplets of water flying. Symbolically flinging off his funk. *I am taking it back. The music is coming back. Caroline is helping.*

Jackson let his feet lift and he floated on his back, his face turned toward the warm summer sunshine. Snippets of lyrics drifted through his mind along with a ghost of a melody as he kicked in a slow, lazy circle. Circle of Fifths, circle of grief, circle of life.

Something. There was something there. He should go back to the trailer and write it . . . *splash!* Jackson lifted his head and grinned. "Hey, River dog!"

Jackson felt almost mellow when he returned to his trailer. Finding yet another schedule change from Ray-Walker waiting for him didn't even make his blood boil. Because in addition to the vague idea for a song, something else had occurred to him somewhere between the river bottom and the surface. He considered the notion as he showered and dressed, and he was still thinking about it as he opened the door of his truck to make a drive into town.

"I'm dropping you off at the hall," he said to River as the dog leapt up into the pickup before Jackson climbed into the driver's seat. "I'm going in for break-fast, and then I have a long list of errands to run. You need to hang at the Fallen Angel this morning."

Big brown eyes gazed at him reproachfully.

"Don't give me that look. Angelica will give you ba-con for breakfast, and her guests will go gooey over you like they always do."

River tilted his head as if considering it, then circled the seat and settled down. Ten minutes later, Jackson drove away from the inn without his dog and with a grocery list for Angelica tucked into his front shirt pocket.

He stopped at the Bluebonnet Café for a plate of pan-cakes before ordering a cinnamon roll to go, the peace offering he planned to take to Caroline. The woman had a sweet tooth that she resisted as a rule, but she did love the Bluebonnet's cinnamon rolls. Forty-five min-utes before The Next Chapter opened its doors, he drained his second cup of coffee, paid his check, and picked up the bakery box. He made the short walk to the bookstore, expecting to find her doing her pre-opening tasks. Sure enough, when he rapped on the window and cupped his hand against the glass to peer inside, he saw her emerge from the back.

She stopped, identified him. Scowled. He held up the bakery box and smiled, tried to mimic that look River had given him earlier with his eyes.

Caroline sighed visibly and walked toward the front door. She flipped the lock, stepped aside, and folded her arms, watching him with a skeptical ex-pression. Jackson dove right into his apology. "I'm sorry. I was grouchy as that green guy on *Sesame Street* last night. Please accept my apology and offer of atonement."

He opened the box as if he were lifting the lid of the jewel case containing a queen's diamond-studded crown. Caroline sighed and said, "You evil man."

"I really am sorry. Forgive me?"

"How can I not? You have a striking resemblance to River right now when he's giving you his pitiful-me look. Bring that box to the break room, and I'll get forks. You have to help me eat it. If I ate a whole one of these rolls all by myself I'd gain ten pounds and go into a sugar coma. Would you like a cup of coffee?"

"Yes, please."

She waited until she'd savored her first two bites of the sinfully delicious treat to ask, "So, want to tell me what last night was all about?"

He told her about Sharon's phone call and the schedule change. "She still holds the end of my chain, and she can jerk it whenever she wants, however hard she wants. There's not a damn thing I can do about it. Most of the time, I'm able to ignore it. But when it's almost time for a visit, when I'm days away from—" He broke off his sentence when a lump of emotion made it hard to speak.

Caroline attempted to finish his thought for him. "Seeing Haley again."

"No." Jackson cleared his throat. "Having to *leave* Haley again. It's the damnedest thing, Caroline. The anticipation of leaving her almost overshadows getting to see her. It casts a great big old black thundercloud over the entire visit. The last day or two of it, especially. And the flight home is brutal. I've never been as lonely in my life as I am when I leave Haley at the end of my time with her."

"Oh, Jackson." She touched his arm. "I'm so sorry. I can't imagine how hard that must be."

"Come with me, Caroline."

She drew back in surprise. "What?"

"Come with me to California. Come meet Haley. I have five days with her. I'm going to take her to Disneyland. We're going to go to the beach. We won't even see Sharon. Come. Come with us. It'll be fun. I want you to meet her. I'd love for you to meet her."

"Oh, Jackson."

He knew right then that she was going to turn him down. He shifted his gaze.

"Jackson, I'd love to meet Haley, but . . ."

"But."

"It's not a good idea, Jackson. For Haley's sake. She's six years old, right?"

"Seven, now."

"And I'm sure she's dying to see her Daddy. She's not going to want to share you. Especially not with another girl."

"But—"

"Have you even ever mentioned me to her?"

"She's not the jealous type," he responded, dodging the question. "She's sweet as can be. Besides, her mother parades the revolving door of her boyfriends in and out of her life all the time."

"Then it's even more important that you are careful about who you introduce to her. And even if that wasn't an issue, I have conflicts of my own. Jackson, I have an author signing this weekend, and I promised Gillian I'd sub for her Sunday-school class this week while she's away on a golf trip with Jeremy."

"Gillian plays golf?" he asked with a grumble in his tone. He stabbed another bite of the cinnamon roll with his fork and ate it, though it tasted more sour than sweet this time around.

"No, but Jeremy does." Caroline laced her fingers and leaned forward. "Honey, I do want to meet your Haley. I very much do. But let's do it in a thoughtful way."

He set down his fork, closed his eyes, and massaged his temples. "Okay. You're right. I know. I just hate this so much. It's the best thing and the worst thing I do. It's so hard, Caroline. So damn hard."

"I know it is. I feel so terrible for you." She rose from her seat and walked around the table, bent down and gave him a hard hug. "You fly out of Austin?"

"Yes. Early Thursday morning. I was going to drive down tomorrow and stay near the airport."

"And you fly back Tuesday?"

"Yes."

"I'll take you to the airport, Jackson. I'll meet your return flight. You can talk about Haley or not talk about her, whatever your heart needs. And sometime during your visit, you can mention your new friend Caroline, and then on one of your phone calls maybe she'll want to talk to me. We can work our way up to my meeting her. Okay?"

He sighed. She was right. He hated it, but she was right. "Okay. It's a deal. Flip for the last bite?"

She looked down and laughed. A full fourth of the roll was left. "It's all yours, Jackson. I need to waddle my way to the front to flip the closed sign to open in a few moments as it is."

On the drive back to the canyon, Jackson thought about what Caroline had said and how she'd said it. She'd called him "honey." That was nice. Really nice. It had just rolled off her lips like she'd meant it. Of course, the waitress at the Bluebonnet Café called him "honey," too, but this was different. Caroline was different.

He wanted her to meet Haley.

He wanted Haley to meet her.

They were the two most important ladies in his life. He loved them both. It was true. A year ago, even six months ago, he'd have sworn on six stacks of Bibles that he'd never fall in love again, but fall he had.

He was in love with Caroline.

Life was good with Caroline Carruthers here in Redemption, Texas, in Enchanted Canyon where troubled souls find peace. It wasn't perfect because Haley was so far away, but it was good. He needed to remember that as he traveled to California and back. He needed to hold onto that.

He loved Caroline and while she hadn't said as much, he was pretty sure she loved him in return. She'd called him "honey."

Caroline—and River—helped him ward off the worst of his bad mood as they took him to Austin and saw him off at the airport. He had a fabulous five days with Haley. They spent two full days at Disney and a third full day at the beach. The other two they spent doing nothing in particular, playing, talking, being silly together, telling jokes, and even singing songs. Jackson told Haley about his new dog River and good friend Caroline, and he could tell by his child's guarded reaction that Caroline's instincts had been on the mark.

Despite his best efforts, the black cloud returned when he kissed his daughter goodbye. Her wails as he walked away ripped fresh wounds in his heart and echoed in his mind all the way to the airport. He was silent as he paid the cab. He responded minimally to the TSA agent who greeted him with a friendly question. He seriously eyed the airport bar as he made his way toward his gate, but he feared if he started down that path, he'd never make it onto his plane.

Then, at the gate, a miracle happened. As he stood blindly staring at the departure sign that read Austin, Texas, a familiar voice said, "Hey, cowboy. Need a hug?"

Caroline, God bless her, had come to take him home.

Chapter Sixteen

Caroline had faced many challenges in her life. She'd tackled some serious life-and-death trials. She'd persevered. She'd emerged if not victorious, then at least still standing.

So why was she trembling in fear at this relatively minor task laid before her? It's ridiculous. It made no sense whatsoever.

"Are you ready?" Jackson asked.

No! her inner self screamed.

"Sure," she said, lifting her chin.

The music started. He emerged from behind the stage onto the empty dance floor at the Last Chance Hall. *It is my last chance,* Caroline thought. *My last chance to bolt for the door.*

As a native Texan, it had been her biggest secret, her greatest shame. She didn't know how to two-step. She'd never learned. She'd listened to pop music in high school and college. Robert introduced her to classical music, but he didn't like to dance. So, she'd never learned. That, apparently, was about to change.

Keen-eyed Jackson had noticed that she always made excuses not to dance at the Last Chance and called her on it. When she finally fessed up to her lack of skill, he'd declared himself her teacher.

She wanted to learn. She did. So why was she so embarrassed about this? "I just don't want to hear any whining when you are nursing your bruised and battered toes."

"Hey, why do you think I wore my steel-toe boots?"

Her eyes went wide as she glanced down at his feet. He laughed. He wore his usual everyday Ropers.

"While you'll looking down there, I'm going to show you my footwork so you'll have an idea of what I'm talking about when I say it. Watch now, darlin'. Basic two-step. It's very simple. I'll start with my left leg first—guys always start with their left—and I'll take a half step, one, and two. Half step, one, two. It's quick quick, slow, slow. Quick quick, slow, slow. That's it. Okay?"

"I guess."

He grinned, grabbed her hand, brought it to his mouth, and kissed it. "You learn to two-step, you'll be dancing all night long, every time you visit the Last Chance. Now, put your hand on the fella's arm here just below his shoulder." He placed it where he wanted it. "Kind of cup it around. Like that. Perfect. The guy places his hand on your shoulder blade like this. Now, see how far apart we're standing?"

She looked down, concentrating hard. How far was that? A foot? Ten inches?

"That's about right unless it's you and me. If it's you and me"—he yanked her tight against him and murmured against her ear—"we'll dance like this. But that's only you and me."

"Jackson!"

Again, he laughed. "Relax, honey. You have this. I am an excellent teacher. Now, the guy always starts with his left leg first. Lady starts with her right leg first. Remember it was a half step first, then a one, two. Quick quick slow, slow. Let's wait for the music . . . coming up . . . ready? Here we go. Quick quick, slow, slow. Quick quick, slow, slow."

She was terrible. Stiff and awkward. She froze up the same way she did like when she needed to do math in public. She got the choreography of the dance step down, but it wasn't pretty. It wasn't dance. It was more Frankenstein stumbling out of the castle. She despaired ever feeling comfortable to go public at the Last Chance. "I can't do this!"

"Sure you can."

But then, Jackson fixed the problem. He distracted her by doing something she'd never heard him do before.

Jackson McBride sang. To her.

Caroline lost herself in the rhythm and the rhyme and the timbre, in the sheer masculine beauty of his voice. She followed him effortlessly, in the half turns, and even in the full turns, and the dance steps became imprinted in her memory. In fact, she knew she'd remember this moment, this dance, for the rest of her life.

Because when the lesson finally ended, when he smiled down into her smiling face and kissed her sweetly on the lips, he said, "See? Ain't no step for a stepper. Or, I guess I should say, a two-stepper."

"I did it."

"Yes, you did. You always do. You have no quit in you, Caroline Carruthers. I love that about you." He cupped her cheek, gazed tenderly down into her eyes, and declared, "I love you. I'm in love with you."

"Oh, Jackson. Me too. I mean I love you too. I love you."

His eyes smiled at her. "Because I taught you to two-step?"

"Of course not. Do you think I'm easy?" She wrapped her hands around his neck and pulled his face down to hers. "You seduced me with song. Sing to me some more, why don't you? Next I want to learn how to waltz."

That Saturday night, Jackson McBride took the stage at the Last Chance Hall for the first time and debuted a new song, a ballad, titled "See That Girl."

The audience went wild.

Jackson took to spending most nights in town at Caroline's. Saturdays, after a night of music and dancing at the dance hall, they stayed overnight together at his trailer. Caroline spoke with Haley on the telephone. Jackson began teaching her to play the guitar. She learned the joy of skinny-dipping in the swimming hole by moonlight. He began looking at house plans and asking her opinion. Neither one of them mentioned marriage. Each agreed they were taking one step at a time. Writing their next chapters.

September brought the return of one of Texas's favorite pastimes—high school football—and on Friday nights, Caroline closed The Next Chapter early. She and Jackson joined the rest of Redemption in rooting on the home team. Angelica proved to be a fierce fan of the game and quite the homer, which became a bit of a problem since the Fallen Angel attracted visiting team boosters as overnight guests, and they didn't always appreciate arriving to Redemption Rattlers window signs and streamers.

Homecoming, the third weekend of September, was a particularly big event with a parade through downtown on the afternoon before the big game. Caroline and her two BFFs Maisy and Gillian, were tied up doing things with the homecoming court. Jackson was due to meet up with her later at the game. For now, he was on float duty. At Angelica's insistence, the Fallen Angel Inn had entered a float supporting the Rattlers, and Jackson was driving the tractor, which was pulling the float built upon a flatbed trailer. The only reason he was wearing a bent halo to match the inn's logo on top of his cowboy hat while doing so was because it settled the college football bet he'd lost with Angelica the previous week.

It was the bent halo that nearly caused the wreck.

When the newcomer to town saw it, he started cackling like a hyena, which drew Jackson's attention. When Jackson identified the source of the out-of-control laughter, he inadvertently jerked the tractor wheel and thus came close to jackknifing the float, a miniature reproduction of the inn with a real-life Angelica performing a royal wave from the chimney on top.

The hyena was his cousin, Tucker.

Finally, he reached the end of the route and was able to park the tractor and trailer. He scrambled down, ready to assist Angelica from her perch and go find his cousin when he heard the grand cackler himself.

"My biggest regret is that my phone was dead so I didn't get a picture of this."

"I thought maybe this halo had messed up the blood supply to my head or something. It *is* you. What the heck are you doing here, Tucker? You home on R&R?"

"I'm home for good. Uncle Sam and I have split the sheets."

"What?"

"I didn't re-up."

Jackson's jaw dropped. Tucker was career military. That's all he'd ever wanted. "What the hell happened?"

Tucker shook his head. "Long story. Gonna need a beer or twelve to tell you about it. First, though, I gotta find a place to bunk. I called the inn but they're booked for the weekend."

Jackson was shaking his head even before Tucker finished speaking. "You can have the trailer. I'll stay at Caroline's. I'm hardly ever there anyway. I've all but moved in with her as it is."

"Oh, yeah?"

"Yeah." Jackson gave him a slow smile and clapped him on the back. "Let's go get one of those beers, and I'll give you the skinny. She and her girlfriends—"

Angelica's voice interrupted from above. "Hello! Excuse me? Excuse me! Jackson, I could use some help here."

Oh, man! Jackson winced. He'd forgotten all about Angelica. *Now there's a first. How can anyone ever forget Angelica?* "I'm so sorry. On my way."

Jackson climbed up on the float in order to lift his innkeeper down from her chimney perch. Then because Tucker had made himself handy, he passed her off to him. "Well well well," she said, "aren't you a pretty fella! Those McBride family genes are a special combination, I daresay. Welcome home, Tucker. Thank you for your service."

She kissed him on the cheek and said, "I'm Angelica Blessing, the Fallen Angel innkeeper. If my cousin Celeste were here she'd say something along the lines of 'Enchanted Canyon is ready to wrap you in its comforting arms and soothe your troubled soul.' I'm not gonna do that. I'm a plain speaker, Tucker McBride. You have a tough row ahead of you to hoe. It's gonna take a powerful amount of work. Might break the blade a time or two. But the blessings you will reap at the harvest will be worth it. I promise. Never forget that you've got family and new friends here in Redemption to help you. Now, set me down."

Stunned, Tucker did as directed. Angelica finger-waved to Jackson, called, "Toddle-do," and sauntered

off into the parade crowd. She was trailing a stream of
yellow crepe paper from her pant leg.

"What the hell was that?" Tucker asked.

Now it was Jackson's turn to do the hyena laugh.
He threw his arm around his cousin's shoulder and led
him toward the nearest bar. Over a couple of local
microbrews, Tucker attempted to explain his change
of heart.

"To be honest, I almost bailed the last time I signed
my contract. It's not in my nature to quit. But I have to
tell you, Jackson, I understand now why the Callahans
preferred to wage war against the drug cartels and
human traffickers from outside the government rather
than from within. The bureaucracy whips your ass."

"So that's what this is about? They've lured you
into working for Callahan Security?"

"No. Not right now, anyway. I'm going to take
some time and try to figure out just what I want to do
when I grow up."

Jackson could tell that there was more—much
more—to this story, but Tucker obviously wasn't ready
to tell it. So he nodded and took a sip of his beer. "Been
there, doing that."

"So, what's the skinny on sweet Caroline?"

Jackson gave his cousin a censored and condensed
summary of his relationship with Caroline. He invited
Tucker to join them at the ball game, but Tucker begged
off. "I've been traveling for days, and I need to see the
inside of my eyelids for about fourteen hours straight at
least. Did you mean what you said about my bunking at
your place?"

"Absolutely." He told Tucker where to find the key,
mentioned the sad state of the contents of his refrigerator, then they finished their beers, exchanged handshakes
and the backslap that served as a hug between the cous-

ins, and Tucker headed for Enchanted Canyon. Jackson went looking for Caroline to give her the news.

That night the first half of the football game was a defensive struggle, ending in a 6–6 tie. Halftime was a pageant with drill-team and marching-band performances, and the homecoming court paraded around the field in classic convertibles. The Rattlers came out in the second half and, as Jackson said to Caroline on the way home from the game, put a whuppin' on the visiting team. It had been a great Texas small-town September Friday. Jackson capped it off by singing a love song to his lady and making sweet, sweaty love to her late into the night.

So both he and Caroline were sleeping in on Saturday morning when his phone rang. He let it go to voice mail. Almost immediately, it started ringing again. This time, he pulled the pillow over his head.

The third time his phone rang, Caroline kicked him. "Just answer it. It's not going to stop."

"Grrr. If it's Tucker, I'm going to kick his ass next time I see him." He thumbed the green button and brought the phone to his ear. "What!"

"Jackson McBride?" the stranger's voice said. "This is Martin Hollis with TMZ. What comment do you have about the crash of Coco's plane?"

Everything inside Jackson went cold. His heart might have stopped.

He sat up, fired out, "What?"

"What comment do you have about the plane crash?"

"What plane crash?"

"Coco's. Oh, man. You haven't heard about it yet?"

His mouth went dry as Big Bend in August. Vaguely aware that Caroline had sat up beside him, her expression wreathed with concern, he closed his eyes and forced out words. "No. I haven't. Tell me."

"Jeez, man. Sorry. Coco played L.A. last night. The band left this morning on two planes. Apparently one of them went down."

"Whose!" Jackson shouted. "Who was on it!"

"It's unclear. I thought maybe you'd know."

Jackson hung up on him.

His hand was shaking, trembling so hard he could hardly scroll through his contacts.

Softly, Caroline asked, "Honey?"

"I don't—" He couldn't . . . he just. . . . He shook his head as he finally found Sharon's contact and placed the call. It went straight to voicemail. "God . . . God . . . God," he prayed aloud. He placed the call again. Same result.

He tried to think of what to do. He rubbed his brow. He couldn't think.

"I'll help you," Caroline offered.

"I don't . . . God. There was a . . . a . . . plane crash . . . but two planes! I don't . . . Ray-Walker. I'll call Ray-Walker." His hand was shaking so hard he couldn't scroll through the contacts.

"Here." Caroline took the phone from his hand. "Ray-Walker what? What's his last name?"

His mind was spinning. He felt frozen. Haley. Haley. Haley.

"Jackson, what is Ray-Walker's last name?"

"Satan. He's listed under Satan."

Caroline cut him a look, but scrolled to the *S*s, placed the call, and handed him the phone. Voicemail again. Dammit. This time, he let it progress to the recording and left a message. "It's Jackson. Somebody damn well better call me immediately."

His phone rang before he could place another call. Another reporter asking for a comment. Another reporter without any new information for him. Caroline reached for the remote, turned on the television and surfed to a news channel. Jackson shook his head. "The entertainment channel. They'll have it first."

He managed to collect himself a bit. He tried Sharon again, got out of bed and pulled on his pants, and began placing calls to members of the band. He had everybody's number. He paced the room as he started working his way through the list, answering every call that came in just in case, dying a little when nobody had a damn bit of news for him. At some point he realized Caroline was on her phone talking to someone.

Despair rolled over him when he dialed Sharon's phone for probably the twentieth time in the nightmare of the past . . . what . . . five minutes? Ten? It felt like an hour. A year.

Caroline said, "I spoke to Boone. He's going to call your Callahan cousins. He said if anyone can find out what's happening, they could."

"Oh, yeah." Relief rolled over Jackson. "I should have thought of them. Good. That's good. He's right."

"He'll call you as soon as he's spoken with them."

"Okay. Okay. I'll keep trying the band. Maybe—" He broke off abruptly when a Breaking News announcement flashed on the TV. He grabbed the remote and turned up the volume.

". . . unconfirmed reports that at least one of two planes carrying music superstar Coco and her entourage crashed in the remote mountainous area somewhere southwest of Las Vegas in the early morning hours. No word of passenger identities or possible survivors is known at this time."

"At least one?" he repeated. "What the—?" He whirled around and met Caroline's gaze, feeling wild. "Both planes? How could that happen? Why would that happen? It doesn't make sense."

"Jackson—"

"That's crazy! I don't believe it." His heart was about to pound out of his chest. "This can't be, Caroline. It's gotta be a—" He broke off as his throat closed.

Caroline placed a comforting hand on his arm just as his phone rang. He recognized the number. "Boone!"

"There's hope, Jackson," his cousin said.

Jackson's knees turned to melted butter. He sank onto the bed and buried his face in his palm.

Boone continued, "Two planes on the same flight plan. The tower in Las Vegas heard a mayday call from plane B. It disappears from radar. Plane A circles back and sees smoke. But that's all we've got so far. We're not one hundred percent sure it was a crash. Not sure about fatalities. Don't know who was on which plane. The Callahans are chasing down that info right now."

"Okay." Jackson raked his fingers through his hair and rubbed the back of his neck. Caroline sat beside him. He took her hand and held it like a lifeline.

"A rancher friend of theirs is sending a copter to pick you up. ETA is twenty-five minutes. It'll bring you to Fort Worth where the Callahans will have their jet ready for you. We'll have you to the site as fast as we possibly can. Are you in town or in the canyon?"

"Town. I'm at Caroline's."

"Okay. Where's the best place to land a bird?"

He didn't know. He couldn't—"The football stadium. Tell him to go to the football stadium."

"Will do."

"And if any more news—"

"You'll be the first to know. They have your number. They'll call you rather than me from this point. Okay?"

"Yeah. Yeah. That's good. Thanks, man."

"Of course. And I told them Caroline might be coming with you."

Jackson met her gaze. "Yes. I hope she will."

"Good luck, man. I'm praying for you."

"Thanks." Jackson sucked in a deep breath, and then blew it out in a rush. "Like you said, there's hope. We don't know anything yet. I don't know . . . oh . . . hey . . . one thing. Tucker is home. Let him know, would you? Call the inn."

"Tucker's home?" Boone repeated, his surprise obvious. "Sure. I'll phone him right away."

They ended the call, and Jackson summarized what he'd learned for Caroline.

"Of course I'll come with you."

She rose and pulled a duffle from her closet and filled it with a change of clothes and toiletries for them both. She gave River food and water, and then left a message on Gillian's phone asking for emergency pet help. Jackson wasn't concerned that she didn't speak to her friend directly. He knew they could count on their friends. They were out the door within ten minutes, in the air within half an hour.

It was one hour and seventeen interminable minutes between the time the reporter said the words "plane crash" and when Luke Callahan called him with the three most beautiful words he'd ever heard: "Haley is alive."

Chapter Seventeen

Caroline watched the relief wash over Jackson, and she sent up a quick prayer of thanks. Haley was safe on the ground in Las Vegas with her mother. But along with the good news, came heartbreak. Four members of Coco's band—longtime friends of Jackson's—her manager, and Haley's nanny had been among the ten souls who'd lost their lives on the plane that went down.

"I spoke with Tyson. He's Sharon's personal chef. Her nanny was worried she might be coming down with something, and she didn't want to give it to Haley. That's why she rode on the other plane," Jackson told Caroline. "Haley is devastated. And Sharon . . . Sharon is a mess. They called in a physician to sedate her."

"Who's taking care of Haley?"

"Good question," Jackson said, worry in his tone. "Someone from the sheriff's office is with her. We're trying to get a phone call set up. Tyson didn't have much more to contribute. He's a wreck himself. Everybody is. The band is a family. This is tragic. Just tragic."

They were less than an hour from Las Vegas when Jackson was finally able to connect with his daughter. It was only when he heard his little girl's voice that tears welled in his eyes and overflowed down his cheeks. He talked to Haley until they were minutes away from Vegas. A short time later he was running toward his daughter and wrapping her in his arms.

If Caroline hadn't already been in love with Jackson, she'd have tumbled for him then and there.

Haley was a little angel of a girl. Strawberry blonde with shoulder-length curls, chubby cheeks, a dusting of freckles across her little pug nose, and her father's green eyes. What concerned Caroline, what she hadn't realized during the phone call on the plane, was that Haley wasn't speaking except to say, "Daddy."

That particular word she said over and over and over. After the initial greeting, he picked her up, and she buried her head against his shoulder as he spoke with the representative from the sheriff's department who had met the plane. Standing next to Jackson, Caroline heard Haley's muffled voice. "Daddy" was a lament, a question, a panicked demand while he was briefed with the latest information about the crash in terms vague enough to convey the facts without causing Haley further trauma.

Throughout the conversation, Jackson patted her back and rocked her like a babe. With a series of questions and decisions, he quietly assumed leadership of Coco's retinue. The authorities were obviously glad to let him do it.

They sat in the back of the SUV for the trip to the hotel where Coco and the other passengers on her plane had been taken, Haley in the middle between her father and Caroline. Jackson attempted to pry his daughter away from his side long enough to introduce her. "Haley, honey. I want you to meet someone. This is my friend, Caroline. The lady you talked to on the phone."

Haley didn't lift her head off Jackson's chest. He shot Caroline a frustrated look.

"Hello, Haley," she said gently, her kind smile meant for both father and daughter. "Your daddy is so glad to see you. He was awfully worried about you. What has happened today is terrible, and I'm so, so sorry."

Now, the girl looked up, and she met Caroline's gaze with eyes that flooded with tears. "My Poppins is dead."

Poppins? Ah, Mary Poppins. Caroline's own eyes filled with tears. "I know, baby. It's just awful."

Haley suddenly released her hold on her father and launched herself at Caroline, clung to her, and sobbed. Jackson looked poleaxed, like he didn't know exactly how he felt to be so quickly abandoned. "You needed a girl hug, didn't you, honey?" she said, as a way of explanation to him.

"Poppins is a girl," Haley sobbed.

Jackson's jaw hardened, and Caroline could almost read his thoughts. *Where's her mother?*

Within minutes, that question was answered, and Caroline was the one left feeling uncertain about being abandoned. Jackson again carried Haley after they entered the hotel through a private entrance that allowed them to avoid the press beginning to gather. They boarded a private elevator, which swept them up to the penthouse. The moment they stepped off the elevator and Coco's gaze lit upon Jackson, Caroline's stomach made an uneasy flip.

His ex-wife looked at him as if her personal savior had just arrived. "Ba-a—by!" she said, stretching it to three syllables.

Caroline hoped the woman was talking to Haley, but she had the sneaking suspicion she wasn't.

"Oh, ba-a-by. You came. You came. Thank God." She threw herself at Jackson, heedless of the fact that he already had his hands full with their daughter. "You know what happened? They're gone! They're all gone! Oh, God, Jackson."

He shifted Haley to one arm and wrapped the other around Coco. "I know. Of course I came."

"Bobby and Shane and Liz and Mary and Randy and Wayne."

"It's terrible."

"And Ray-Walker! Oh, Baby, Ray-Walker!"

"I'm so sorry, Sharon."

"What will I do?" she wailed. "What will we do?" She touched her daughter's head. "What will we do without Ray-Walker and our Poppins?"

"We will figure it out, Shar," Jackson crooned in a tone Caroline had never heard from him before. "We will figure it out."

Coco dragged him over to a nearby sofa where she launched into a tear-filled account of the day's events, never letting go of Jackson, never acknowledging Caroline's presence. One or two of the half dozen other people in the room nodded to Caroline, but no one approached her. They all waited to speak with Jackson once Coco gave them the opportunity.

Caroline drifted over to one of the floor-to-ceiling windows and gazed down upon the Las Vegas strip, trying not to feel anything but supportive toward Jackson. This wasn't about her. The man had his hands full. She had no reason to be jealous. She was not going to be one of those women.

Still, when she did turn to look at the trio—Jackson seated with his left arm around Haley, Coco on his right, her head resting on his shoulder, her hand lying possessively on his thigh—something ugly stirred inside Caroline. They looked like such a family.

And she needed to get a break from it, or she *was*

going to become one of those women. She was better than that.

She needed to freshen up. At some point in the past little bit, someone had brought their duffle up. It sat just inside the door. Quietly, she crossed the room, lifted the bag, and went in search of a bathroom.

The hotel suite was huge, and she had plenty of rooms from which to choose. She picked the bedroom-and-bath combination that was the farthest away from what was obviously the master suite. The long, hot shower did her a world of good. So did a fresh blowout and new application of makeup.

She stroked lipstick across her lips, and then blotted it with a tissue. To her reflection in the mirror, she softly said, "Like Mama always said, you can take the girl out of Texas, but you can't take Texas out of the girl."

She exited the bathroom and stopped short. Jackson sat at the foot of the bed. Rising, he gave her a solemn look. "I'm sorry. I was a jerk. I totally ignored you."

I really do love this man. "No, you weren't a jerk. That was an extraordinary moment, and I'd be a real B if I got my panties in a twist about it. I came to support you, Jackson, not make things more difficult."

He sighed and opened his arms, and she went into them gladly. He held onto tight, swayed slowly side to side. Breathed deeply as if he found the very scent of her somehow sustaining. "Thank you. Thank you, Caroline. Have I told you today how much I love you?"

She smiled. "No, I don't believe you have."

He sang it to her in a melody that she'd heard him composing on her back porch last week. "To the moon, to the stars, and to worlds yet unknown. I love you, there and back. My love to you, there and back."

She sighed. "It doesn't seem fair that I can't sing you a love song."

"Honey, you sing me a love song every time you look at me and smile." He drew back, kissed her gently, and said, "I hate like hell to break this up, but I need a shower, too. I'm doing a press conference in twenty-five minutes."

"*You* are doing it?"

"Yeah. Somebody has to speak for the band, and Sharon damn sure can't. She wigged out and had the doctor give her pills. Scares the crap out of me, Caroline. She's weak to begin with. A situation like this is how a person gets hooked on crap."

"Where's Haley?"

"She fell asleep. Naturally," he hastened to add.

"She's a beautiful little girl, Jackson."

"Yeah. She is"—his throat closed up and he cleared it before finishing—"isn't she? Those freckles are new this summer."

"They're too cute. Did you have freckles where you were young?"

"No. She gets those from her mother." The frown returned to Jackson's brow. "She's going to be so lost without Mary. She's been her nanny since Haley was two. It sounds terrible to say, but losing her Poppins will be worse for Haley than losing Sharon would have been. She'll need help, more than what Sharon will be able to give her."

He grimaced and shook his head. "This so sucks."

"Go take your shower, Jackson. You could probably use something to eat, too. I saw trays of food. I'll make sandwiches for us. Okay?"

"Thanks."

The press conference ended up being delayed for

forty-five minutes because Coco decided the show absolutely positively must go on. In other words, she attended the event, escorted by Jackson, whom she leaned on both physically and emotionally throughout.

Caroline took Haley down to the swimming pool to play while it took place and watched it on YouTube later. It was a heartbreaking performance. Though, performance wasn't the proper word because Coco hadn't been acting. Her devastation and helplessness was real. Caroline understood the devastation. The helplessness, not so much.

However, she told herself she wasn't going to judge. People grieved differently, and nobody had the right to tell someone else how to go about it. Hadn't she learned that lesson personally? Still, being around Coco necessitated Caroline calling upon all her maturity reserves. And as the first day drew to a close, no end to the need was in sight.

Everyone turned to Jackson for direction—families of the deceased, surviving band members and crew and their families, corporate staff in Nashville, and even household staff there and at both of Coco's vacation homes. Jackson stepped right into the role of decision maker and never skipped a beat.

By all appearances, Coco was not only content for him to assume the mantle, she thrust it upon him.

If Jackson had been designated decision maker, as their second day in Las Vegas drew to a close, Caroline recognized that she had assumed the part of Poppins, acting as the new nanny for Haley. Not that she minded. Haley was a sad little sweetheart who was lost as she could be right now. Jackson was giving her lots of love and comfort and attention. Her mother seemed to take more comfort from Haley than give it, but Caroline admitted that could be a little harsh.

Long after they went to bed that second night, Jackson lay tossing and turning in the bed. She knew he was exhausted. He'd caught only a few hours of sleep the night before, and today had been particularly draining as he'd led the families in hammering out an agreement on how the band would memorialize its lost members.

Finally, she rolled onto her side and asked, "Want to talk about it?"

"No. I don't want to think about it." He exhaled a heavy sigh into the darkness. "Unfortunately, I can't stop."

He sat up and slung his feet over the side of the bed, which triggered muted floor lighting. He sat hunched over, his elbows on his knees, his head dropped forward. "Today was . . . oh, Caroline. So much heartbreak in that room. And trying to come to a consensus, nothing was going to make everyone happy. Some of those people will never be happy again. Damn. Randy had four kids. Two boys and two girls. Mary was her parents' only child. And Paul—he's one of our sound guys—he's a basket case because he's the one Mary switched seats with right before everyone boarded. He bitched and whined because he was supposed to be on the other plane—usually played cards with our drummer. Now the guilt is about to eat him alive."

"The whole thing is tragic." She went up onto her knees behind him and began massaging the tight muscles of his shoulders and neck. "Are they any closer to figuring out what happened to the plane?"

"Some sort of mechanical malfunction, but pinpointing exactly what will take some time. I hope they will be able to tell us exactly what happened. Otherwise, we'll never get half those people back on an airplane."

Caroline's fingers stilled for just a moment as she braced herself, then she dug a little harder with her massage as she said, "Haley told me today that she doesn't want to fly home. That she's going to go in the bus with you and her mom."

"Yea-ah." He groaned the word. "I was going to talk to you about that tomorrow. Nobody in the group is in a real hurry to get on a plane. I've got Sharon's bus dead-heading here. They'll arrive sometime tonight. The memorial will be in Nashville on Saturday. Randy's wife is the only one who wants a funeral first. That'll be in Tulsa on Thursday. Sharon is adamant against getting on a plane, and if Haley's feeling that way, too, well, I can't leave her."

"No, you can't."

"I can't ask you to come on the bus."

You can't? Her hands slid from his shoulders. She sat back on her heels.

Then Jackson twisted around and pulled her down onto her back. He rose above her. His eyes glittered as he spoke fiercely. "Don't think I haven't noticed how Sharon is taking advantage of you. You're not the new nanny. I haven't been in the position to call her on it, and I figure you've been okay with it for a couple of days because you wanted to help and you've been a godsend where Haley's concerned. But enough is enough, Caroline. You have a business of your own to tend to. If I recall the calendar correctly, you have another author signing this weekend. I can't—I won't—ask you to put your life on hold for another week because my child's mother needs help being a mother."

Caroline didn't know how to respond to that. She couldn't argue with his reasoning. She reached up and cupped his cheek. "I love you, Jackson. I want to help you any way I can."

He pressed a kiss against her palm. "I have to take

care of them. Not forever, but I have to help them get through this next week."

"I know."

"You are so precious to me." He lowered his head and kissed her, slowly, sweetly, and tenderly. When he finally lifted his mouth from hers, he stared down into her eyes for a long moment. "Before I met you, I never knew just how sexy strong is."

He made love to her then, as slowly and sweetly and tenderly as his kiss. In doing so, he applied that special Jackson McBride balm to her bruised emotions.

First thing in the morning, at Caroline's request, Jackson booked a seat for her on a commercial flight to Austin due to leave a little before noon. Before Caroline left the hotel for the airport, Coco thanked her graciously for her help and wished her safe travels. Jackson and Hayley rode with her to the airport. At the curb, she knelt down and gave Haley a big hug. "I'm so glad I finally got to meet you, Haley. I put my phone number in your phone, and I want you to feel free to call me whenever you want to talk—as long as it's okay with your mom and dad, that is."

"Okay. I will. Will you come see me again, Miss Caroline?"

Caroline glanced at Jackson. He answered for her. "She sure will."

"Good."

"Goodbye, sweetheart." Then Caroline gave Jackson a fierce, hard hug. "Good luck. Call me. If you need anything, just ask."

"I will." He leaned down and kissed her. "Thank you, Caroline. For everything. I don't think I'd have made it through all this without you."

"You would have, but I'm glad I was able to help."

"Help doesn't begin to describe it. You did more than

help. You saved my sanity. I love you, Caroline. Travel safe. Call me when you get home."

"I will. Love you too."

"River is with Tucker, but if you miss him . . ."

"I do miss him. I'll bring him to town. You come get him, get us, just as soon as you get home."

"That's a plan. It shouldn't be long. A day or two after the memorial, at the latest, I figure."

"Okay." She bit her lower lip as she smiled at him.

"So, see you later, lady." He touched her cheek.

It was sort of a standoff, then, neither one of them wanting to turn away first. Finally, Caroline lifted her chin, squared her shoulders, and said, "Goodbye, Jackson."

She turned and walked into the Las Vegas airport where slot machines pinged and bells rang and falling coins jangled. McCarran International Airport was a crowded, bustling place, one of the busier airports in the world. Waiting to go through security and then walking to her gate, Caroline had rarely felt quite so alone.

Jackson spent much of the road trip with a phone glued to his ear as he ironed out details for the memorial. At the request of the families, the service itself was to be invitation only, but they'd agreed to allow it to be televised live. These had been performers, after all. Jackson was pleased with the program they'd come up with. A mix of speakers and music, it wasn't anything he would have wanted for himself, but for Coco's band, it was appropriate.

Haley spent much of the ride glued to her tablet. Another time, he would have done something about that—using technology as a babysitter was a particular pet peeve of his—but these weren't normal circumstances. Sharon slept. And slept. And slept.

Another time, he'd have done something about that, too.

Except, he thought that right now, sleeping was probably the best thing for her. She seemed to have cried out all of her tears. Now when she was awake she was either always in motion in a manic way or sitting in her seat, staring out the window in a vacant, zombie stare.

Neither way was good for Haley. He almost wished he'd pushed for sending his daughter to Texas with Caroline. He could probably have gotten Sharon to agree to it. Hell, even today, she looked at him to make all of her decisions.

Just like she'd done before Ray-Walker had come into their lives.

"Daddy?"

The sweet word was balm for his troubled soul. *Need to get back to Enchanted Canyon ASAP.* Haley, too, had been napping in the row of seats across the aisle from him, but now she was sitting up and rubbing her eyes. "Yeah, baby?"

"Would you play the guitar for me?"

"I don't have my guitar with me, sweetheart."

"Austin has his." Before he framed a response, she'd scrambled out of her seat and up the aisle four rows to where the band's lead guitarist sat. "Austin, can my daddy use your guitar?"

Jackson couldn't help but wince. Austin Tyree simply didn't share his Martin. "Sure, little lady."

Well, the world has changed in the past couple of days, hasn't it?

"Thanks," Jackson said moments later as Tyree handed over his instrument. He spent a few minutes tuning it, and then looked at Haley who had returned to her seat and now sat cross-legged watching him closely, her eyes big and sad and solemn. "What song would you like to hear?"

"The angel song."

"Angel song?"

"The one that Poppins liked for you to play for her. We sing it in church? It's her favorite song."

"Ahh." The angel song was "Amazing Grace."

He took just a moment and did a couple of warm-up riffs, testing both the instrument and his own resolve, because the memory of playing the hymn for Haley's Poppins was so alive that he wasn't sure he could pull this off. Once he felt ready, he segued into the first verse, keeping his concentration keen on his daughter. Would she find comfort in the hymn? Or would it cut her to the core and make her grief worse? He could see it going either way.

He'd rather pitch Austin Tyree's prized possession out onto the blacktop rather than make this situation any worse for Haley. But it was okay, because she clasped her hands together, closed her eyes, and smiled. It was almost as if she could hear her beloved angel singing.

And then Jackson realized that's exactly what she was hearing.

Her mother was standing in the aisle two rows away. The heavenly voice of the incomparable Coco sang,

". . . And grace my fears relieved;
How precious did that grace appear
The hour I first believed.
Through many dangers, toils and snares,
I have already come;
'Tis grace hath brought me safe thus far,
And grace will lead me home."

Jackson closed his eyes and was lost. In the song, in the sound. Her sound. Their sound. It pulsed through

him like a heartbeat that had been shocked back to life
after having lain silent and dead.

"The Lord has promised good to me,
His Word my hope secures;
He will my Shield and Portion be,
As long as life endures.
Yea, when this flesh and heart shall fail,
And mortal life shall cease,
I shall possess, within the veil,
A life of joy and peace.
The earth shall soon dissolve like snow,
The sun forbear to shine;
But God, who called me here below,
Will be forever mine.
When we've been there ten thousand years,
Bright shining as the sun,
We've no less days to sing God's praise
Than when we'd first begun."

He played the complicated bridge pattern that followed the last verse without skipping a beat, and opened
his eyes to see Sharon kneeling beside their daughter,
holding Haley's hand, watching him, and imploring
him to join her.

Together, Jackson and Sharon sang,

"Amazing grace! How sweet the sound
That saved a wretch like me!
I once was lost, but now am found;
Was blind, but now I see."

Haley watched with her hands clasped prayerfully
in front of her mouth. When the final note died, rapidly

blinking back tears, she beamed at her parents and declared, "That was wonderful. So wonderful! I never heard you sing together before and that was one of my special wishes. I didn't think it would ever come true, but it did! I'll have to tell Caroline."

Caroline.

Her name jolted Jackson back to the reality of the here and now. He blinked, gave his head a little shake, and stared at his daughter as she continued to bubble.

"It was actually one of her special dented-angel wishes that she was saving for a special occasion, but she gave it to me to use because I had a penny that I got when I bought Poppins a surprise ice-cream cone so that was a love penny. Love pennies have more power anyway so it was already starting out extra good. When I told Caroline what my wish would be, she said she wanted to give her wish to me to use for it because you were part of it, Daddy. And she's your special friend and now I'm her friend and Mommy, she said you sing like an angel and Poppins is an angel and a lady named Angel told her about the special wish so it all just seemed perfect. Even though she warned me that the Angel lady said it might take a really long time for the bent wishes to come true."

A lady named Angel, Jackson thought. Angelica. Dented angel, Fallen Angel. Okay, now this was making some sense.

Haley continued. "So, Caroline squeezed my hand and gave me her wish and I held my love penny and made my wish and threw it into the wish fountain and now it's come true! Really, really fast!" Haley took hold of one of her father's hands and one of her mother's hands. "Isn't that wonderful?"

"I think it's fabulous," Sharon declared, smiling

tenderly at Haley. Both females looked expectantly toward Jackson.

He had the sensation that he'd just stepped onto a meadow riddled with buried land mines. "Wonderful."

Sharon reached over and gave his knee a squeeze. "It's the Circle of Fifths, Jackson. Our circle of life." Then she closed her eyes and swayed, began to hum an unfamiliar melody. "Mmmm . . . mmm . . . mmm. Mmm . . . mmm . . . mmm. Mmmm . . . mmm . . . mmm. Wishes for my angel. New star in the sky. Da . . . da . . . da . . . da. Da! Da! Go with me here, Jackson. Something something. See you tonight."

They worked it through. In less than an hour, they'd finished the song. Four complete verses, a chorus, and a bridge. She stood as she sang it from the top, a lament of loss and pain that everyone on that bus had experienced. The music was mostly his, the words theirs. She sang for every single person on that bus, and she sang from their collective hearts, from their collective souls.

"I wish I wish I wish . . .

I could hold you again . . . tonight."

As the final line faded away, the bus was silent. The song was beautiful. It was powerful. It was perfect.

The bus erupted in applause.

Jackson knew they'd just written a hit.

Sharon—Coco—beamed at him and said, "Jackson, we're back!"

He closed his eyes. *Ah, hell, Caroline. What have I just done?*

Chapter Eighteen

On the fifteenth of November, Caroline stared at her silent phone in her silent cottage and said aloud to Jackson's silently sleeping dog, "Well, River dog, it *is* my next chapter."

And her next chapter be hanged if she'd spend Thanksgiving Day alone again this year. She had a fence she'd like to mend and this was as good a time as any to take a first stab at that. She picked up the phone and made a next-chapter gesture by reaching out to her past. "Hello, Elizabeth," she said when her former sister-in-law answered. "It's Caroline. I know it's late notice, but I'm calling to invite you and George to join me in Redemption for Thanksgiving dinner. I'd love to have you join me. I believe it's my turn to cook."

"Oh," Robert's sister said. "Oh, Caroline! Well, yes. Yes, I would like that. George and I would like that very much."

Caroline heard the tears in Elizabeth's voice, and that triggered tears to pool in her own eyes. Thanksgiving always had been a special holiday for Robert and his sister filled with traditions from their childhood that the two had taken care to continue. Caroline was certain that last year had been terribly difficult for Elizabeth.

Her own effort to run from the holiday by spending the day hiking in Peru had been an abject failure. Physical exertion hadn't stopped the physical ache of her grief, an ache she believed would have been lessened had it been acknowledged and shared that day.

"What would you like me to bring?" Elizabeth asked.

Caroline blinked away her tears. "Well, it's not Thanksgiving without your sweet potato pie. I'd love for you to bring that."

"I'll be happy to do so. Thrilled, in fact. Caroline, I—" Elizabeth's voice choked up.

Caroline waited, her own throat tight.

Finally, Elizabeth said, "I've been meaning to call you. Honestly, I've been trying to work up the nerve. I owe you an apology. During my brother's illness, I took out my fear and grief on you. I treated you badly, and you didn't deserve it. I'm sorry. I hope you will forgive me."

"Of course," Caroline said. "It was a hard time for everyone, Elizabeth, and heaven knows I could have been kinder to you, too."

"You were an excellent wife to Robert. He loved you very much and I know you loved him and did your best for him."

Caroline closed her eyes. These were words she'd needed to hear, and they healed a wounded place inside her.

The conversation continued for a few more minutes, and Caroline ended the call glad that she'd made it. Next, she placed calls to Angelica, Maisy, two of her employees, and her next-door neighbor. By noon, she had a guest list of ten—a comfortable number for her little cottage, she decided.

She spent the afternoon pondering her menu and making a point of not brooding about the dearth of phone calls coming from Tennessee. Okay, maybe she did brood some, but she didn't spend all her time staring at the phone, waiting for it to ring. Willing it to ring. It never rang.

In all fairness, he had warned her not to expect to hear from him when he'd called to tell her that he was headed up to the Smokey Mountains to do some song-writing.

With Sharon.

They were in the midst of a creative storm born out of the shared tragedy of the plane crash.

Okay.

Caroline had watched the memorial service so she'd witnessed the truth of that. They'd ended the program with a song that Coco and Jackson had written for Haley's nanny, one that Coco had announced to world had been inspired by the kindness shown to Haley in the wake of the tragedy by a friend of theirs named Caroline. She'd dedicated the song to angels every-where.

Haley had joined her parents onstage for the song, sitting at their feet while they performed. The song was hauntingly beautiful and had touched Caroline deeply. Then, when Jackson added his vocals to Coco's and they sang "Amazing Grace" to end the program, Caroline hadn't been able to hold back the tears. The hymn . . . the occasion . . . and yes, the picture of a reunited family caused her stomach to sink.

She loved Jackson. She trusted Jackson. She *wasn't* a jealous woman. But she'd be a fool not to recognize that their situation had changed. She had every right to be a little concerned. When she confessed as much to Gillian and Maisy at their next girl's night out, her friends who had also watched the memorial show agreed that she'd be crazy not to be just a little uneasy.

And that had been before he'd called to tell about his and Coco's imminent departure on a creative getaway to the singer's mountain retreat. Her isolated mountain retreat, where apparently as part of her back-to-nature worldview she'd removed both cell and Internet service.

That had been seven days ago. Seven days of silence. A week of total blackout. And with every day that passed, Caroline's uneasiness grew, her thoughts became more unsettled, her imaginings more bleak and sometimes, slipping into ugly.

She loved him. She trusted him.

She decided to cook Thanksgiving dinner.

And she spent the next five phone-call-free days spinning in a similar vicious circle. Trust to suspicion. Patience to what her grandmother used to call blue funk. What was that music term Jackson said that Coco was using as her talisman? Circle of Fifths?

Well, for Caroline it was a Circle of Blue Funk. Blue headed toward black. The circle was obviously shaped like a vortex and Caroline was a nickel spinning around and around rolling inexorably toward the center, the black hole of suspicion and doubt and ugly imaginings.

Was he ghosting her? Would she never hear from him again?

No. Jackson wouldn't do that. He'd at least send her a text to dump her.

"Stop it," she said in the grocery store on the Tuesday evening before Thanksgiving as she marked off carrots on her shopping list, then scanned the produce aisle for the green beans. She'd already had a long day, having worked late at the shop getting everything ready for the anticipated Black Friday rush, but she wasn't in any hurry to go home, so she dawdled. She bought two packages of butter shaped like turkeys and put a ridiculous amount of thought into her choices of cheese for the cheese tray she planned to set out before dinner.

And the wine. What wine to serve?

She settled on "lots."

She didn't arrive home until well after ten. She let River out into the backyard, and then went to work unloading her car. It was almost ten thirty before she put the last of the groceries away, and River still hadn't scratched at the back door indicating that he was ready to come back in.

"You better not be messing with your old friend again," she murmured as she opened the door to call him. He'd tangled with a skunk four days ago and while the dishwashing detergent-hydrogen peroxide bath she'd given him had helped, she still caught whiffs of the stink. "River? River! Come on back in."

He sprinted around the side of the house and bounded up the steps, all but knocking her down as he rushed inside. "Careful!" she scolded, scowling after him. Instead of heading directly toward his water bowl like he normally did following a trip outside, he disappeared into the front of the house. Caroline sighed, expecting she'd find him at the front window. She'd have to remember to clean the slobber off of it before Thursday.

She took one last look around her kitchen to make sure she hadn't missed putting anything away, then pulled the stopper from the bottle of wine she'd opened last night and poured herself a glass. She'd take it and the novel she'd started to the bathroom and enjoy a nice, relaxing, distracting soak. She'd lose herself in ancient Rome and not think about the Smokey Mountains at all.

At least not until she pulled the plug on her bath and the water began circling the drain. Like a vortex. Circle of Dirty Water. Of Blue Funk. Of—

"Arf . . . arf . . . arf . . . arf . . . arf . . . arf." Crash!

Caroline sighed. Had that dog just knocked over her lamp?

As Jackson turned the corner onto Caroline's street, the glow of lamplight in her windows drew him like a magnet. She was home. Thank goodness. And by all appearances, still awake. Even better. Not that he wouldn't have awakened her, but he didn't want to scare her, just surprise her.

She'd be happy to see him. He'd brought flowers and everything.

Then why was he nervous?

Oh, gee. Maybe because he hadn't called her? Because if he'd called her, he would have had to tell her his news? And he didn't want to tell her? Not over the phone, anyway. *Hell, McBride. You are deep in the cow patties now, and you know it.*

True, that. No getting around it. Even a woman as wonderful and generous and understanding as Caroline wasn't going to be happy about the new developments in his life.

Pulling his truck into her drive, he shifted into park and shut off the engine. He wanted to leap from the truck and run to her door and burst inside yelling her name. He imagined sweeping her into his arms and kissing her senseless and carrying her off to bed. Then after they made sweet, sweaty love he could say, "By the way, sweetheart . . ."

He dragged his hand down his face, blew out a heavy sigh, picked up the two-dozen red roses he'd purchased at the grocery store ten minutes ago, and exited his truck. At the sound of River's excited barking, a smidgen of his tension eased. No matter what else happened, he'd still have the love of man's best friend.

Except that River was a really smart dog, and he'd been living with Caroline for a while now. *She's been the hand feeding him, not you.*

Should have bought a box of dog treats when he picked up the flowers.

He heard a crash from inside as he rang the doorbell to give her a head's up just before he slipped his key in the lock, opened the door, and stepped inside.

She stood in the threshold between the kitchen and the living room wearing jeans and a sweater and an expression he couldn't read. Caroline. Beautiful, beautiful Caroline. Their gazes locked. In that instant, everything else faded from his consciousness.

Home. I'm home.

River raced around the room yapping and jumping and crashing into things. Jackson absently reached down and grabbed the dog, held him, scratched him behind the ears and murmured some sort of greeting as that unique scent of Caroline Carruthers' home swirled around him—cinnamon and sunshine.

Home. I'm home.

Finally, he released River and held out his arms and smiled. "Surprise!"

He wanted her to rush across the room and jump into his arms and wrap her legs around his waist and plant a big old wet one on his lips. She stayed right where she was and folded her arms. *Okay, then.*

"This is definitely a surprise," she said, her tone flat.

"A good one, I hope." He gave her an encouraging smile.

She tapped her foot. "I guess you lost your phone?"

"I told you Sharon doesn't have service in the mountains."

She glanced away. Shrugged.

Jackson sighed. He lifted his right boot, shoved River

out of his way, and walked slowly toward her. "I couldn't have reached you before about one o'clock this afternoon. I honestly thought you'd like to be surprised."

"Why the roses?"

Jackson glanced down at the bouquet in his hand, then back up at her. "Because it's what guys do? They bring girls flowers."

Her chin came up. "Big bouquets like that are for guilty consciences."

"They were on sale."

That happened to be true, though price wasn't what had motivated him to purchase the second dozen. He *did* have a guilty conscience. Sort of. Except "guilty" wasn't really the right word. He had not done anything of which he needed to be ashamed. He just had a situation. News.

He should tell her now. Just come right out and say it and get it over with. If he had any balls at all, that's what he'd do.

But those Bambi eyes of hers castrated him. She was looking at him as if he had . . . W*hoa! Wait a minute.* Now his chin came up. "Dammit, Caroline, you don't really think I went off to the mountains and slept with Sharon, do you?"

She closed her eyes.

"Caroline?" He tossed the roses onto a nearby chair and braced his hands on his hips. "If that's what you think it's really gonna piss me off. I love you. I committed to you. I'm a man of my word, and I don't the hell cheat."

"I know that," she said in a little voice.

"Then why . . . ?" He waved his hand in small circles toward the tears that had escaped her eyes to trail down her cheeks.

Her chin came up. "You didn't call me."

"I couldn't!" Jackson threw out his hands. "I told you that ahead of time."

"That's just the past twelve days! You've hardly called me at all since you've been in Nashville."

He grimaced. *Guilty. Guilty. Guilty.* "I know I didn't call enough. It's been crazy. Everything's been crazy. Seems like I spent thirty hours a day on the telephone, and when I got a chance to speak to you it was two in the morning Texas time. I didn't want to wake you."

"That's no excuse. I was probably lying awake fretting about why you hadn't called. The few times I did hear from you left me unsettled, Jackson." Caroline wrapped her arms around herself. "I'm not acting like myself, and I don't like this me very much. I'll admit to some insecurity. At the memorial when you and Coco performed and Haley joined you onstage, you were a family, Jackson. I think I felt threatened."

Yep. I am knee deep in the cow patties now.

"You're right. I was wrong not to call more. I'm sorry." He took the final few steps to her, wrapped his arms around her, and held her tight. He buried his face in her hair, smelled her shampoo.

Home. I'm home.

Now he just had to figure out a way to stay here.

"I'm sorry, love. I want you to understand about my running off to the mountains with my ex. I let her talk me into going up there because we really did have some special work mojo happening. Because of the accident, I think. It was burning in both of us, and we were connecting. When that happens, as an artist you have to respect it. But it was the music, Caroline. The music. Not personal. Nothing personal. Okay?"

She didn't speak, but she did nod. He took it.

"My mistake was not ordering a satellite phone or messenger pigeon so that I could contact you. You have every right to be pissed at me about that." He felt her smile against his shoulder, and some of his tension eased.

He tightened his hold on her and rocked her. "I won't pretend that this situation isn't complicated, but you should never, ever doubt my love for you. We will work things out. You have to believe that. You need to believe me. You need to believe in me. Hear me?"

"I hear."

"Promise?"

"I promise."

"Good. I'm going to hold you to that." He placed his fingers beneath her chin and tilted her face up to his. *Tell her.* "Caroline?"

"Yes?"

I've missed you. "Do I finally get a welcome-home kiss?"

A slow smile spread across her face, and the wicked gleam that sparked in her eyes was the most appealing thing he'd seen in a month of Sundays. Jackson didn't want to think about complications any longer.

She circled her lips with her tongue. "Maybe. Are you finally gonna give me my flowers?"

"Maybe." He swallowed hard. "I'm sort of having second thoughts about it though."

"Oh?"

"For one thing, those roses are Texas dozens, which means there are fifteen roses instead of twelve. It occurs to me that thirty roses have lots of petals—plenty to make a nice little blanket for you to lie on. Naked. For me to look at."

"Hmm. I don't know about that, McBride. Seems

like that would make these more your roses than my roses."

"Well. Yeah, you do have a point." He dipped his head and nuzzled her neck. "More's the pity."

She arched against him and gave a hum of pleasure as he nibbled her earlobe. "I do have a counterproposal to offer."

"Let's hear it."

She licked the skin revealed by the V of his shirt. "You lie naked on the rose petals for me to look at."

Jackson stilled momentarily, and then drew back. "You are full of surprises."

"It's a night for them, I suppose. Do we have a deal, McBride?"

"Seal it with a welcome-home kiss, Carruthers."

She did with so much enthusiasm that they both forgot all about the rose petals until after he'd scooped her up into his arms and carried her off to the bedroom. They were both already half naked, and he was kissing her flat belly as he peeled off her slacks, when she suddenly pushed at his shoulders and said, "Wait! We forgot the flowers!"

Jackson looked up, his expression pained. "Do you know how long it takes to pluck a rose, Caroline? Much less thirty of them?"

"Are you trying to renege on our agreement?"

He licked a circle around her navel, and his hands continued their quest. "Just renegotiate. How about we save the flowers for tomorrow? I could bring a couple more bundles and add something to hit all the sensual bases. With rose petals you have the sense of sight and scent and touch covered, so maybe add taste and sound in? What do you say?"

She wiggled and rolled and managed to maneuver

him onto his back. She rubbed herself sensuously against him, then waggled her brows and teased. "Gonna drive a hard bargain, aren't you, McBride?"

"Or die trying. Or die if I don't get to try soon. Caroline, what—"

"McBride?"

"Hmm?"

"You talk too much. Put that tongue to better use."

"Yes ma'am." They were the last words he spoke in quite a long time.

When they finally lay spent and sated in each other's arms and Jackson sensed Caroline drifting toward sleep, he knew he could delay his news no longer. Trailing his thumb slowly up and down her arm, he said, "Honey?"

"Hmmm?"

"I can't stay tonight. I have to go back to the canyon."

Sleepily, she said, "Okay." Then, once his words sank in, she stirred against him, opened her eyes. "What? You're leaving? Why? Is something wrong at the inn? Tucker came by the shop this afternoon. He didn't mention anything."

"No." He sighed and rolled over onto his side then propped himself up on his elbow so that he could watch her. "It's that complicated situation I spoke about earlier."

He watched her eyes grow wary. *Waist-deep cow patties, McBride.* "Maybe I should have told you before I took you to bed. Maybe I should have told you the minute I walked in the door. Hell, maybe I should have called and told you before I ever left Tennessee. Or maybe this is the right way to do it, when you're lying here beside me after we've made love. You need to know that I love you, Caroline. Somehow, some way, I will make this work."

"What are you trying to tell me?"

"I didn't come home alone, Caroline. I brought Haley with me. We will be staying at the inn."

"You did?" A smile flittered on her lips. "That's wonderful, Jackson."

Well, yeah. Just wait. I'm not done with the telling yet. "Her mother tagged along to Texas, too."

Chapter Nineteen

Thanksgiving Day dawned sunny with temperatures expected to rise to the mid-sixties by the afternoon. Weather-wise, it should be a spectacular day. Beyond that, Caroline wasn't prepared to make any predictions.

Her guest list for Thanksgiving dinner had swelled to thirteen. What a lucky number! Coco was coming and bringing cranberry sauce. The kind her grandmother always served. Ocean Spray, straight from the can.

Bless her heart.

The last time Caroline's emotions had been this jumbled she'd been going through puberty. She was truly happy for Jackson. He had Haley back in his life. He was writing songs again and pleased with the work he produced. The revival of the Last Chance Hall continued to rock along, Jackson's cousin having stepped up in his absence to take care of the day-to-day operations. And, the man was getting laid. Yesterday he'd shown up with four-dozen roses, and she hadn't the willpower to resist. Jackson McBride had it pretty darned good.

Considering that he was living with his ex-wife.

That's where the jumbled-emotion part started coming in. Coco had checked into the Fallen Angel Inn, and she was insisting that Jackson stay there, too, rather than return to the trailer that Tucker had offered to vacate. Haley needed her father close, Coco had insisted. Jackson couldn't argue the point. Neither could Caroline, but she didn't have to like it.

She punched the Pulse button on the food processor and sent the onion spinning. Her sympathy for the singer had just about reached her limits. *Pulse. Pulse.* No woman was that helpless. *Pulse. Pulse. Pulse.* She was such a performer. *Pulse. Pulse. Pulse. Pulse.* And Jackson . . . could he not see through her act?

Caroline glanced into her food processor bowl and groaned. She'd pulverized her onions into mush.

Her eyes teared as she scraped the mess into the trash—strong onions—and she fetched more from her pantry, paying closer attention to her chopping this time. She'd just added the perfectly chopped onions to her dressing when her front doorbell rang. She glanced at the clock. Nine forty-five. Way too early for guests.

She wiped her hands on a dishtowel and headed for the door. "Angelica!"

The older woman had her long red hair piled in ringlets high on the back of her head and arranged in a style reminiscent of turkey tail feathers. Today's ankle-length gypsy skirt was vertical color blocks of orange, brown, russet, and gold. Her long-sleeved knit shirt was harvest gold, and her braided-rope belt matched her skirt. Her dangling gold earrings spelled "Gobble" and "Gobble."

"This is a nice surprise," Caroline said as she opened the door.

Angelica swept inside pulling a collapsible cart filled with grocery bags and small kitchen appliances. "I came to cook with you. I know it's nervy of me, but you are a generous soul, Caroline Carruthers, and I've always thought that half the fun of Thanksgiving was food prep with those with whom you planned to share the feast. Besides, Cuckoo for Cocoa Puffs is driving me bonkers, and according to some—namely my cousin who suggested I find somewhere else to be this morning—I'm already halfway around that bend."

The breakfast cereal? Somehow, she didn't think that's what Angelica was talking about.

"Do you know what she did this morning?"

Caroline knew she probably shouldn't ask, but really, Thanksgiving wasn't a day for willpower, was it? "I take it the 'she' you're talking about is not Celeste?"

Angelica sniffed. "Not hardly. Celeste is running in the Redemption Turkey Trot 5K race this morning. She made her angel food cake yesterday so she is free as a dove until one o'clock when we're all due to arrive here. I'm talking about the Fallen Angel's newest"—she cleared her throat.—"guest."

"What did Coco do?"

"She decided it was time to teach Haley to make a pie. In my kitchen. On Thanksgiving Day."

"Oh, dear."

"It was all I could do not to knock her candy into her yams, I'm telling you. I realize that one could make the case that I'm committing the same sin by invading your kitchen this morning, but I know your heart, Caroline. I am welcome in your kitchen. Am I right?"

"Of course! I'm thrilled to have you here, and I agree with you about sharing meal prep on Thanksgiving."

Angelica made a sweeping gesture with her hand. "There you go." She pulled an apron from her cart and tied it on.

Caroline read the message emblazoned across the front and grinned. "'Get your fat pants ready.' That's great."

"I brought an apron for you, too. It says 'Gobble till you wobble.'"

"Perfect. I love it. Thank you."

While Caroline exchanged her plain apron for Angelica's holiday gift, the innkeeper unloaded her cart onto the kitchen table. "Thank heavens I made my bread yesterday and could leave this morning. I know I'm getting ahead on my holidays with this metaphor, but there's simply no room at the inn. And it's only been two days! How am I going to manage two months?"

"Two months?"

"Over two. She's booked every room that wasn't already reserved until Valentine's Day. Tried to get me to cancel those, but I am a woman of my word."

"Valentine's Day? Why Valentine's Day?"

Angelica drew Caroline's chef's knife from the block and studied the blade's edge. "I don't know. Something about circles and first dates. She's a piece of work, Caroline. I know she's been through a trauma, but she's a Southern girl. Where's her grit? Where's the steel in her magnolia? Why, thank goodness our Jackson is as stout as a Bois D'arc barn beam. The way she leans on him shames me to my feminist core. A lesser man would fall right over."

She eyed the celery Caroline had lying on her countertop. "Can I help you chop that?"

"Be my guest. It's washed and ready."

"I brought my own board." Angelica pulled a wooden cutting board shaped like angel's wings from her cart.

"That's cute," Caroline observed.

"Celeste gave this to me to roll out dough. I like using it as a cutting board because it collects dings and dents that way. Dings and dents suit me. They're part of me. I'm a dinged-and-dented sort of girl."

Caroline smiled. "I can relate."

"There's nothing wrong with a few dings and dents. Nothing against my cousin. Celeste Blessing is a special woman, and the world is a better place with her in it, but I think that sometimes, imperfect suits a little more perfectly than perfect does. The thing that those of us who are less than perfect have going for us is that we have room to change and grow. I think that makes us interesting people, don't you?"

"Angelica, you are definitely one of the most interesting people I've ever met."

"Thank you, dear. You're sweet as pecan pie to say that. Speaking of which, guess what kind of pie that woman invaded my kitchen to make?" She forged ahead without giving Caroline a chance to guess the answer. "Pudding pie. From a box. With a graham cracker crust. Also from a box. Forgive me for being judgmental, but she kicked me out of my own kitchen on Thanksgiving morning to make pudding pie! Even River is appalled."

Caroline didn't try to hold back her smile. "Why didn't you tell her no?"

Angelica heaved a heavy sigh. "Because of Haley. That poor, dear, sweet little girl. She's lost without her Poppins, and her mother is trying. It's a pitiful effort, but she's trying. What else could I do? What else can any of us do? It's a tough situation, sticky as Karo on the kitchen floor, that's for sure."

"Jackson says he'll find a way to make it work," Caroline said.

"He's a fine man, our Jackson. He loves you."

"He does. I know that. He loves Haley, too, and her needs are huge right now. We all want Jackson to do what is best for her. I'm in this relationship for the long haul with Jackson, and I can be patient."

"You are a fine woman, Caroline. A good match for Jackson."

"Thank you." She accepted the compliment with a nod, and then eyed the pies lined up on the buffet— pecan, pumpkin, cherry, apple, buttermilk, and banana cream. All homemade. From scratch. No crusts from a can or a box or the freezer.

Bless her heart.

"Angelica?"

"Yes, dear?"

"Just because I'm prepared to be patient doesn't mean I'm a pushover. I'm ready to go Colonel William B. Travis at the Alamo if necessary."

Though a newcomer to Texas, Angelica was familiar with the area's historical lore. "You're going to draw a line in the sand?"

"I am. We're in my territory. Today, Coco better keep her puddin' pie out of my kitchen."

For a holiday that was all about the turkey, this one sure involved a lot of cats, Jackson observed as he met Tucker's gaze and topped off their wine glasses—again— with the Napa pinot noir that had been his contribution to the meal.

Jackson had made a serious mistake when he'd accepted Tucker's suggestion shortly after their arrival at Caroline's house to turn the phrase "Bless Your Heart" into a private drinking game. At the rate things were going, they'd both be blotto before halftime of the Cowboys game. Shoot, they'd even had to toss back a gulp because Celeste of all people threw down a BYH. Celeste!

Both men held up their glasses in silent toast, threw

back a drink, then returned to their task. McBride men traditionally handled KP duty following holiday dinners and today was no exception. Frankly, they'd both been glad to retreat from the battlefield.

"I know it's a Thanksgiving tradition to bitch about women having to use china that you can't put in the dishwasher," Tucker observed a moment later as Jackson handed him a dinner plate to dry. "But I have to be honest. I've missed this."

"How long has it been since you've been home for a holiday?"

"Four years."

"You should have made the trip to Eternity Springs with the rest of the clan."

"Nah. I was honestly glad to have an excuse to stay here. I love the fam-damn-ily—don't get me wrong—but there's too many of 'em. I'm going to have to work up to showing up to one of the big gatherings."

Jackson gave his cousin a sidelong look. In their youth, Tucker had been the most outgoing of the three cousins. Their grandfather used to say that Tucker had never met a stranger. That had certainly changed. Today's Tucker had walls high as mountains. Frosty walls, at that. *Wonder what happened to you, cuz?*

His musings were interrupted when Caroline's brother-in-law wandered into the kitchen carrying a dessert plate and wearing a mildly sheepish look. "Y'all are making me look bad. Better give me a dish towel, or I'll be hearing about it all the way back to Austin."

Jackson nodded toward the drawer where Caroline kept her clean towels. "Second from the bottom. Glad to have the help."

They talked college football as they worked their way through the china. Before long, the other two male members of the dinner party joined them, and they finished the dishes—and two more bottles of wine—in rapid order. The other guys had picked up on the drinking game and wanted in.

By the time they all hung up their dishtowels and rejoined the felines—females—Jackson had received commiserating back pats from all the guys. He didn't know whether that made him feel better or worse.

As Caroline's neighbors and friends from the bookstore said their goodbyes, Jackson's gaze shifted between the women in his life. He didn't know what the hell he was going to do. He felt like the wishbone from the carcass of ol' Tom, the star of today's show. Caroline and Sharon could each take an end and Bless His Heart until they split him in two and one of them got the big end and declared herself the winner.

"Daddy?"

Haley slid her hand inside of his. Immediately, Jackson felt better. "Yes, Little Bit?"

"Could we go to the park?"

Escape! "Sure. I could use some exercise." The neighborhood park was a block away and had old-fashioned playground equipment—a slide, swings, a merry-go-round, a teeter-totter, and a jungle gym.

"I'll tag along," Sharon said.

Of course you will. Jackson stifled a sigh. "Caroline, join us?"

She shook her head and gave him a brittle smile. "No. I have guests."

"Go!" said Elizabeth. "Don't stay on our account. George and I were just about to head out ourselves."

"We were?" George murmured.

Elizabeth elbowed him in the side and continued, "Traffic into Austin will be a nightmare if we wait much later."

They went around the room speaking to everyone,

saving Caroline for last. "Thank you so much for inviting us. It meant the world to me. It's been a lovely day."

"Yes, it has. I'm so glad you came, Elizabeth. I needed
my family with me."

Moisture glistened in the older woman's eyes. She
squeezed Caroline's hand. "I'll see you in two weeks for
the lunch we've planned."

"Yes."

As soon as the car pulled away from the curb, Haley
tugged on Jackson's shirt. "Now can we go, Daddy?"

Before he could open his mouth, the women who
remained at Caroline's all chimed in.

"Run along," said Celeste.

"I'm no guest," Maisy said. "Go to the park, Caroline. I'm watching football."

"Me too." Angelica made a shooing motion with
her hand. "Celeste and I have a bet riding on the Cowboys."

"Well, I guess a little fresh air might do me good,"
Caroline said, reaching around to untie her apron.

Angelica said, "You deserve it. Why, you've worked
your fingers to the bone providing this delicious meal.
The pies especially were"—she kissed her fingertips
and saluted—"*magnifique!* And all from scratch!"

Sharon shoved to her feet. Her chin came up, her eyes
blazed, and in full Coco, she snapped, "You people. You
small-town people. This is ridiculous. I'm just about
tired of being made to feel like an outsider. Jackson—"

"Enough!" he snapped.

"I just want to go down the slide," Haley said in a
little voice. "There were some other kids playing there
earlier."

Jackson wanted to scream at the sky. Instead, he
smiled at Haley, but spoke to Caroline. "Caroline, honey,
would you mind taking Haley on to the park? Sharon

and I will join you in a bit. We need to make a run to the store first."

"A run to the store!" Sharon turned her diva glare on him. "What for?"

"A can of fake snow," Jackson drawled.

Tucker snorted. It was a McBride family putdown about family. Sharon knew it and she obviously remembered it because her eyes narrowed. Tucker's lips twitched. He lifted the beer he'd switched to when he'd started watching football and said, "Bless your heart."

"Can we go, Caroline?" Haley said, oblivious to the undercurrents. "Please?"

Caroline gave Jackson a long look, and then said, "Sure, honey."

After Caroline and his daughter went out the front door, Jackson hauled Sharon out the back. "Jackson, what are you doing?" she demanded. "We're not really going to the store. What is this all about?"

"Actually, I think we will go to a store. You and I need to talk, and we need some privacy to do it. The shop is closed today. We can go there. We'll walk."

"What shop?"

"The Next Chapter."

"Caroline's bookstore?

"Yes."

"You'll take me to *her* bookstore?"

"Yes. It's the perfect place. You and I need to figure out our next chapter. It's time. The right time. The right place. Redemption, Texas."

"Redemption," she repeated in a murmur. "I could use some of that." Then to his surprise, she went quiet.

As they walked the short distance to the bookstore, the feisty spirit she'd put on display today seemed to drain from her. He sensed that she was once again reverting to the needy woman she'd been ever since the crash. He led her to the alley behind the shop and used the key Caroline had given him to unlock the door. He walked inside, flipped on the lights in the storeroom, and then gestured for his ex-wife to take a seat at the workbench.

He took a seat across from her and said, "Sharon, we have to figure this out. This situation is not going to work."

"It's not fair of you to rush me. We've only been back two days."

"You can take all the time you need. I'm not trying to chase you out of the inn. I wasn't kidding about the canyon. I think there is something special about the place, and I think it might just work its magic on you. It's a good thing that you and I are getting along again. Seriously, I'm really happy about it, but I can't—I won't—have you thinking there's gonna be a do-over. We are not turning back the clock. You and I are not getting back together. Ever. That ship has sailed."

"Yes!" she agreed, surprising him. "Around the globe. In a circle."

Oh, hell.

"It's our circle. Our Circle of Fifths. Our circle—"

"Broke. It's broken. Our knot slipped or the rope frayed or it wasn't a circle to begin with. I think life is more of a road than a circle, Sharon. You and I traveled it together for a while, but we're on different routes right now."

She shook her head, denying his words. "The songs we wrote, Jackson. They're *good*."

"Yes, they are. But—"

She reached for his hand and grasped it hard. "You've always been a great songwriter. The songs in the past . . . you put my name on them, but they were yours. I admit it. I'll tell the lawyers and give you the royalties. But

Poppins' ballad and the songs up in the mountains are *ours*. I helped you. I contributed. Those are our songs and they're fabulous. They're going to be big hits."

Jackson was damn near speechless. Once upon a time, he'd have given a limb to hear her admit what she'd just admitted. Funny how priorities change.

"I think you're wrong about the circle, Jackson. We're not broken. This is how it was meant to be. We are better than we were. You can manage the band. Help us find replacements. I hate to think about it, but it has to be done. You are the perfect person to do it."

I don't want to do it. I don't want to manage the band again.

"It could be so good again. Remember? It was good. We were good back then. The circle doesn't have to be broken. We need you, Jackson. I need you." Entreaty glistened in the tears in her eyes. "I can't do this without you. Please, we can be a family again. The three of us. It's the way it's supposed to be. I know it is. This mountain album is the best work we've ever done."

Oh, Sharon. "Just because we can work together again doesn't mean we should live together."

"Why not!" She shoved to her feet and braced her hands on the table and leaned toward him. "Why not, Jackson? Why not! Haley would love it. Don't you want to do what's best for Haley?"

"You know I do." He stood, too. Leaned inward, too. He had to reach her. She had to hear him. For once, they had to communicate. "And here's something I've come to realize in the past month, something I didn't clearly see before now. So do you, Sharon. You want what's best for Haley, too."

Tears pooled in her eyes. "I love her."

"I know you do." He came around the table and

placed his hands on her shoulders. Softly, honestly, he said, "You love Haley, Sharon, but you don't love me."

"I do love you!"

"No."

"I do! You were my first! You know me, the heart of me. We share the same roots and grew in the same soil side by side. You support me, Jackson. You're my strength. You anchor me to my bedrock. I do love you. I need you. Please, Jackson."

"Sharon." He gave her shoulders a gentle little shake. "Don't do this. You're scared. That's what this is. That's all this is. You're scared, because the ground has been ripped out from underneath you. I'm the devil you know, so I'm safe. That's understandable. But you *don't* love me, and Sharon, I don't love you. Not the way we'd need to love each other to be married."

She blinked rapidly. Her tears spilled and slid slowly down her cheeks. "Not the way you love Caroline?"

He felt like she was asking him to drive a stake through her heart. Sharon was beautiful, one of the most talented people on the planet. She was one of the wealthiest people on the planet. How can a person with so much going for her be so insecure? So pitiful? So fragile?

Caroline could teach her a thing or two.

He didn't want to hurt Sharon, but she needed to accept reality. "Not the way I love Caroline."

"Are you going to marry her?"

Well, I'm not going to tell you before I ask her, that's for damn sure.

He let his avoidance of the question answer it. "Let's sit down, and let's talk about Haley."

He guided her down to her seat and pulled his chair around so that he'd be seated to her side rather than across from her. He took her hand. "I've had an idea. I'll admit I haven't given it a lot of thought—in fact, it's only just occurred to me—but maybe we can talk it through together, and decide if it will work for us. The three of us."

"Don't you mean the four of us?" she asked with just enough snide to her tone that he had to swallow a sharp retort.

"We need to do something about Haley's education."

"She's way ahead, Jackson." Sharon swiped away the wetness from her cheeks. "We have time to find a new nanny."

"What if we didn't try? Not right away, anyway. Finding the right someone to follow Mary is going to be an almost impossible job. Haley will resist anyone trying to fill Poppins' shoes."

"I know. She needs time to heal. That's why you brought us here."

"What if we filled that healing time in a different way? You heard her earlier. She wanted to play with other kids in the park. That was the appeal. Let's send her to school, Sharon. Here in Redemption. Let her be around other children. I think it would be really good for her."

Sharon pulled her hand free of his, sat back in her chair, and crossed her arms. She sat without speaking for a full half minute before asking, "You'd send her to public school?"

"Sure. The school system here is highly rated."

"But what about security? You know I don't take her out in public without private security."

"Redemption isn't Nashville, thank God. It's a small town where people keep an eye out for one another. I think she'd be just fine. In fact, I think it'd be the best thing we could do for her. Give her normal for a time, Sharon. Let her be a small-town little girl who walks to school and plays in the park and takes piano lessons on Wednesdays."

"Jackson, she's been taking piano lessons for three years already. She's probably more accomplished than you on the instrument at this point."

"Really?" Now was not the time to be annoyed that he hadn't known that. He plowed ahead. "Get a house in town, Sharon. Send Haley to school here for the rest of the year."

"I can't live without private security."

"You can in Redemption."

"You won't be there to protect us. Will you? You're not planning to live with us?"

"No. But I'll be nearby. Give yourself normal for a time. I think it would be good for both of you."

She wrinkled her nose. "It's a small town in Texas. Don't you remember how hard I fought to get out of a small town in Texas?"

"I do." He nodded, and then shrugged. "But maybe you should think about your circle, Sharon. Maybe it's bringing you back for a reason."

"I thought you said it broke."

"*Our* circle broke. Not yours."

Sharon stood up and began pacing the storeroom. Pausing beside Caroline's desk, she picked up a pen imprinted with The Next Chapter logo and clicked it open, shut, open, shut. "I thought you said we needed to be inside the canyon for the enchantment to work."

"It's a ten-minute drive. You can spend plenty of time there. Stay weekends at the Fallen Angel."

"So Angelica would only *think* she'd gotten rid of me?" she asked innocently.

Jackson couldn't help but laugh. "You two don't exactly rub well together."

"I'll not nominate her for innkeeper of the year."

Click. Click. Click. "What about the band?"

"The band?"

"Will you manage?"

She's negotiating. His heartbeat sped up. "I will help you, but I'm not the right person for the job. Just with the changes in technology, the business is changing at a breakneck pace. I haven't kept up with it. You were right to hire Ray-Walker when you did. You need an R-W two-point-oh now. That ain't me."

He didn't miss the mulish look on her face, so he was quick to continue. "Now, musicians are something else entirely. I can find you musicians, Sharon. I will find them. We'll want the right guys to record the mountain album."

"Guys and gals," she corrected. "You know I want women in my band."

"Guys and gals. My bad."

Click. Click. Click. Click. Click. "I don't know, Jackson. I'll have to think about this. This isn't what you said when you convinced me to come to Texas. It feels a bit like bait and switch. We were all going to live together at the inn like a family, and now you want to split us up and make me live by myself."

"No," he said, summoning his patience. "I want to send Haley to school. The house was only a suggestion because I think it'd work out better for everyone and you'd be happier in a house in the long run. But if you want to stay at the inn and butt heads with Angelica, fine."

She lifted her chin and challenged him. "You're not going to be there."

She's still negotiating. You know that tone. "No. I'm going to be with Caroline."

"You're choosing her over Haley."

"No, that's not what I'm doing, and I'm not letting you write that narrative. Get back on point. I want to send Haley to school in Redemption through the end of this school year. I'll help you hire a new manager. I'll help you find musicians who fit. What else do you want?"

It caught him off guard when she burst into tears. "I want Ray-Walker. And Poppins. And Bobby and Shane and Liz and Randy and Wayne. I want the crash to never have happened. I want to have stayed in L.A. for another day like they wanted."

"I know. I know. I'm sorry." He took her in his arms and held her. "I'm sorry. I wish that was in my power to give, Sharon. I really do."

She cried and cried and cried, sobbed like he hadn't seen her sob since those first few days following the crash. Jackson was at a loss. Was it good that she was letting this emotion out? Or was it a bad thing?

At least she wasn't all drugged up. He knew that. That was part of the reason why he'd agreed to go to the mountains with her in the first place. Drugs scared him. He'd seen too many lives ruined—too much talent wasted—and it haunted him. Ironically, drug abuse had been one thing that he and Sharon agreed on until the end. It simply wasn't allowed in their band.

But she'd been vulnerable in the wake of the crash, and she'd taken the drugs doctors had prescribed. He couldn't blame her, but he'd feared it becoming a problem for her.

So he'd made sure the pill bottles got left behind when they headed for the hills, then he distracted her by working her ass hard in a place where she didn't have easy access to refills. But dammit, had he screwed up? He wasn't a doctor. He was just a concerned ex-husband. A worried father.

"What can I do, Sharon?"

"You'll have to pick her up in the mornings and take her to school. I don't want her walking. Even in Redemption."

He went still. *Yes? She's saying yes?* Jackson cleared his throat. "Okay."

Speaking against his shoulder, she said, "And I'm not sure about the house. I may want to stay at the inn, and if I do, you'll still have to come pick Haley up and probably bring her home. I don't know what I'll do about staff. If it's not the three of us . . . I just don't know, Jackson. I'm not committing to anything beyond school."

"But you're committing to school."

"If you're committing to the band."

"Under the terms I outlined?"

She pulled away, not entirely out of his arms, but far enough so that she could look up into his face. "I think for the sake of the Circle we should seal it with a kiss, Jackson McBride. A kiss to say goodbye. I don't think we ever did that. We shouted. We screamed. We slammed doors. We were never nice."

"No, we weren't nice. Suing you was downright mean."

"That one hurt, Jackson."

"I know. I'm sorry, Sharon. I should not have done that."

"Music to my ears, McBride." Her mouth lifted in a bittersweet smile. "So, would she mind, your Caroline?"

"A kiss to say goodbye?" he murmured. "No. I don't think she'll mind. She's a generous woman, my Caroline."

Sharon reached up and cupped Jackson's cheek. "She's a lucky woman. You're a good man. Better than I deserved. Be happy, Jackson."

Their lips met. The kiss was brief. It was sweet. It healed something broken.

When Jackson lifted his head, two items on the wall above Caroline's desk drew his gaze like a magnet. The first was a framed photograph from the Chamber of Commerce of Caroline at the bookstore's ribbon cutting. She was looking right at the camera. Seemed to be looking right at him. Her sparkling eyes and beaming smile warmed him and welcomed and called to him.

The second was a framed photograph of her store's sign.

The Next Chapter
Redemption, Texas

Funny. He'd never really paid attention to her logo. An oval encircled the words. Another circle. *Welcome home, Jackson.*

A few minutes later, as they stepped into the crisp autumn afternoon, Jackson had a smile on his face and more hope in his heart than he'd had in years. Thanksgiving Day had lived up to its name. Sharon had said yes to him.

They arrived at the park to find Caroline chatting with a group of parents watching a gaggle of children playing tag. Jackson introduced Sharon as Coco. As he'd expected, the parents got past the celebrity shine pretty quick and talk turned to a usual topic for November—the Texas high school football playoffs. When the game of tag broke up, Haley begged for Jackson to push her on the swing. "You come, too, Caroline," she said. "Daddy can push you."

Caroline glanced at Sharon.

"Mama doesn't like to swing. It makes her tummy seasick."

"Actually, Jackson, if you'll loan me your truck, I think I'll go on back to the inn. I have a tune circling around my mind. I'd like to work on it while it's perking."

"Sure." He pulled the keys from his pocket and tossed them to her. "Here you go."

Jackson didn't let anybody drive his truck, so this unusual response left Caroline gaping at him in shock. But before he could do more than give her a sheepish grin, Haley grabbed their hands and pulled them toward the swing set.

They played for fifteen more minutes before walking home, the three of them hand in hand in hand. Haley said, "This has been the best Thanksgiving. I wish we could have Thanksgiving at your house every year, Caroline."

Pleasure gleamed in Caroline's eyes as she met Jackson's gaze. "That would be lovely."

"I'm really glad you're my daddy's girlfriend."

Caroline brought her free hand to her chest. To her heart. "Me too, Haley. Me too."

Jackson blew her a kiss, and a few minutes later he climbed the steps to her front porch happier than he'd been in a very long time.

Welcome home.

They entered the house to find Tucker asleep on Caroline's couch. Maisy and Celeste were in the kitchen debating whether they'd try cherry or pecan pie next. Angelica barely spared them glance. The Cowboys were down by seven to the Redskins with less than a minute to play in the fourth quarter.

Angelica's loud cheer when the Cowboys intercepted a pass woke Tucker and brought Maisy and Celeste back to the living room. Angelica drew a giggling Haley into a wild dance when the Cowboys scored with seconds on the clock. "Fixin' to be a tie ball game," Tucker observed. "We're going to overtime."

Jackson watched for a moment, and then shook his head. "Coach should go for two."

Aghast, Angelica exclaimed, "What? Go for two? You're crazy. They don't go for two in the NFL."

"It's not against the rules."

Tucker gave him a disgusted look. "You take the point. Tie the game. Fail to make two and lose the game, your coach's ass will be grass."

"I know. I still think they should go for two."

Caroline observed. "Someone has called a time-out. Something's going on."

"Why do you think they should go for two, Daddy?"

"Because he's crazy," Maisy observed.

Celeste folded her arms, pursed her lips, and thumped her index finger against them. She winked at Jackson.

For some reason, that made him want to laugh. "Because, Haley, sometimes in life, you put it all on the line and go for the win. Today is Thanksgiving Day."

Maisy shook her head. "If this were the old days and this were the Aggies playing the Longhorns for a year's worth of bragging rights, I'd agree with you. But the Cowboys have a possibility of making the playoffs. You can't risk that."

"Sure you can. Sometimes, you absolutely should. Because something I've learned in the past year or so is that life isn't always about the safe play. Sometimes, you take the risk. Sometimes, you throw caution to the wind and move to a new place and open a bookstore."

Now, finally, he'd dragged Caroline's attention away from the football game.

"Sometimes—even if it means calling an audible— you go for the win. It's Thanksgiving Day. A little while ago I got a yes to question that is nothing short of a miracle. I am filled with thanksgiving for my friends, my family, and because I'm back in Texas, for football."

"Amen," Tucker agreed.

"So it seems only appropriate that since the momentum of the game is going my way, I go with my gut and make my call. Team Jackson is going for two."

He took hold of Caroline's hand and went down on one knee. "Caroline, will you marry me?"

Haley gasped. Although his attention was focused on Caroline, Jackson did take note of the reactions from the others in the room. Most importantly, Haley's eyes lit with excitement. She clasped her hands prayerfully. Tucker grinned and took a sip of his beer. Maisy's chin dropped, and she covered her mouth with her hands.

Angelica tore her gaze away from the football game where the Cowboys were lined up without a kicker in the backfield. With a downright devilish gleam in her eyes, she winked at him and said, "Score, Jackson. Score."

"We could elope," Jackson suggested as he lay with Caroline in the hammock at one of their favorite places in the canyon, a picnic spot he'd named Sunset Point for obvious reasons. After his public marriage proposal on top of a day spent with a crowd, they'd both desired private time. He'd been the one to suggest Sunset Point. This evening's sky promised to be a barnburner, and the idea of hiking after the day's indulgence had appealed to them both. Plus, he'd promised her romance, which also appealed after a marriage proposal that had been anything but romantic.

Not that Caroline was complaining. The moment

might not have been romantic, but it had been joyous. Haley's squeal of delight had been the prettiest music she'd ever heard—and having listened to Jackson sing to her, she'd heard a lot of beautiful music.

"No, we're not going to elope. Haley would be heartbroken."

"Okay, you're right about that. But June? Why do we have to wait until June? That's a long time away."

"Quit pouting. It's hardly any time when it comes to wedding planning. The absolute earliest I'd want to try is April, but Maisy's been planning her April in Paris trip for over a year, and I want her to be my maid of honor."

"What about May?"

"Gillian is going on her honeymoon in May."

"I thought she's getting married in February."

"She is. They're delaying their honeymoon."

"Oh." He turned his head and nibbled her ear. "I don't want to do that. We will honeymoon in June, okay?"

"Okay."

"Unless I can talk you into eloping on Saturday."

"We're not eloping on Saturday."

Jackson sighed heavily. "It's hot here in June."

Caroline grinned. She could tell from his tone that his heart wasn't really in this protest, but he'd given her a perfect opening for an idea she'd been mulling during the hike. "I know. So, what would you think about a destination wedding?"

"Honey, I'll marry you anywhere you want. You're thinking of a beach somewhere?"

"No, the mountains. Eternity Springs, to be precise. Angelica happened to mention that Celeste had an unexpected cancellation for her honeymoon cottage at Angel's Rest for the second week of June, and it's supposed to be a fabulous place to honeymoon. Since so much of your family has property there, it would be convenient."

"I like it. I like that idea a lot." He lifted his head and kissed her hard and quick. "Boone showed us pictures of the Angel's Rest honeymoon cottage when we were designing ours at the Fallen Angel. It's beyond awesome."

"So we set the date for that Saturday? I believe it's the ninth."

"If this Saturday is out, that Saturday works for me."

"Good." Happiness warmed her like the summer sun. "We can drop by the inn on our way back to town tonight and speak to Celeste directly. Wouldn't want someone else to book it."

"Tomorrow will be soon enough. Think about it, honey. If Angelica suggested it to you, she won't let anyone else get the jump on us."

"True."

"June ninth. That's a good day for an anniversary. Wonder what day of the week it'll be when we celebrate our fiftieth?"

"Our fiftieth wedding anniversary?" Caroline laughed. "What made your mind go there?"

"I don't know. I'm feeling golden. Seriously. What are the chances that Sharon would have taken a wrong turn in the neighborhood on her way back to the canyon this afternoon and stopped when she saw a house for sale?"

"I can't believe she knocked on the door and asked to see it."

"That I can believe. When she has her Coco on, she doesn't wait for anything. Do you think your neighborhood will adjust all right to having a celebrity on the block?"

"As long as she keeps her grass mowed, it'll work out just fine."

"I'll be sure to add hiring a lawn management service for her to my to-do list."

"Better put housekeeping at the top of the list," Caroline advised. "The best lady in town just let her clients know that she's quitting after Christmas. We have cleaning-lady wars going on in Redemption right now. Wow, Jackson, look at the sky."

"Talk about golden."

"It's like a glimpse into heaven," she murmured as a dozen shades of gold lit up the western horizon.

"You think Robert is up there wishing you well?"

A swish of evening breeze rustled the fallen leaves upon the ground. A smile ghosted across Caroline's lips. "I do. You know, I really truly do."

After that, she and Jackson fell into a companionable silence, watching the sun set behind the rim of Enchanted Canyon on this glorious Thanksgiving Day. He shifted their weight enough to keep the hammock softly swaying. They watched without speaking as the golden sky caught fire in a dramatic burst of vibrant orange and red and scarlet before fading steadily to pink and rose, mauve and purple.

The stars began to pop. Twilight faded toward night and Jackson said, "I'm gonna sing you a song, Caroline."

"Perfect." He'd promised romance. She couldn't think of anything more romantic.

"I've debated this more than once since we started seeing each other. I've resisted, because I'm sure it's not original, and I hate like hell to be hokey."

"You're never hokey."

"I'm pretty sure this crosses the line. I could sing one of my own songs, but sometimes, someone else's lyrics are just right. Someone else's song fits the moment."

"Then that's the song I want to hear."

"Even if it is hokey and it's football season in Texas instead of baseball season in Boston?"

Caroline laughed, knowing then what he was going to do. No, it wasn't original, but he was right. This song was as perfect as the moment. And as the stars at night popped big and bright in the sky above an enchanted canyon deep in the heart of Texas, Jackson McBride sang "Sweet Caroline" to his bride-to-be.

Epilogue

JUNE 8
ETERNITY SPRINGS, COLORADO

"I'm the flower girl and I have a basket that's going to have rose petals in it and I drop them as I walk up the aisle," Haley told the boy who was skipping rocks on Hummingbird Lake. "Only it's not an aisle like in a church because we're getting married down by the lake. They leave a gap between the chairs, and I walk down that throwing my rose petals. That's the aisle. And River Dog is gonna be the ring bearer only he's not carrying the real rings because my Daddy doesn't trust him not to jump in the lake. River loves water."

"River is a cool dog," ten-year-old Reilly Murphy said. "I like him."

"Thanks."

"He's not as cool as my dog, though. Sinatra is the best dog ever. He has blue eyes."

"Really? I've never seen a dog with blue eyes."

"He's pretty special." Generously, Reilly added, "Your mom sings really good. My mom is really excited that she is going to sing at the rehearsal party tonight."

Haley shrugged. "We will see if she actually does it.

She's been bad about saying she's going to sing and then not doing it."

"Does your mom have a dog?"

"No."

"Maybe she should get one. Having one teaches responsibility."

Haley shrugged. "She needs someone to do my daddy's job, first. She doesn't like anyone he picks to take his place. He's a fit to be tied."

Reilly frowned. "What does that mean? I never understood what that means."

Haley wasn't exactly sure, either. Her daddy said it when he knew she was around. When he thought she couldn't hear him, he used words she wasn't supposed to know. "Is there a spot to find good throwing rocks? We have one of those back home by our pond."

"Yeah. Come on. It's just a little ways. I'll show you."

Haley glanced back toward the house where Caroline watched her from the front porch. She shouted, "I'm going to get skipping rocks with my new friend. It's not far."

"Stay within sight and listen for me," Caroline called back. "Your dad will be here soon, and we'll need to start getting ready for the rehearsal."

"Okay."

From a rocking chair on the porch of the house she shared with her "bride tribe" at the Callahan family's compound along the lake, Caroline watched Haley follow the boy along the bank for a short distance. When the children bent and began harvesting a wealth of flat rocks for their game without appearing to be in danger of falling into the chilly water, she relaxed. Haley was a good swimmer, but this water was cold. Besides, eventually, they would begin this wedding rehearsal.

The groom would return along with his best man. The guess was would they bring her bridesmaid back with them? Or had Gillian done a disappearing act?

"Have you heard any more from Jackson?" Maisy asked, stepping outside with a steaming mug of coffee in her hand.

"No."

"I'm so sorry, Caroline. I feel terrible. This is all my fault."

"No. Stop it. It is not your fault."

"I'm the one who overlooked her bag in our tent while she was busy helping you pack up your gown after the bridal photos. I should have been the one to run back up to Stardance River Camp to retrieve it. I wouldn't have gotten lost."

"We don't know that is what has happened," Caroline said softly, worriedly.

It was however the best of the possibilities. Gillian had left here three hours ago and should have been back within the hour. They'd begun to worry when she was half an hour late. When phone calls went to voicemail, their worry escalated. Discovering the phone plugged into the charger in Gillian's bedroom took their concern up another notch.

Gillian was not herself these days. Understandably. She was putting on a brave face, but she wasn't fooling anybody. It would be hard for any bride who'd been left at the altar only a few months ago to be part of this weekend's festivities. Caroline had carefully broached the subject of Gillian's possibly skipping this wedding, assuring her friend that she'd understand, but Gillian wouldn't hear of it.

But man, she appeared as brittle as glass these days.

"Maybe she just had a flat tire and is waiting for

someone to come along and change it for her," she suggested. "Gillian is not one to get her hands greasy."

"True. Or ruin her manicure two hours before a big event," Maisy agreed. "However, it also isn't like her to go anywhere without her phone."

Caroline chewed on her lower lip. "This isn't good."

"I really don't think there's any reason to worry, Caroline. Why don't you call Jackson again?"

She shook her head. "He said he'd let me know the second he knew anything. He's tense enough as it is. I don't want to add to the stress."

Maisy pursed her lips. "Jackson was cool as a cucumber compared to Tucker. What's the deal with him and Gillian anyway? They've been sniping at each other since we left Texas."

"I don't know. I love Tucker, don't get me wrong, but Jackson's cousin is—"

"Yummy!" Maisy interrupted, gesturing with her coffee cup.

Boone McBride had just come into view, walking from the direction of the outdoor stage accompanied by Luke Callahan and Coco. "I believe we were speaking of the other cousin," Caroline said dryly.

"Too many cousins around here today to keep track of everybody. Maybe Boone has heard something. I'll go ask." Maisy handed Caroline her coffee and skipped down the porch steps to meet the focus of her flirtations.

The trio halted at Maisy's approach. They spoke a moment before Boone shrugged, and he and Maisy veered off toward the lake. Luke and Coco continued on toward her. "Where's Haley?" Coco asked.

Caroline gestured toward the lake. "Skipping stones with a new friend."

"That's Devin and Jenna Murphy's boy, Reilly," Luke said. "Caroline, you met them last summer."

"Oh, that's Reilly?" Smiling she took a closer look at the boy. "He's the one who has a Christmas wishing tree in the forest at Angel's Rest, isn't he? It stays decorated year round? I thought it might be fun to try to find it while we're staying there."

Luke nodded, and then said, "Your little girl looks happy."

"Yes, she does." Caroline and Coco spoke simultaneously, and then shared a look. Coco shrugged and added, "She thrives being around other children. Maisy said something's happened to Gillian? Is that why Jackson missed the sound check?"

Caroline explained about Gillian's disappearance, then added, "Jackson said Martin has everything well in hand for your performance tomorrow. He thinks Martin will be an excellent manager."

"Maybe." Coco shrugged and scowled.

Luke proved his mental acuity by making a quick escape. Coco took a seat in the rocker beside Caroline's and two women sat without speaking for a time, rocking and watching Haley. Then Caroline said, "I've said this before, but I want to say it again now that it's just the two of us. I'm really honored that you are going to sing at our wedding, Coco. It means so much to Jackson and to me."

"I'm doing it for Haley," she quickly pointed out.

A smile fluttered on Caroline's lips. "I know."

Except, that wasn't the whole truth. In the past seven months, Sharon had made a place for herself in Jackson and Caroline's Redemption, Texas family. And she was grateful for it. Even if she'd never come right out and admit to it.

"I can't believe you are honeymooning for a month." Coco pushed out of her rocker and began to pace the porch. "I really don't think Jackson and I discussed that when we agreed on Haley's schedule for the next year."

Yes, you did.

"It's not responsible of him to go away for so long. We have special circumstances. Haley is accustomed to having him around. He takes care of things for her. He is always there to solve her problems. He is always there when she needs him. Haley will—"

"Be fine," Caroline said, standing. She walked over to Sharon and spoke more to the point. "*You* will be fine. You can do this. You are stronger than you think."

Sharon's throat worked. Tears pooled in her eyes. "I'm not strong."

"You are, too. You are here, aren't you? How many women have the grits to come to their ex-husband's wedding? Not just attend, but celebrate it like you are doing."

"That's pride, not strength."

"It's both. Look, you took a terrible blow last fall, and you are still standing. You're wobbly, but you're standing. That impresses me. I don't know that I could have done it."

"You? Wonder Woman Caroline?" Sharon folded her arms defensively.

"Wonder Woman! Hah. You should have seen me when Robert first shared his diagnosis. I went into a fetal position that I didn't crawl out of for months."

"But you did crawl out of it."

"I did. Because by that time Robert was the wobbly one and he needed someone to support him. We didn't have a Bois D'Arc like Jackson in our lives to step up and help. So I sucked it up and I stood. You're doing it, too, Sharon. You are. You just need to trust yourself."

She made a *phfftt* sound. "Now you sound like Angelica."

"No, that sounds like Celeste. Angelica would tell you to go throw your pity-pot off the top of Enchanted Rock."

Sharon snorted. "During a full moon."

Caroline grinned. "While naked."

The women shared a smile, and then Sharon's gaze drifted back toward the lake where her daughter sent a rock skipping across Hummingbird Lake four times, then threw up her arms in victory. "Girl power."

"We've got it. We just have to believe in it."

"Maybe I should write a song about that."

"You can do it, Coco. I know you can."

The conversation was interrupted by the arrival of two vehicles—Jackson's truck and *whew!* Gillian's Mercedes. Before Jackson pulled into his parking spot, the sedan had sent gravel flying as it screeched to a stop. Both the passenger's side and driver's side doors were flung open. Tucker, his face a thundercloud, climbed from behind the wheel as Gillian, her expression just as dark vaulted from her seat. Both doors slammed and the combatants marched off in opposite directions.

"Well," Coco said. "There's a story there."

Jackson opened the door of his truck and climbed slowly to the ground. Meeting Caroline's questioning gaze, he grimaced and slowly shook his head. Walking toward them, he said, "Long story. I'll tell you later. Right now, I need a shower and maybe a beer. Then we have a wedding to rehearse. And a party. Sharon, how did the sound check go?"

She glanced at Caroline and winked. "Don't worry about it, McBride. I have it handled."

JUNE 9TH
THE HONEYMOON COTTAGE AT ANGEL'S REST
ETERNITY SPRINGS, COLORADO

"This has been the most perfect day," Caroline murmured as she rested her head against her husband's naked chest and tipped her face toward the stars. Around them, steam rose from the bubbling outdoor spa.

Jackson reached over to the champagne bucket set into the built in cooler at the spa's edge and topped off their glasses. "It was a fun wedding."

"I can't believe River went into the lake."

"I called it."

"Yes, you did. Haley was the cutest flower girl ever born."

"She's a performer like her mother. Such drama with those flower petals."

"Our guests were smitten."

"Can you imagine what she's going to be like in ten years? I'd better start practicing my mean dad glare now to keep the hairy-legged boys away."

"Ten years?" Caroline sniffed. "You'll be lucky to have six."

"No-o-o," he groaned. "Let's change the subject."

His hand started to wander, though the shift in subject wasn't all that different. Soon, Caroline was the one who was groaning. They spent much of their wedding night and the first week of their marriage beneath the Colorado stars, before flying to the South Pacific for the balance of their month alone at a beach beyond reach for anything short of a dire emergency.

It was, they both declared, the perfect honeymoon, but when it was time to return to Redemption, to the canyon and the dance hall and bookstore, to River Dog, and to Haley, they were ready. More than ready.

Ready for the next, next chapter. The next verse.

Jackson had a title for it already.

He called it "Coming Home."

Don't miss the next book in the
Eternity Springs:
The McBrides of Texas series
by **Emily March**

Tucker

Coming in February 2020!